DAYS

GORDON WAUGH

Stoater
Books

Published in 2018 by Stoater Books

ISBN Paperback: 978-1-9993227-0-0
Ebook:978-1-9993227-1-7

A CIP catalogue copy of this book can be found
in the British Library.

Published with the help of Indie Authors World
www.indieauthorsworld.com

IndieAuthors
World

Dedicated to my wife Jean, with love

Many thanks to Jim Kennedy
a true champion.

To   Teresa.

Best Wishes

Gordon Waugh.

Dedicated to my wife Jean, with love

Many thanks to Jim Kennedy
a true champion.

To Teresa.

Best Wishes

Gordon Waugh.

ACKNOWLEDGEMENT

The ability to write a book is, they say in everyone. That may well be so but in my case it would never have happened without the constant support I received from countless friends and family over the years.

In the end it took a great deal of work and encouragement from Sinclair and Kim Macleod at Indie Authors World to get me over the line. Without their expertise I would never have been able to get the job done, they were quite simply magnificent.

Also I must make mention of Suze Clarke-Morris, who had the unenviable task of editing my manuscript. She showed a great deal of patience in her dealings with me and her advice was invaluable in the production of this book.

My sincere, grateful thanks to each and everyone who helped me along the way, allowing me to fulfil a long held dream.

CHAPTER ONE

Back in the summer of 1980, Mary McLeod found herself boarding a plane in Cape Town, South Africa bound for Heathrow Airport in the United Kingdom. Her ultimate destination was Edinburgh and home. Not that she had a home to go back to exactly, but she would deal with that when she arrived. For now, apart from what she was wearing, she had a small suitcase with one or two other items of clothing and jewellery, as well as a few hundred Rand. All her worldly possessions.

It was sweateringly hot and Mary couldn't wait for the aircraft to take off. Her only regret in going was having to leave her twelve year old daughter Aimi behind, who was at boarding school in Johannesburg. The whole family had left Scotland eight years earlier for a, so called, better life in South Africa. This never materialised.

Mary's husband, Reginald McLeod was a banker, who it turned out had an eye for the ladies. Life had not been easy for Mary trying to raise a bright child in a strange country whilst her husband was hardly ever at home. And when he was he paid little or no attention to her or the child. Reginald had a string of affairs all in an effort to scramble up the social ladder. It was hardly surprising then that, more by way of retaliation than anything else, Mary, who was still an attractive woman, engaged in an affair of her own. She chose one of the bank's younger employees. It didn't last long and was intended only to annoy Reginald.

Unfortunately it ended with her falling pregnant at the age of forty. To say Reginald was outraged would be a gross understatement. He was livid and demanded she get rid of the child immediately. It seemed he had double standards. He could behave in whichever way he pleased but his wife, well, that was not on. Mary went against his wishes and indeed the advice of her doctor. Having a child at her age was risky but she was going to keep it.

Ever the devoted husband, Reginald seized this opportunity to inform her he was suing for divorce and throwing her out of their home. There was no chance of her living with the child's father, so Mary had little choice but to return to Edinburgh.

Reginald refused to let Mary take Aimi, not just because she was settled in boarding school but also because it was just the way he was, a nasty, spiteful individual. Mary didn't argue, she had a good relationship with her daughter and Aimi realised her mum's only option was to return to Scotland. She was doing what was right to protect her unborn child. It was then that Mary realised, possibly for the first time in her life, what a wonderful daughter she had in Aimi.

So Mary found herself on a plane bound for Great Britain. Her future was uncertain but surely better than the life she had endured in South Africa. As the plane soared into the sky, Mary closed her eyes and dreamed of home. It took what seemed like an eternity to eventually reach Heathrow.

Mary then caught the connecting flight to Edinburgh some fifty minutes later. Just before midnight her plane landed at Edinburgh Airport and Mary was pleased to see that it was raining. A proper welcome home, good old Scottish weather.

As promised her brother Archie was there to meet her, umbrella in hand. He was all that was left of her family in Scotland. A confirmed bachelor, he was headmaster of a private boys school, a posh place for rich people in Perthshire. Archie was a former pupil of the school as was Mary's ex husband, Reginald. That was how they'd met in the first place.

Archie smiled at his sister, kissed her on both cheeks and gave her a hug. A great feeling of relief came over her, as she always felt safe in his company. He whisked her away to a hotel in Edinburgh city centre for a couple of days, to allow her to recover from her journey. Mary had to admit she was totally exhausted after her long trip but was glad to be back.

Archie had arranged for her to view a small house in Leith which he hoped would suit her needs. It was a little small but Mary was in no position to quibble and was happy enough with the property. It had potential. Archie didn't receive a fabulous salary, unlike Reginald but he told her he was quite willing to purchase the house to give her a start. Mary was more than grateful and knew she could make things work. He also insisted on paying her a small monthly allowance until she was able to get back on her feet which was lovely of him.

There had always been a great affection between Mary and her brother. They were twins, however Archie was all of ten minutes older than her. He had always played the part of big brother. Although he was hardly what could be described as a man's man, he always seemed to do the right thing. She believed that his pupils all thought the world of him.

As soon as she could Mary moved into the tiny house and set about cleaning and decorating it from top to bottom. She soon had it ship shape. The beauty of the house being so small was she did not require much in the way of furniture to fill it, which was just as well as funds were tight.

Mary often smiled to herself when she remembered the evening of her first day in her new home. She had been exhausted but happy and the child she was carrying gave a kick of approval. Given her age Mary had worried about having a baby but she needn't have. Right on her due date, she gave birth to a beautiful baby girl who weighed in at 6 pounds 2 ounces, with a mass of dark hair and dark features like her mother. Aimi had been very blonde, taking after her father. She named her baby Isla and asked her brother Archie if he would be her godfather. He was delighted to accept. Now she was divorced Mary reverted back to her maiden name, Buchanan.

CHAPTER TWO

By October, the same year, summer was a distant memory and winter had almost arrived. That night a chill wind blew across the city of Glasgow. It was bitterly cold, a dark and miserable place.

Any respectable person would have long since been indoors, huddled up beside a roaring fireside or wrapped up warm in bed but then Josephine Jardine wasn't looked upon as a respectable person. She was a twenty-five year old prostitute with a drug habit who was afraid to go home to her drunken, abusive boyfriend without any money. She had done alright for such a miserable day but her habit had taken up most of the money she had earned.

It began to rain heavily around midnight, the Georgian buildings turning into dark slate like mirrors, reflecting what little moonlight there was on to the soaked pavements below.

Josie as Josephine preferred to be called, found herself sheltering in the doorway of an office building in Blythswood Square, just at the corner with Douglas Street. Even her best friend, Sadie Gleason, had packed up and gone home long ago.

They had been on the game together since their early teens when they first met in council care. From the start there was a bond between them and they became the best of friends. They relied upon each other through thick and thin. Even now they lived close to one another just off the Saltmarket in Glasgow. Sadie had her own place, whilst Josie lived with her alcoholic boyfriend, Bobby McGowan and their five year old son, Matthew, or Matty as he was known. Josie's oldest son, Tommy Jardine who was ten and from a previous relationship also lived with them.

It was just approaching one o'clock in the morning and Josie thought to herself, just another couple of punters and she could go home. She smoked her last cigarette and pulled her black imitation leather coat around her slim body in an effort to keep warm. Her spirits lifted for a moment as she saw a figure walking towards her through the park. Hopefully it would be a new customer.

"Well, hello Josie," a voice echoed across the deserted street.

She knew immediately who it was, her worst nightmare. He had appeared in this area about six months before and from the beginning he had harassed just about every one of the prostitutes at one time or another .Usually in this part of town he was spoiled for choice as this was normally one of the busiest locations to find a 'girl' in Glasgow. But tonight wasn't normal, it was a dreich, wet October Tuesday. It was just Josie's bad luck that he had come across her. The man was a sexual predator. She would humour him and hopefully he would go away.

Wednesday was half day at Curries, one of the smallest bookshops in Glasgow. Hamish Currie, the owner, was hoping to drive up to visit friends in Callander when the shop closed at lunchtime. His wee bookshop, which catered for a select clientele, was on Blythswood Square just at the corner with Douglas Street and was a basement premises in a building owned by a well known insurance company.

Having parked his MG sports car, which was his pride and joy, Hamish descended the stairs to his shop and saw that there was a large bundle blocking the doorway. At first he thought it was yet another black bin bag of rubbish. He was used to rubbish being dumped outside the shop because people were so inconsiderate.

On closer inspection however, to his horror, he realised it was not a bin bag at all but the body of a young woman, dressed in an imitation leather coat. He immediately phoned the police. He would not be visiting his friends in Callander that day.

Despite the best efforts of Strathclyde Police no one was ever arrested for the murder of Josephine Jardine. Someone had strangled the poor woman with her own tights, having first sexually assaulted her. The partially clothed body had been left in a heap in the shop doorway.

With the passage of time her death became just another statistic. Yet another unsolved prostitute murder. Was anyone really that bothered?

Just a few days after Josie had died, her boyfriend Bobby McGowan disappeared and was never seen or heard from again. Rumour had it that on hearing the news about Josie he had gone on a bender and drowned in the River Clyde. Some thought that perhaps the oldest boy, Tommy, who was a big lad for his age with a quick temper, may have killed McGowan as he had been prone to handing out beatings to the two boys for no other reason than he could.

In any event Tommy and Matty were placed into council care and the next few years were not easy for either of the boys. Tommy was more than able to look after himself. Because of the lifestyle of his mother and Bobby McGowan he had been used to taking care of himself and his wee brother sometimes for days on end. Matty was different altogether. He was a skinny child and rather slow of thought.

When Josie died and then Bobby McGowan disappeared, Josie's pal Sadie Gleason had tried to adopt the boys to keep them out of the system which she and Josie had been brought up in, but the authorities in their wisdom, deemed her to be an unfit person.

Over the years Sadie was still the only person that Tommy and Matty could turn to if they were in any kind of trouble or needed help. If they ran away from any of the care homes in which they were staying, and they often did, the police always knew that eventually they would turn up at Sadie's flat. She would clean them up, feed them and more often than not buy them some new clothing. As it turned out she ended up looking out for the lads for far more years than their own mother had. Sadie didn't mind, she loved the boys as though they were her own. She would do anything for them and there was no way she would let her old friend Josie down. Over the years Tommy and Matty came to love Sadie in return. Tommy especially made sure she had the little luxuries that she perhaps could not afford herself.

When the lads left care they were placed in a flat in the high rise complex in Red Road, Springburn. Tommy kept their heads above water by wheeling and dealing from the back of an old Ford Transit van. He would buy and sell anything that would turn a profit. Whatever he could get his hands on. Sometimes his business dealings were less than legal but he was hardly a criminal. He was more of a Jack the lad and soon earned himself the reputation of being a decent bloke. Someone who could be trusted.

Unfortunately Matty had fallen in with a bad crowd and like so many his age became hooked on drugs. Tommy and

Sadie did what they could to help him but he was soon shoplifting to try to feed his habit. All this resulted in an ever-lengthening criminal record as a petty thief. Tommy and Sadie thought that he may have turned the corner when he met and moved in with his girlfriend Shirley. She had a young daughter Cheryl, from another relationship and had been left alone when she fell pregnant. The father disappeared never to be seen again. Bringing up Cheryl was not a problem to Matty though, as he loved the wee girl. All three of them lived in a flat in another high-rise complex in Balgrayhill Road, Springburn and for a time everything was good.

The problem with drug addiction is that once you are hooked it can be so difficult trying to shake off the habit. It was not long before Matty fell back into his old ways and if anything Shirley was even worse.

Their situation worsened, getting completely out of hand when Matty started working for the Graham family. Then the wheels really came off. To be honest it was surprising that they lasted so long before disaster struck. All along they were an accident just waiting to happen. What was to come later would affect Matty for many years.

CHAPTER THREE

The Graham clan were one of the major crime families operating in Glasgow. They were based on the North side of the city but their business interests stretched not just across the city but throughout the whole of Scotland.

The head of the family, Frank Graham Snr., was sixty-five years old and not very tall but was a stocky, evil wee man. In his younger days he had been involved with some very unsavoury characters and had a pathological hatred of authority. He had done time in prison for a couple of violent assaults and was suspected of having been involved in more than a few murders for which he was never even charged let alone stood trial. He ruled his family with an iron fist.

His wife Agnes Graham, Nan to her friends, was also in her mid sixties. A wizened wee woman with dyed jet black hair, she always had a pound of makeup caked on her face and wore bright red lipstick. Agnes looked like something from a horror movie and was a right nasty piece of work to boot. It is thought that she had been a prostitute back in the day, although she had no previous convictions and nobody dared to ask her.

Frank Snr. and Agnes lived in a ground floor council flat in a rundown building. They had raised their family in the flat but were shortly to move to a brand new development just along the road.

Despite the fact that neither of them had worked a day in their lives the flat was furnished with the very best quality furniture and they wanted for nothing. The two of them were both revered and hated in equal measure by the locals. Nobody messed with the Grahams. They were treated like royalty by their family and associates. No matter where they went they were always chauffeur driven.

Frank Graham Jnr., the eldest son, was forty-three years old and in his early years he had been involved in house-breakings and vehicle crime, under the watchful eye of his proud father. He now lived about a mile from his parents but in a different world. He owned a large stone built detached house in an exclusive estate. The property had extensive grounds. Everything was covered by alarms and CCTV. Frank had married his childhood sweetheart Sharon and they had a daughter Annette who was currently at university in America. Frank Jnr. doted on his family.

All the family were involved in the drug trade and Frank did his business from the lounge bar of a pub called The Railway Inn. Unsurprisingly it had taken its name from the nearby railway depot. His close associate and minder, Cammy Wilson was never far away. He and Frank had been pals for years going all the way back to school. Cammy had gone on to become a promising heavyweight boxer until a road accident ended his career. He was devoted to Frank for looking after him and would do anything for him. He was very good at his job and kept Frank Jnr. safe, was very handy with his fists and not afraid to use a gun if required to do so.

Frank's wife, Sharon ran her own business, a hairdressers and beauty salon in the nearby Willow Shopping Centre. It was quite simply called 'Sharon's' and on the face of it seemed totally legitimate.

Jamie Graham had just turned forty and revelled in the nickname 'The Man.' He lived just on the outskirts of Glasgow but still near enough to his parents and the hub of their business. He lived with his wife Michelle on a fancy housing estate. They had no kids.

The house was situated at the end of a cul de sac looking back along the whole length of the street. Not that Jamie was paranoid, he just liked to see who was coming. He was very security conscious so his property too was well alarmed and covered by state of the art CCTV cameras. Michelle ran a florist called 'Flower Power' also in the Willow Shopping Centre.

When he was younger Jamie like his elder brother was involved in all aspects of the family business, theft, stolen cars, housebreaking. Somehow though Jamie was a bit different, with other ideas for expanding their criminal activities. Early on, he disappeared south of the border to Liverpool, Manchester and London. From then on the Graham family became heavily involved in the drugs trade. Jamie ran the show and they were now one of the main suppliers in Glasgow and beyond.

He was also like his father in one regard, he was not averse to a little violence and it was rumoured that he was available, at the right price, for the odd maiming or even murder. It was common knowledge that he always carried a gun and wore a Kevlar bullet proof vest when out in public.

Although he had his own driver, in all his business dealings, his two main henchmen for all the violence were his younger brothers, Billy and Bobby Graham. They were thirty-five years old. Both had a cocaine habit and loved a bit of aggravation. They lived the life, plenty of money, flash cars and a beautiful river side apartment in the centre of Glasgow.

They were supposed to be identical twins and indeed had been until an incident in a night club ten years earlier. Both had huge egos and thought they were untouchable because of the family.

It had been Billy who, one Friday night whilst he had been drunk as usual, tried to grab a woman in the Carousel club in the city centre and had said the wrong thing to the young lady. Her boyfriend had taken offence and during the resulting fight Billy had accidentally sustained a freak injury to his face which left him needing over one hundred stitches. He would never be a pretty boy again.

His mother was apoplectic, someone had scarred her wee boy and must pay. Frank Snr. thought this was the ideal opportunity to send a message and at the same time show off his skills.

The identity of the person who had been fighting with Billy was quickly established. Frank Snr. had urgent enquiries made to learn his whereabouts. It was not too difficult given the vast criminal network the family ran. That very same evening the man was abducted at gunpoint by a couple of the Graham's associates.

Needless to say the man was delivered into the hands of Frank Graham Snr. What happened next is just rumour and speculation. It is alleged that Frank used a razor to skin the man alive before eventually killing him. Whatever happened, the man was never seen again.

The message went out loud and clear. Do not mess with the Graham family or you will suffer the consequences.

The only sister in the Graham clan was Margaret. She was thirty-eight years old but looked much younger. Margaret was an absolute stunner and where she got her looks from was anyone's guess given her parents.

The smart money was on her being adopted. No doubt about it. At 5' 10", slim with long auburn hair she could stop traffic. Margaret had however inherited some of her parents traits, she swore like a trooper and hated the police. She lived in the house right next door to her brother Jamie with her boyfriend Craig Strachan. They also had no children.

She ran the public house right across the road from the Willow Shopping Centre. The pub was aptly named 'The Crooked Man'. There was absolutely no chance of it being run legitimately nor the taxi company, 'Willow Cabs', which Craig ran at the rear of the centre. Both businesses were purely used by the family to launder money from their extensive drug empire. This meant that nearly all the family ran businesses very close to one another.

Craig Strachan was well matched to Margaret in that he was a tall, good looking guy. He could probably have been a male model. As it was, in his youth he had been a car thief and spent time in a young offenders institute. He thought because of his association with the Graham family that he was a gangster but he lacked one thing. He had no bottle.

Also he liked booze a little too much, as well as the odd line of cocaine. Perhaps one day that would become a problem and get him in trouble.

CHAPTER FOUR

I t was early morning on 27 September 2001. The following day was the start of the September weekend holiday. The weather forecast was predictable, sunny patches with scattered showers.

Detective Chief Inspector Sandy Morton sat at his desk within Stewart Street Police Office in Glasgow. Nursing a mug of coffee, he was taking a final look at an operational report. It's author Detective Sergeant Moira Clarkson sat opposite her 'gaffer' awaiting his comments.

As the new Millennium had approached the ongoing problem with drug dealing and drug abuse had reached epidemic proportions. Nowhere was this more prevalent than in the West of Scotland. The Chief Constable of Strathclyde Police had declared war on the drug barons and their associates.

In response to this call to arms Detective Superintendent Malcolm Sinclair had charged Sandy Morton with putting together a team to combat the problem in the city centre of Glasgow. The DCI had chosen well, so well in fact that after only two years, he had just lost his Detective Inspector who had been promoted to a post in Ayrshire.

DS Moira Clarkson would be the lead on the team's next, most important raid. Moira was a forty year old, single woman who had been recruited from the drug squad. Her experience was essential in developing the rest of the team. Sandy worried how long he could hold on to her before she too was promoted.

Detective Constable Kenny Brown had been appointed from the ranks of 'A' Division CID, as he knew the area like the back of his hand. All his nine years service had been spent patrolling the city centre. The twenty eight year old was already on a high having recently discovered that his wife was expecting their first child in the new year.

DCs Paul Corrigan and Gerry Lynch came as a box set. They had joined the job on the same day twelve years before and had worked in 'D' Division, Springburn. Sandy Morton had been their shift inspector. Both had been handpicked for the team. Not only did they have knowledge of the Graham family and their associates, they also each held a black belt in Taekwondo and were certainly more than able to handle any aggravation that came their way. Paul was married with a young son. Gerry had a long time girlfriend Audrey Jennings who also happened to be a DC working at 'A' Division. Their relationship was a source of much humour in the office as their colleagues all agreed that they should have married long ago.

David O'Neill and Rona McLean were both uniformed officers seconded into the group. David was only nineteen years old and baby faced. Rona was actually twenty-five and a university graduate but looked much younger. They had been invaluable to the team being able to get much closer to people and premises before raids, due to their youthful appearance.

All of the team were well aware of the Graham family. They were one of the main players when it came to dealing drugs in the city centre. For over two years, The Central or 'A' Division, Plain Clothes Crime Unit, to give them their full title, had policed the area with much success. Making inroads into the Graham's business and causing untold disruption.

It was no surprise that their Detective Inspector had been promoted. Now after the receipt of intelligence from a reliable registered informant, things were beginning to look up. The next raid would hopefully hit right to the heart of the Grahams and seriously affect them. Sandy Morton closed the folder and stood.

"That's good work Moira," he said, "really good. Let's go brief the troops and get this show on the road."

DS Clarkson followed the gaffer along the corridor to the conference room. Sandy Morton walked straight over to the dais and prepared to address those assembled. Moira Clarkson stood at the doorway to prevent anyone not involved entering the briefing. Everyone was present and the team were joined by two uniformed (Armed Firearms Officers) or AFOs.

DCI Morton outlined the target and the premises. "At exactly 11.00am today we will attend the Railway Inn in Springburn and gain entry to the lounge bar. Hopefully there should only be one occupant, Frank Graham Jnr., as his minder Cammy Wilson will be otherwise engaged at Glasgow District Court answering a few parking and speeding tickets. I do not envisage any problems gaining entry to the premises as it should be open for business. If necessary DC Corrigan, being the fittest amongst you, will be in possession of the metal battering ram to force the door. As you will have observed we are joined by two uniform officers who are both AFOs. They are there purely for your safety should Graham be armed as his minder is missing. David O'Neill is already taking up a position to observe the target premises. Rona McLean is on Cammy Wilson and will give us regular updates on his situation.

"First thing is detaining the suspect. We will then carry out a thorough search of the premises. Our source has intimated that there should be a large stash of drugs and cash hidden in a safe situated in the wall of the toilet, just to the side of the cistern. We will go through the motions before being really surprised at coming across the stash.

"Apparently so confident is he at not being turned over, Mr Graham does not lock the safe whilst he is on the premises. Let's go and make his day. We will rendezvous at Springburn Police Office at 10.30am and await my signal to go. That is all, unless there are any questions?"

There were none.

DS Clarkson took her team to their office to pick up all the gear they required and stow it in the vehicles they were to use. An unmarked Ford Escort and an old Comer van. The two uniformed AFOs left in their marked police car. They were all heading off to pick up some breakfast before the 'turn' and would be at Springburn Police Office in plenty of time.

At 10.30am DCI Morton gathered his team together again in Springburn Office.

"Right folks, I have an update from Rona McLean. A very angry Cammy Wilson is going to trial pleading not guilty to all these alleged traffic offences. Once he does go to trial the Procurator Fiscal will desert the case due to some technical error. By then you will hopefully have completed your business.

"Latest from David O'Neill is that the landlord is on the premises at the Railway Inn but he is under strict instructions never to enter the lounge, no matter what is going on. Our target is still at home but expected to be on the move shortly. As you all know he only lives about ten minutes away from the pub."

The team checked all their equipment yet again. A couple visited the toilet. Adrenaline was beginning to kick in. If this job came off it would be a big deal. It didn't matter how many times they went on jobs like this, it affected people in different ways. Some took it in their stride, others got excited. Nobody wanted to get excited today just in case firearms were involved. The hope was for a simple in and out with a positive result.

DCI Morton came back into the room.

"Okay team, our target is on the move. Get set and await my signal."

They all went out into the back yard and boarded their respective vehicles. Just a short time later the DCI's voice came over the radio.

"Target on site, you have a go, repeat you have a go."

The three vehicles emerged from the back of the police office. It was only a matter of a few hundred yards to the Railway Inn. Somehow it seemed quieter than usual. Traffic was light and there were very few people walking about. The pub sat in front of an old railway yard which was now disused. There were plans to redevelop the area but at present the building stood alone. The door leading to the lounge bar was down a cobbled street at the side of the building. The only sign of life was Frank Graham's top of the range Mercedes Benz parked at the door to the lounge. It looked completely out of place. Quickly and efficiently the officers alighted their vehicles. Gerry Lynch tried the lounge door, it was unlocked. Entry was gained with no problem at all. The look on Frank Jnr.'s face was a picture. He was shocked into silence. A quick search found he was unarmed and there was no other person on the premises. Even the landlord had gone to the cash and carry.

DS Clarkson read over to him the contents of the search warrant. He still had not spoken. They then began to search the premises. It was a good day. The source had been spot on. Gerry Lynch and Paul Corrigan recovered one and a half kilos of cocaine and almost £20,000 in cash from the safe in the toilet which had indeed been unlocked.

The team were in and out long before a raging Cammy Wilson climbed into his car outside

Glasgow District Court to head back out to Springburn. It was not until he got back to the Railway Inn that he learned what had happened.

"Bastards!" was all he could say. He knew that he and Frank had been set up.

As he had been arrested in another Division, DS Clarkson and her team took Frank Graham to Baird Street Police Office. He was cautioned and charged with offences under the Misuse of Drugs Act and detained overnight to appear at court the next morning. That was the easy part taken care of, now came the writing up of the case and proving it in court.

Later Sandy Morton recalled saying it all seemed too easy.

As he sat in a cell Frank was fuming. The last thing he needed was to go to prison. Unfortunately, that is exactly what was going to be happening to him. He had been caught in the possession of and concerned in the supply of a large quantity of controlled drugs. He knew he would only serve half the sentence he received if found guilty but given the value of the drugs he had been found with he was expecting a hefty one. That is unless his QC, Maurice Henshaw, could manage to pull a rabbit out of the hat.

Frank Jnr. was angry. What was the point of having a bent copper on the books if he couldn't even give them the heads up when a drug search was about to go down. As far as he was concerned he had been suckered and set up by the polis. Yes, he was very angry but much worse, he was embarrassed. What had occurred was a massive loss of face and made the family look stupid. At least he'd have the pleasure of knowing that some of those who put him in prison would be punished. The family would see to that. In the meantime someone had better get Henshaw over from Edinburgh. Frank knew the score, he was unlikely to say anything but it was always better to have a Queen's Counsel in your corner, especially one who owed the family big time.

CHAPTER FIVE

Maurice Henshaw was one of the best known solicitors in Scotland, a pillar of society. He was a man who seemed to have everything. His father, the 4th Lord Dunbeth, had for many years been a very successful wine merchant in Edinburgh. Maurice had a mother who doted on her only child. It was fair to say he grew up to be a spoiled brat. The family lived between an estate in East Perthshire called Balmuir and a large town house in Edinburgh.

When Maurice was eight years old his father insisted that the boy be sent to boarding school in an attempt to instil some discipline into him. His mother eventually agreed but only if he were sent to Woodcroft House a private school for boys which was virtually next door to the Dunbeth estate. She just could not bear to be too far away from her 'darling boy'. So in 1948, Maurice Henshaw enrolled at Woodcroft House. There was no doubt he was good looking and tall for his age, with sandy blonde hair and piercing blue eyes, but there was something disturbing about the boy.

From the outset he gathered around him a small gang of which he had to be the leader. At first they committed minor indiscretions, such as stealing sweets from the tuck shop. Then they moved on to bullying and assaulting fellow pupils. As the group got older their conduct worsened and they found alcohol and girls. They were responsible for committing many sordid acts against young women from the nearby village.

On many occasions Maurice's father had to interject personally to make problems go away. Sometimes he had to part with large amounts of cash before the complaints were withdrawn. By the time Maurice left the school at eighteen it was safe to say that the staff at Woodcroft House, as well as the local community, must have been delighted to see the back of him and his cronies.

Despite everything Maurice Henshaw had a brilliant mind and was accepted at Glasgow University to study law. Whilst living in Glasgow he stayed in a house owned by his family in Buckingham Terrace just off Great Western Road and quite near to the university itself. During the five years in Glasgow the house saw many a raucous party at which Maurice became infamous for his treatment of the women who attended.

On gaining his degree he took up practice in Edinburgh and had a meteoric rise to fame. He was known for his great oratory. In just a few years he was appointed as a Queen's Counsel, at that time the youngest in the country.

In 1978 upon the death of his father he became the 5th Lord Dunbeth. Maurice had been living in Edinburgh but moved back to Balmuir to be with his mother until she passed away the following year. Later in that same year, Maurice married Vivien Grainger, the daughter of a multi-millionaire businessman from Edinburgh who owned numerous department stores dotted about the country. Vivien was much younger than Maurice and was pregnant when they married.

They eventually had two sons William and James, like their father both were now former pupils of Woodcroft House. The boys were the spitting image of Maurice with their sandy blonde hair and piercing blue eyes.

When the Scottish Parliamentary elections took place in 1999 Maurice stood for election in East Perthshire as a Conservative candidate. He was duly elected to Holyrood and not surprisingly became his party's spokesperson on law and order. A clever man, he was a brilliant solicitor and politician.

There was just one major problem with Maurice Henshaw that would not go away, women. He loved, no he craved, the feeling of abusing them, both physically and mentally. He got a buzz from it. He cared not who they were, some poor creature dragged off the street or a lady from society. It made no difference to him as long as he sated his perverse appetite. And what an appetite it was. From the start of his sexual perversion Henshaw had always used drugs to subdue his victims. Somehow taking great delight in being in control. All these women had been treated appallingly. As he had gotten older he had needed some sort of stimulus to aid his debauchery. This was how he had come to be involved with a criminal gang in Glasgow called the Graham family and a certain police officer.

For many years they had worked closely together and on occasions when they required

representation at court Lord Dunbeth QC was there to help. In exchange Henshaw received not only date rape drugs from the Grahams but also any amount of top grade cocaine on request and an endless supply of female company. Nothing was too much trouble for his Lordship.

CHAPTER SIX

Six years after Mary Buchanan had returned home to Scotland her eldest daughter, Aimi had left school and enrolled at university in Johannesburg to study medicine. She was an excellent student and it was no surprise when she gained her degree and became a doctor.

Occasionally through the years studying at university Aimi had managed to con money from her father and used it to visit her mother. Each time she visited for only a few days which was never long enough. Once Aimi became a doctor it was more difficult, as she felt a certain responsibility towards her patients and seemed to rush back to tend to them in South Africa. When she did visit Aimi got on well with her younger sister and Isla loved her.

As the years passed Isla also grew to be a very attractive young woman. She studied hard at school encouraged all the way by her mother and uncle, Mary had initially taken a number of small jobs, to make sure Isla got everything she needed and to get her own life back on an even keel.

Through nothing more than hard work Mary managed to save some money and taken out a mortgage on a small flat, also in Leith. This property needed a complete makeover and Mary set about the task with gusto. Six months later she sold the small house Archie had bought her for a tidy profit. She was able to repay her brother and had a little nest egg left.

Mary and Isla moved into the small flat. It was to be the first of many moves as Mary bought cheaply, mainly rundown properties, renovated them and moved on, each time selling them for a profit. By the time Isla was due to leave school Mary was a very successful property developer and they were now living in a very nice spacious house in Edinburgh.

Mary and Archie expected that when the time came Isla would go to university, probably to study medicine like her big sister or perhaps law. The thing was, Isla really had no interest in university. Her passion was politics and she wanted to begin right away at the bottom of the ladder and learn everything from the grass roots up.

Despite leaving school with a barrowful of 'O' and 'A' grade certificates she would not change her mind. Not even Aimi, whom she looked up to, could influence her decision. Her mother and Archie were disappointed and not too pleased. Even more so when she told them for whom she was going to be working.

Isla had applied for a job at the office of one of Scotland's most flamboyant new politicians in Edinburgh. Maurice Henshaw QC was one of Scotland's most famous legal minds and now a member of the Scottish Parliament. Isla was to be a political assistant to the man himself. Mary hid her disappointment, just happy that Isla was doing something that she wanted to do. Uncle Archie was less pleased but would not say why.

***

As the world welcomed in 2001, Mary and Isla found themselves waiting at the arrivals gate at Edinburgh airport. At Christmas, Mary had received a card from Aimi which had given her the nicest surprise of her life. Aimi had written a short note to tell her mother she was coming back to Scotland to work. It was late on Friday night when Aimi arrived from South Africa via Heathrow. It had been a long journey and she was shattered.

Mary let her daughter sleep most of Saturday. When she finally awakened Aimi was starving. The three of them went out for dinner and Aimi explained all about her new job. Isla was so happy to see her big sister again and thought she was looking really well. She had a fantastic tan which looked even better with her having blonde hair. Mary was slightly emotional having her two girls together for what was really the first time. Over dinner Ami explained that she had been offered and had accepted a contract working with Strathclyde police in Glasgow.

"It all sounds very grand," she said. "My title is Deputy Chief Medical Officer and I will be based at their offices at the Occupational Health and Welfare Centre in the grounds of Glasgow Caledonian University." She went on to tell her mother and sister that her contract started at the beginning of April. Her remit was to see to the health and welfare of almost eight thousand police officers and civilian employees, throughout the whole region of Strathclyde.

The staff offered all sorts of treatments and therapies to officers and civilian staff suffering from a variety of complaints from stress to injuries received whilst on duty.

Also part of Aimi's job description was to carry out all the post mortem examinations in relation to sudden or suspicious deaths reported to the Procurator Fiscal in Glasgow.

This was one of the main reasons she had been appointed, as she had the reputation of being a top pathologist.

For the next couple of weeks the three women enjoyed each other's company, eating out, shopping and just getting to know one another again. All too soon it was over and Aimi travelled through to Glasgow by train staying overnight in city centre hotel.

The next day she had an appointment at 10.30am to meet an agent to view houses and flats. The two women met on time and Aimi was shown several different properties in the city centre, all of which were very nice. After some deliberation she decided on a modern, fully furnished two bedroom apartment on the second floor of a building overlooking the River Clyde. Apart from the great view it was only a short drive to her new office and less than a five minute walk to the City Mortuary. She paid six month's rent in advance and moved in straight away. The rest of her possessions would follow shortly. All she needed now was a car.

Having moved into her apartment Aimi wasted no time in having her mother and Isla over from Edinburgh to see what they thought of her new home. They both loved it. The view was stunning and the shopping in Glasgow was great as well. They both made plans to return again as soon as possible. As it turned out Isla would be back sooner than she thought.

CHAPTER SEVEN

sla had now been working at Lord Dunbeth's Office in Edinburgh for a while and she loved the work. She had learned so much and indeed had not ruled out the possibility of one day standing for parliament herself.

The one thing Isla did not care for was Lord Dunbeth himself. She didn't know exactly what it was about him but she did not trust him. There were lots of rumours in the office regarding inappropriate behaviour and of people who complained tending to be sacked rather than their complaint being looked into. Nothing of that nature had ever happened to Isla but she was still wary of him.

Having been elected to the first Scottish Parliament in 1999, Henshaw had built up a good reputation and was well liked by those he represented. The next election was still a couple of years away but already his office was gearing up to fight for him to keep his seat. Isla had been a team leader for a group who had in recent weeks been out and about on the streets of East Perthshire canvassing opinion. No stone would be left unturned in an effort to get Lord Dunbeth re-elected.

During the last week in April, Graham Smythe, Lord Dunbeth's secretary, invited Isla to attend the recording of a television show which was due to be filmed at the Scottish Television Studio in Glasgow on Friday 27th April. It was to be aired on the evening of the following Sunday.

"I realise that this is a weekend," Smythe told her," but Lord Dunbeth believes it will enable you to see another side of the political spectrum and he wants to reward you for all your hard work".

Had she been going with just Lord Dunbeth she would have declined, but Graham Smythe told her that he was also attending and that if she wished she could stay with her sister over the holiday weekend. Isla was happy to accept the offer and telephoned Aimi to let her know she was coming.

On the Friday afternoon Lord Dunbeth's chauffeur duly arrived at the office in Edinburgh about 4pm and uplifted his passengers. He was driving a dark blue Mercedes Benz saloon, Reg. No. LD2, one of Dunbeth's private number plates. En route to Glasgow Lord Dunbeth and Graham were deep in conversation discussing the forthcoming programme. Isla did not think either of them was aware of her being in the car.

They arrived at the studio just before 5pm. Lord Dunbeth went straight into make up with the others participating in the programme. Isla and Graham were introduced to the show's presenter Jim Delaney, who gave them a quick tour of the studio before he too was also called to make up.

An hour later the audience began taking their seats. Lord Dunbeth emerged from the makeup room sharing a joke with the person who was representing the Labour party and seemed to be in good spirits. But when the lights dimmed and the cameras began rolling the gloves came off. No more laughing and joking.

A lively debate took place at which, as usual, each different party engaged in slagging the others. In the end who came out on top depended on which party people supported. All Isla knew was that she had thoroughly enjoyed it.

After the show the chauffeur was waiting and as they got into the vehicle Lord Dunbeth mentioned that he had forgotten to say to Smythe that he needed to be back in Edinburgh early the next morning. Even although it was a holiday weekend he had an urgent briefing to attend as he was due to appear for the defence at a murder trial at the High Court.

Isla was disappointed that she would have to stay at the hotel and not with Aimi. She phoned her sister to let her know that her plans had changed and Aimi suggested that they have dinner together. She knew a lovely Italian restaurant quite close to the hotel at which Isla was staying. Aimi said she would grab a taxi and meet her there in thirty minutes. That was ideal for Isla.

It was 9pm when they reached the hotel. Graham arranged a room for Isla and had her small suitcase taken there. He then joined Lord Dunbeth for dinner. Isla walked along the street to meet Aimi. It had been a long day and she had not eaten for some time.

During dinner Isla was excited to tell Aimi all about her time at the television studio and how she had really enjoyed the experience. They only had a couple of glasses of wine each with the meal. It was soon time for Isla to leave as they were all to be up early the following morning. She promised to telephone Aimi as soon as she got back to Edinburgh. Isla waved goodbye to Aimi's taxi and started walking back towards the hotel. It had been lovely to see her big sister again and spend quality time together.

What Isla was unaware of was that she was being watched.

When she reached the hotel Isla went to the bar and ordered herself a coffee. She sat quietly for five minutes, finished her drink and headed for the lift. That was the last thing Isla Buchanan remembered.

When Isla awakened she had no idea where she was or what had happened to her. All she knew was that she was not in her hotel room but in a back street alley somewhere. It was daylight but everything was quiet so it must be early in the morning. She was naked and in agony, her whole body ached.

Somehow Isla managed to get to her feet and with great difficulty staggered towards a doorway which looked like the entry to flats. There was a small window at the side of the door. She saw herself and could not believe what peered back at her. She looked like someone who had been involved in a car crash.

Her right eye was swollen and closed, her body was a mass of cuts and bruises and she was bleeding heavily from some severe wounds. The magnitude of the situation suddenly hit her.... she had been brutally raped.... Isla screamed, then fainted. When she regained consciousness she was in hospital with a police officer seated at her bedside. Not that Isla would have known where she was.

It appeared that Isla had suffered a mental breakdown, brought on by the trauma of what had happened to her. She was unable to speak. The only way they had been able to identify her was from her handbag which was found by the police discarded in the alleyway, together with her clothing, which was in shreds.

Her mother had been contacted and was on her way from Edinburgh. When Mary had taken the phone call from the police she had nearly fainted herself. She had thought Isla was staying with Aimi. Mary had managed to compose herself long enough to phone Archie and Aimi to let them know what had happened. When Mary and Archie arrived at the hospital Aimi had been there for some time and was able to update them on Isla's condition.

The police investigation had been handed to Detective Constable William Robertson.

Unfortunately, Isla had to undergo the usual intrusive but necessary full examination. Blood was taken from her, all her injuries catalogued and treated, swabs were taken and she was given a 'morning after' pill to prevent pregnancy. Isla was oblivious to all this. The tests subsequently failed to reveal any trace of a so called date rape drug.

Aimi went and spoke to the doctor in charge of Isla's case and then returned to her mum

and uncle. "Listen," she said, "there is nothing more we can do here tonight, Mum. I'm sorry to say this but you look awful so I suggest the two of you come back to my place for the night. We can get a night's sleep and see what's to be done tomorrow."

Aimi had taken charge and both Mary and Archie were glad of her being there. They followed her out of the hospital without complaint, back to her river side apartment. On arriving at her flat Aimi showed them where they would be sleeping and after a nightcap they retired for the night. She had noticed that her mother looked really tired and so had slipped a sedative in her drink to ensure she slept.

Aimi sat in the living room for some time looking out over the River Clyde trying to make sense of what had occurred. How could this have happened to Isla? There were so many questions and no answers. As she sat watching lights dancing across the water Aimi came to a decision. Her mother and sister would have to stay with her until Isla was well enough to return to Edinburgh. How long that would be for, no one knew - just as long as it took.

CHAPTER EIGHT

The next morning Archie Buchanan was up early. He had slept soundly which was not surprising given all the worry and the drive down to Glasgow from Perthshire. He was amazed to find Aimi already up and dressed.

"Uncle Archie," she said, "I was just going to leave you a note. I've just checked my messages and I'm afraid I have an urgent post mortem to do this morning. Once it's finished I'll give my boss Dr McKay a phone to see if he can arrange cover and I'll be back as soon as possible. Could you stay here until Mum wakes up? I don't like leaving her on her own and I didn't want to disturb her as she looked awful last night. She seemed twenty years older".

"Of course," Archie replied. "I don't have to rush back, I will wait and if we are not here when you get home we will be at the hospital."

"Thanks Uncle Archie," Aimi said kissing him on the cheek before grabbing her bag and rushing out of the door.

Aimi performed the post mortem examination and telephoned her boss to explain the situation regarding Isla. He fully understood her predicament and told her to take some time off. As she had only been in the job a few weeks Aimi thanked him but declined his kind offer. She would manage. She got home again around noon. As she walked through the front door her mother was just stirring and Archie was making coffee. Once Mary had come around and eaten breakfast she showered and dressed. Then they all went back to the hospital to see Isla. When they arrived Aimi excused herself and went to speak with the doctor. Archie and Mary sat by Isla's bed. She was asleep.

"It will be all right now, Mary," Archie said. "Aimi will take care of Isla and if anyone can make her better she can."

"I do hope you're right, Archie," Mary replied looking at her youngest daughter lying on the bed like a broken doll.

It was thirty minutes later before Aimi returned.

"Right everything is arranged," she said in as cheerful a voice as she could muster.

"As you both know Isla has been raped and seriously assaulted. Some of her injuries are quite nasty and will no doubt take time to heal, but heal they will. My concern is her mental state. There is no knowing how long it will take or indeed if she will ever snap out of the state of mind she is in at present. Hopefully with love and care we shall get our Isla back again."

Aimi went on to explain that she intended to take her mother and Isla to live with her in the apartment for as long as it takes. She would not listen to any arguments from her mother but to be fair, Mary was in no real state to argue. The whole experience had wearied her.

"You need care as well before you kill yourself," Aimi scolded her. "We will each have our own bedroom and I will get a hospital bed and put Isla near the big window in the lounge overlooking the River Clyde. I will get a private nursing agency first thing tomorrow and arrange 24/7 care. Once the doctors say Isla is fit enough to be moved we will have her home." Mary felt as though a great weight had lifted off her shoulder and burst into tears. She was so proud of Aimi, she had turned out to be a wonderful daughter. The three of them went back to the apartment, and after a bite to eat Archie left to drive back to Perthshire. Aimi promised to keep him updated.

That night as they sat quietly, Mary said, "Aimi, I think I should sell my house in Edinburgh to help pay for all this treatment Isla will require."

"No you will not," Aimi replied. "I don't mind you staying with me until Isla is better and then you can go back home. You never know I might get a boyfriend," she joked. "Seriously, Mum, I sold my apartment in Johannesburg for a small fortune and made a packet on it. There is no need to worry about cash. Let's just concentrate on getting Isla better."

Just a week later the bed and nurses were in place and the hospital allowed Isla home to her mother and sister. She was still not speaking.

As far as finding the culprit for the attack on Isla, things were moving along slowly. Lord Dunbeth and Graham Smythe had been interviewed and their statements were almost identical. They outlined their trip from Edinburgh to Glasgow and the televised political debate. Thereafter they had dined together while Isla Buchanan had gone to meet her sister. As Lord Dunbeth had an urgent meeting in Edinburgh the next morning they had retired early around 10.30pm. They had not seen Isla again.

Graham added that Isla was supposed to have been going to stay somewhere in Glasgow with her sister but due to

Lord Dunbeth's change in itinerary he had booked her a room at the hotel. He assumed she would have been in it. When the hotel staff checked her room her small suitcase was there but there was no trace of Isla and the room appeared unused.

Lord Dunbeth had been forced to leave for Edinburgh but Smythe had remained in an effort to trace Isla. When she had not appeared by lunchtime he reported her as a missing person to the police. It was they who were able to inform him of the attack on Isla. He had visited the hospital and spoken to Isla's relatives before returning by train to Edinburgh.

What Graham Smythe did not know was that the previous evening after dinner, Lord Dunbeth had gone to his room and used his mobile phone to contact Billy and Bobby Graham. He had wanted some cocaine and if possible someone to 'play' with.

About an hour later the twins had arrived with his cocaine and also literally carrying a young woman between them. She was obviously in a drugged state. At first Dunbeth did not recognise Isla. It was only when the twins threw her on the bed that he did. At first he was, to say the least, not very pleased and asked whereabouts they had picked her up. Not wishing to have Dunbeth think they were a pair of lazy bastards, who had drugged her coffee in the downstairs bar, Billy said they had picked her up along the road from the hotel. Dunbeth seemed happy enough with his answer and confessed to the brothers that he had fancied Isla for some time. He asked them to return in an hour. Billy and Bobby went downstairs to the bar.

Sixty minutes later they returned to Lord Dunbeth's room and removed Isla. They took her down in the staff lift and secreted her out of the hotel's back door. It was their plan to dump her in an alleyway about half a mile away. Both could see that the woman was in quite a bad way physically already but that wasn't new. Dunbeth always seemed to leave his women in this state. She had been beaten and raped.

That did not stop the twins also having their fun with her, taking it in turns before throwing her naked body and her possessions into the alley. They had no idea who she was and could not care less whether she lived or died. No way was anyone going to link her to them anyway.

CHAPTER NINE

The weeks slipped by slowly and gradually Isla improved physically under the care of the dedicated nurses. There was no doubt that the care and treatment was expensive but it would hopefully all be worth it in the end. Unfortunately Isla was still unable to speak. Aimi was delighted with the improvement but somewhat frustrated at the lack of progress in the police investigation.

Aimi was not enamoured with the officer in charge of the case, Detective Constable Robertson. She felt he was just lazy and downright rude. His colleague Audrey Jennings had been appointed as a liaison with the family. This had pleased Aimi no end, as in the short time she had been in her job, Audrey had become a friend. They were about the same age and enjoyed the same things.

They had first met in the mortuary, of all places, when Audrey was looking into a suspicious death. Knowing Aimi was just back in Scotland after several years abroad she had invited her out for a glass of wine. The friendship flourished from then on. Aimi had even met Audrey's boyfriend Gerry Lynch who was also a Detective Constable. They all got on really well and Gerry had joked about getting her a boyfriend, if he could find anyone as good as himself. It was now more or less a given that the girls would go out for a drink or a meal regularly. Sometimes Gerry would sit with Isla so that the girls could also take Mary for a break.

At first Mary had hung around the flat all day when Isla was first brought home from the hospital. She soon realised that all she did was just getting in the way. Eventually she took to going out for a walk or into town for lunch and really looked forward to her nights out with Aimi and Audrey.

Later in the year Gerry was not around so much. Audrey told her friend the truth, that he was working.

"His squad have been really busy lately but hopefully all the hard work will soon come to fruition."

She was right, as near the end of September, Gerry and his colleagues arrested Frank Graham Jnr. for possession of a large amount of controlled drugs. The value of which was so high he would be appearing at the High Court in Glasgow on trial.

The autumn months were fairly quiet and people were gearing up for Christmas. After work one night Aimi went into the city centre to do a little shopping, when she got home she found her mother crying.

"What's wrong, Mum?" she asked,

"Nothing darling," Mary replied, "just the opposite. I'm crying because I'm happy. Just the best thing happened today. Isla spoke."

Aimi rushed to give her mum a hug and then went over to Isla's bed. She was asleep. A break through at last, she thought.

"That's great news Mum. What did she say?" she asked.

Mary was choked up and hugged Aimi as she managed to say,

"Just one word - Mum."

Both women burst into tears and held each other. It was the best Christmas present ever. That Christmas Uncle Archie came down for the holidays. The family had a wonderful time together. Isla had managed to speak a bit more and was improving daily.

Audrey Jennings spent quite some time trying to get her to remember what had happened to her. But she was unable to help the police with their enquiries. Despite her best efforts, she could not remember anything about the night she was attacked that would help. Isla had recalled having dinner with her sister and Aimi leaving the restaurant in a taxi, but nothing more. Whatever had happened her mind had simply blanked out the whole horrific experience as though it had never occurred in the first place.

CHAPTER TEN

The trial of Frank Graham Jnr. started early in December 2001. Despite Maurice Henshaw QC leading his defence team and also an aborted attempt to bribe members of the jury, things did not go well.

Henshaw was his usual self in court, making attempts to belittle the evidence presented on behalf of the Crown. He even made a pitiful attempt to claim that Frank was merely a customer in the premises out for a quiet drink, when he was set upon by a band of ruffians, who turned out to be plain clothes police officers. That was all well and good but the defence had no explanation as to why Frank's fingerprints were all over the drugs and money recovered from the hidden safe in the toilet. The jury agreed and in no time at all found Frank Graham guilty as charged. He was remanded in custody over the Christmas period and was due to be sentenced early in January. That day had come.

What a way to start 2002.

As darkness fell there was a hint of snow in the air and it would fall later that night. Sandy Morton's team couldn't care less. Today they had just had one of their best results ever. Over the years they had gnawed away at drug dealing and more especially disrupting the business dealings of the Graham family. Morton had described this mob, on more than one occasion, as a gang of toe rags. Today at his sentencing hearing, Frank Graham had been sent to prison for ten years, having been found guilty of being concerned in the sale and supply of controlled drugs.

This was a cause for celebration, hence the crime unit and their boss, DCI Sandy Morton, were in one of their favourite watering holes celebrating big time. Not to miss any of the fun and probably in an attempt to feel like a real policeman just one last time, Detective Superintendent Malcolm Sinclair had tagged along to bask in the glory. He was on the wind down to retirement and known to enjoy the odd half of whisky or two. He did not have the nickname 'Malky the Alky' for nothing.

Also present were Kenny Brown, Gerry Lynch, Paul Corrigan and Moira Clarkson. Last but by no means least was David O'Neill. He looked somewhat out of place being several years younger than the rest and was one of the babies of the group along with his colleague Rona McLean. Speaking of babies, Kenny only had a couple of orange juices before excusing himself from the celebration to visit his wife in hospital. She was due to give birth to their first child any day. Rona McLean was also missing from the night as she was in the middle of a course at the Scottish Police College.

Those who were left ensured that the night went really well and the drinks flowed. By the end Det. Supt. Sinclair was asleep in the corner. However, help was at hand as Audrey Jennings had been despatched from the office to make sure everyone got home in one piece.

She took Sinclair and Morton home first as they both lived close to one another in Baillieston, then dropped Paul

Corrigan at his home in Bishopbriggs, before returning to get her boyfriend Gerry Lynch. Tonight he would be staying at her flat in the West End.

DS Clarkson did not drink and so simply drove herself home to Paisley.

David O'Neill walked home as he lived in a city centre flat just five minutes away from the pub. By the look of them all, Audrey reckoned that there would be more than a couple with sore heads in the morning but, to be fair, the squad had deserved their wee celebration. It had been a great result taking one of the Graham family out of the equation for some considerable time.

It was around 3am when Gerry's mobile phone rang. He was in no fit state to answer it, snoring his head off, crashed out fully dressed on Audrey's settee. He had been so drunk he hadn't even made it to bed. Sleepily, it was Audrey who answered the phone and then she was suddenly alert and wide awake. How she had managed to rouse Gerry she would never know. He was now strapped into her Vauxhall Corsa and heading for Easterhouse.

Gerry was deathly pale and it had nothing to do with drink. Despite being thirty-one years of age, Gerry still lived with his parents in Easterhouse. He had never married, partly because he and Audrey had not sorted themselves out, and partly out of loyalty to his parents. Audrey understood.

His father, Colin was disabled having been injured many years earlier, whilst working in the building trade. Gerry was only ten years old when it happened and struggled to come to terms with the situation that the family had found themselves in. His mother, Anne was an angel. She had struggled to bring him up almost single-handed and care for her husband. All this and two jobs as well.

They all lived in a semi-detached house on Lochend Road close to Easterhouse Police Office. It had all been a bit of a struggle managing until Gerry was able to earn some money and find the finances to help out. Eventually he had spent quite a lot of time and money carrying out renovations to the ground floor. They had an extension built at the back of the house. This had enlarged the kitchen and they had turned the dining room into a bedroom for his father with an en suite wet room. Most of the work was carried out by Gerry under the direction of his dad.

Now despite the snow, which was falling quite heavily, they sped along Edinburgh Road. As they did so Gerry said a silent prayer.

Immediately Audrey turned into the street and they saw the fire engines and police vehicles, Gerry knew it was bad news and that his prayer had not been answered. Where his home had stood was now just a tangled mess of burnt timber, smouldering under the gallons of water used to extinguish the blaze. Only the outer brick walls remained.

Gerry did not even try to get out of Audrey's car. There was no point. He knew what the outcome was. His parents were gone forever, killed in the inferno that had been their home for all of his life. The worst thing was, it was down to him. His black BMW was still parked outside the house. This had been no accident. It had been a deliberate attack meant for Gerry and his parents had been the victims. He was distraught.

On the orders of the senior police officer at the scene Audrey drove Gerry back to her flat. Neither of them would get any more sleep tonight. They would be at Stewart Street Police Office in just a few hours time.

At 9am the room was deathly silent. Nobody could find any words. Det. Supt. Sinclair accompanied by DCI Sandy Morton entered the main CID Office. Sinclair remained standing, while Sandy took a seat with the rest of the officers. With a tear in his eye and his voice trembling with emotion Sinclair outlined to all those present, the full extent of the horrors which had occurred in the early hours.

Colin and Anne Lynch, Gerry's parents, had lost their lives when their home had been the subject of an arson attack. It transpired that Gerry's mother could probably have escaped the blaze but had stayed to try to help her disabled husband. Their remains had been found at the back kitchen door, they had so nearly made it to safety but this was of no comfort to Gerry. He blamed himself. Those responsible had seen his car parked outside the house and wrongly assumed that he too was also inside.

Moira Clarkson had been driving herself home when her car was forced off the road, by what witnesses said was a black coloured 4x4 vehicle, which made no effort to stop at the scene. Moira's car had tumbled down an embankment. She had suffered multiple injuries and was pronounced dead on arrival at hospital.

Young David O'Neill was in the intensive care unit at Glasgow Royal Infirmary. He had received a severe beating and been stabbed four times. His condition was serious but stable. He had fortunately been found just yards from his own front door by a tramp who had been looking for shelter from the snow and raised the alarm. He could just as easily have be dead. When interviewed later, David was unable to say who had attacked him as it had happened so quickly.

All those present were now in no doubt about what had occurred and the consensus was that the Graham family were responsible. Cowardly attacks by way of revenge for one of their own having been sent down. Proving it was going to be difficult, if not nigh on impossible.

Sinclair added that he believed that Kenny Brown had escaped by leaving early to visit his wife. The only reason anyone could come up with as to why Paul Corrigan had been missed was that those responsible had probably failed to recognise him. They must have thought he was one of the gaffers when he left with them and Audrey. Paul was usually very easy to pick out as he had a shock of red hair, but had been wearing a woollen tammie and heavy coat because of the cold weather. This failure to identify him probably saved his life.

Sinclair went on, "I spoke with the Chief Constable first thing this morning."

He coughed and looked as though he was about to pass out before continuing.

"I know that you will want to get back at the Grahams, nobody more so than me but.... this is now out of my hands and comes straight from the horse's mouth at headquarters. As of now it will be someone else's problem. The Squad is disbanded with immediate effect and all officers are to be reassigned to normal CID duties."

Sandy Morton felt very sorry for Sinclair. He was finishing up shortly and this was no way to leave the job he had served for almost forty years. In his time he had been one of the very best detectives in the city. As the detective superintendent left to return to his own office, the remnants of the team just looked at one another, eventually realising there was nothing more really to say and the gathering broke up.

CHAPTER ELEVEN

That very same morning over on the north side of Glasgow, Jamie Graham took a telephone call. He replaced the receiver and smiled at those assembled. It wasn't just the Central Crime Squad that were meeting today. It was the practice of the Graham clan that they meet on a monthly basis at their parents flat to discuss family business.

Today Frank Graham Snr. had called a special meeting. The family were not happy at Frank Jnr. being imprisoned for such a lengthy period and indeed their legal team were already planning an appeal.

As Frank Snr. had said "They are getting paid enough so they better earn it. That QC Henshaw is bloody useless."

In the eventuality of things not going their way at young Frank's trial, they had put in place plans to deal with those responsible.

Jamie let the family know the result of his phone call and most seemed very happy.

But not Frank Snr.

As far as he was concerned they had only been fifty percent successful. One dead, one critical, great but more had escaped. The fact that a couple of parents had died, was neither here nor there, they were just collateral damage. Frank was more than annoyed that his eldest son was in prison, and he wanted to know what had gone wrong with attempts to tamper with the jury.

Such was the way of the Graham family, born criminals one and all.

That morning by the end of their meeting the Grahams had resolved to eliminate the rest of the targets they had missed. Frank Snr. delegated Jamie to get things sorted by any means possible. Only when the Central Crime Squad had been wiped out would he be happy.

CHAPTER TWELVE

Gerry spent the next few weeks at Audrey's. He was finding it hard to come to terms with the loss of his parents. They had visited the site of the fire to retrieve his car. The stench of acrid smoke still hung in the air. The premises had been totally destroyed. Gerry had not only lost both his parents but didn't even have any photographs or mementos of their family life together. Nothing was left. He had only the clothes he was wearing. All that remained was a pile of charred, blackened wood.

Gerry simply broke down in floods of tears, his shoulders shaking as he wept uncontrollably. Audrey had to get uniform officers from Easterhouse Police Office to drive Gerry's car back to her flat in the West End.

After visiting his own doctor as well as the police casualty surgeon he was placed on extended sick leave. It was hoped that with peace and quiet as well as a few weeks rest, Gerry might get over his anguish and return to duty as good as new. But it didn't happen. Unfortunately, no matter what anyone else said to him to the contrary, Gerry blamed himself for his parent's death and he became submerged in depression.

He had been prescribed tranquillisers by the doctors and had began drinking heavily. A recipe for disaster.

His condition and state of mind were causing problems between himself and Audrey. She found it increasingly difficult, trying to balance working full time, whilst watching the man she loved disintegrating before her eyes.

Soon he was totally out of control on the slippery slope to oblivion. Even daily visits from his best friend Paul Corrigan did not help. In his stupor Gerry would recognise Audrey and Paul but sometimes couldn't even remember their names. Aimi McLeod had called round to the flat a few times, not only in an official capacity but also as a friend. She had tried to speak to Gerry but to no avail. Her advice to Audrey was that Gerry needed to be admitted to a hospital to get specialist treatment if he was to get better. Something drastic had to be done or they would lose Gerry forever.

Paul Corrigan tried to speak to Gerry in an effort to bring him back to reality. They had been friends from the day they had both joined the police back in1991. Paul lived in Bishopbriggs with his wife Jackie and their ten year old son Scott, who worshipped Gerry. Since being a young lad himself Paul had been a Partick Thistle supporter. His dad had taken him to watch 'The Jags' and now he wanted to make sure that his son was a supporter too. He took Scott to Firhill as often as he could and, of course, Uncle Gerry had to come as well.

Paul and Gerry were so competitive in everything they did. Both liked sport and loved nothing better than challenging each other in whatever it was they took on. Working together, training together, they were inseparable. Brothers could not have been closer.

Paul reminded Gerry of how, after returning from police college in Fife they had met a new colleague on their shift, Jim Kennedy. Back in 1983 Jim had been World Champion in his weight category in Taekwondo. No mean achievement at that time. The lads had been intrigued by this sport which they had never tried before. Paul laughed when he recalled how smug he and Gerry had been with Jim, boasting about how fit they both were after being at college.

Jim explained to them that if they were serious about the sport he would set them a programme of training for them which, if they adhered to it, would mean they should obtain their black belts in about three years.

He made it sound easy, although it was anything but. Training consisted of running five miles a day. for six days a week and attending three Taekwondo instruction classes per week in the evenings at a school in Kirkintilloch. Jim was now an instructor there in his spare time. He explained to them that from a beginner to black belt first dan there were ten different grades, or kups. They would also have to compete regularly in competitions. He recommended they join a boxing club to sharpen up on fitness and punching skills and they had to go there twice a week into the bargain. Jim said if they could keep up this punishing regime then they would attain the black belt in three years. It took them almost five years. He had forgotten to mention that sometimes police work got in the way.

When Paul spoke to Gerry it did seem to cheer him up for a while, before he regressed back into his depression and his bottle of malt whisky. Audrey was almost at the end of her tether and the hardest part was still to come.

***

Somehow between them, Audrey and Paul got Gerry through his parents' funeral. It was excruciatingly hard. There were hundreds of mourners at Daldowie Crematorium, neighbours of the couple who had known them for years, as well as a large number of Gerry's colleagues from the police force. Later Gerry could not recall speaking to a single person.

The funeral of Moira Clarkson had also taken place in Paisley. Audrey stayed at home with Gerry whilst the rest of their colleagues, including Paul attended. There was no point in Gerry attending.

As for the rest of the team, Paul had started back on the normal CID shifts. He was not stupid. He and his gaffer were taking no chances. For some time Sandy Morton had an unmarked car and two armed plain clothes officers watching the Corrigan family home during the night. Paul was much more aware of all those around him and kept himself alert at all times. He never mentioned any of this to his wife Jackie or his son Scott, not wishing to alarm them.

Little did he or Sandy Morton know it at that time, but Jamie Graham was well aware of all the precautions being taken. He had an informant within the police who was passing him all the relevant information. Not only on those still in the job but also on the other members of the squad who had either been forced to leave through ill health or had decided on their own to move on to pastures new.

Kenny Brown's wife had given birth to a healthy baby girl. Mother and baby were happily back in the family home. After much soul searching and not without a little prodding from his wife, Kenny had reluctantly decided to put in his papers and resign from the force. His wife was too afraid that something might happen to him if he remained in the job and given the new arrival he felt he had no option. He would now be trying his hand at selling cars for his father-in-law. The job had lost a good officer.

David O'Neill was still in hospital making a good recovery. Unfortunately he had lost a kidney. He too would soon be out of the job on an ill health pension, much to the relief of his parents. They hoped he would now return to university to study to become a solicitor.

Rona McLean was kept on at the training centre in Kincardine on a two year secondment. She would later be promoted and move to a job in Edinburgh.

Jamie Graham had all this information. His source ensured he was kept fully updated. They were still grovelling over being unable to warn the family about the raid on Frank Jnr. What Jamie did with the information was up to him, he had to decide who to target and who was no longer a threat to his family.

CHAPTER THIRTEEN

One Sunday morning early shift, Paul Corrigan was called into Sandy Morton's office. Sandy was only in to try and catch up on a mountain of paperwork. It was supposed to be his day off.

Of all the officers at the Central working in the CID, Detective Constable William Robertson was the least well liked. Not only by all uniform officers, but also his colleagues in the CID. Usually he was required to take out all the new starts as nobody wanted to work with him. Putting it plainly, Robertson was not a very nice person. Besides being a bigot, he gave all the female officers he came across a hard time. He was prone to make some very offensive remarks. It was a mystery how he had survived in the job given his attitude.

All this aside, DC Robertson had been forced to come to the DCI that morning to tell him that he had received intelligence from a source that needed urgent attention. The indications were that there was a large quantity of drugs stashed in the home of Joseph Patterson, a known dealer, at the flats in Dundasvale Court.

Robertson informed DCI Morton that he had taken the liberty of obtaining a search warrant. He further explained that Patterson was alleged to use firearms. There were only a new detective constable, who had just started midweek and a young aide available to assist. Robertson asked if it was possible for DC Corrigan to help out as he was firearms trained and as yet the others obviously were not. Paul did not really fancy the idea but' seeing no real way of getting out of it, he reluctantly agreed. He was directed to the detective sergeants' room where Robertson was mustering and briefing his troops. As Paul entered the room Robertson handed him a Glock 9mm, handgun, holster and harness.

"I took the trouble of drawing you a weapon to save time," he said.

Paul noted that Robertson was carrying an identical weapon.

Armed with the search warrant the four officers drove to Dundasvale Court in an unmarked police car. They approached Patterson's flat which was situated on the ground floor and knocked on the door, identifying themselves as they did so. Paul and DC Robertson stood ready to draw their weapons if required.

Joseph Patterson answered the door and when they explained their business he allowed them into his flat without any problem at all. Straight away Paul felt that something was not quite right but began assisting his two younger colleagues in searching the flat from top to bottom. They found absolutely nothing. No drugs, no firearms, nothing. Either the intelligence was wrong or Patterson had been given prior warning from someone of their pending arrival and had cleaned out his flat before the police arrived. It wasn't the first time that had happened.

Paul was not very happy, something was just not right about the whole set up. DC Robertson instructed the two younger men to pack up their things and take them out to the car. Without

question they began gathering up all the clipboards, evidence bags, production labels and the like and headed out to the vehicle. Just as the two young officers reached the car they heard the sound of three shots being fired from within Joseph Patterson's flat. They ran back into the building not knowing what to expect.

Joseph Patterson was slumped against the settee with two bullet wounds in his chest. He was obviously already dead and beyond help. So too was Paul Corrigan. He lay near the fireplace blood pouring from a wound in his head at the right temple, his handgun still in his right hand. DC Robertson was sitting on the floor and looked to be in a severe state of shock.

Later that same day Jamie Graham took a phone call at the family meeting. He then announced that Detective Constable Paul Corrigan was dead and therefore could be crossed off the list. The news went down very well with all those present.

At the subsequent enquiry conducted by two senior CID officers from another police force, the two younger officers could only state what they had heard and seen. Detective Constable Robertson's evidence carried the most weight as he was an eye witness to the events that had taken place. He stated that for no apparent reason DC Corrigan had drawn his weapon and without warning shot Joseph Patterson twice in the chest killing him instantly. Without saying a word Detective Constable Corrigan had then immediately turned his gun on himself and shot himself in the head .

Given the evidence available the enquiry had no option but to rule that DC Corrigan had murdered Joseph Patterson before committing suicide by shooting himself. The Patterson family subsequently received compensation from Strathclyde Police. His mother a well known prostitute in the city centre could now retire. It was a very large sum of money.

When Gerry was given the news about the death of his friend he just couldn't believe it. This seemed to be one step too far for him. It was the final straw and he just shut down and ceased to function. It was as though someone had switched off his brain. Nothing and nobody could get through to him. He seemed to be in an almost catatonic state. A broken man. There was certainly nothing more that Audrey could do for him. He was beyond her help.

As the doctor at the hospital explained to Audrey.

"He is in a dark place and there will be many dark days ahead. Who knows if or when he will snap out of it."

Gerry was a very sick man. In the end the doctor was right. He would eventually come out of it but it would take a very long time, more than three years in fact. Three years in which he was detained in hospital in Glasgow whilst making numerous visits to the police convalescence home, Castle Brae, in Auchterader.

Eventually after all the various lotions, potions, therapies and even electric shock treatment had been tried, the powers that be sent him to a sanatorium by the sea on the Kintyre Peninsula near Campbeltown to recover.

Throughout his treatment, as a friend, Aimi McLeod had kept an eye on his progress. Gerry was actually the patient of her boss Dr McKay. The long recovery process continued.

Gerry spent many days sitting quietly just gazing out across the water, watching the sea birds and gathering back a sense of tranquillity into his life. Part of his training with Jim Kennedy had involved meditation and breathing exercises and he made use of these to aid his recovery. There were also many sessions with the resident psychologist in an attempt to get to the bottom of his problems.

Neither Audrey or Sandy Morton were encouraged to visit him in Argyll. The doctors felt he had a far better chance of recovery if he could at first clear his mind in isolation. To do so he was to have no contact with anything or anybody from his past.

As Gerry sat looking out across the water, day after day, he thought of many things. How he had loved his parents and tried to do his best by them, especially after his dad's accident. He felt somehow obliged to stay at home and look after them. Every time he thought about how they had died he felt a pain in his heart, as though stabbed by a dagger. It hurt and he didn't know if the pain would ever go away.

These thoughts then led him to recall the Graham family and the hatred he had for each and every one of them. Sometimes all he had on his mind was revenge and how he would eliminate them one by one once he was allowed out of the hospital. He spent hours plotting in his mind how he would go about eliminating them.

Some days when he was in a more relaxed mood he thought about Audrey. He remembered the first time he had met her. He and Paul had just transferred to Stewart Street Police Office to join a plain clothes squad which DCI Sandy Morton was putting together. They had seen this tall, dark haired woman sitting in the CID office and both thought the very same thing, "I hope she's in the team."

Paul would pull his chain all the time over Audrey. He had almost had to bully Gerry into asking her out. Gerry was too shy to ask her. The man who could punch his way through walls and fight ten men if required, in order to get the job done, was a big softie too shy to ask the lassie out. Gerry smiled remembering how his old pal had kidded him on. In the end, he had somehow summoned up the courage and asked her if she fancied a drink after work. He could recall her exact words.

"You took your time asking Lynch."

They had more or less been an item ever since. Gerry's parents were fed up telling him to marry the girl, before someone else grabbed her. They thought the world of Audrey and she them. This was possibly due to the fact that Audrey no longer had parents, she had been orphaned when she was quite young. Her parents had died in a car accident which Audrey had somehow survived. That had been years ago and she had no real recollection of them. She had been brought up in care and had astonished everyone with her academic prowess. It was very unusual for somebody in her position to shine at school the way she had.

Gerry would sometimes get quite morose when thinking about how he had let her down. That was when the staff would tell him that he thought too much. He should try to clear his mind and think of the future. Easier said than done.

Apart from hoping that he could somehow rekindle his relationship with Audrey, Gerry had one other overwhelming desire. He wanted to get well enough to resume the job he loved so much. The longer he stayed in hospital in Argyll the more he felt his chances diminished. It was not until towards end of his stay in Argyll, as he was eventually getting better that Gerry got a visit from none other than the Chief Medical Officer of Strathclyde Police, Doctor Donald McKay. Over the time he had been ill they had met on many occasions.

What Dr McKay had to say that day came as no surprise but it was not what he wanted to hear. Gerry was being medically discharged from the force. Dr. McKay was very nice about it but really it was the only decision that could be reached. The simple fact of the matter was that although Gerry had no problems physically, mentally he was unfit for duty. He had made giant strides back to normality but after all his time, they worried that he wouldn't be able to cope under stress. Although he had been half expecting it for some time, to actually hear he was no longer a police officer hurt. The fact he would eventually receive a small pension was no consolation. He had no worries on that score as Gerry had found that he was quite well placed financially from insurance policies his parents had held. No, he was sad because he had just loved his job so much. He did accept that the doctors had made the right decision as he had no idea how he would react if put under pressure. One thing was for sure he would find out.

Eventually the time came when Gerry felt much better mentally. He was ready to face the world again, if only he could rid himself of a recurring nightmare. He would awaken covered in sweat and see his parents in their home with his friend Paul. A man, who Gerry assumed was himself, stood in the doorway of the blazing building. He felt he needed to help and as they ran towards him in this dream he shot all three dead.

This dream had been interpreted, by those more qualified, that he felt responsible for all three deaths and was guilty at having survived himself. He was assured that his anguish would at some point abate. He hoped it would stop sooner rather than later.

There was no doubt that whilst he had been recuperating he had spent many days looking out to sea and thinking about lots of things. Thinking about his parents, his friend Paul Corrigan, Audrey the woman who loved him and whom he had also let down so badly.

He knew things may get better. As to whether his guilt would ever go away, that was another matter. Of all the many things he had contemplated during his time in hospital there was one thing which he simply could not come to terms with. Gerry still would not and could not believe his old friend had done what they had said, such an act was just not in the Paul Corrigan he had known. He vowed to make it his business to find out the truth when he returned to Glasgow.

Something else which did concern him greatly was, what he was going to do now for a living. But one thing he was sure of was that, someway, somehow, the Graham family would pay for all the pain and grief they had caused to his family and friends.

Paul's wife Jackie had long since sold up and moved to England with her son Scott. Gerry was not surprised they moved away. He felt for them both trying to get on with their lives but having the stigma of being related to a murderer hanging over them.

He had been unable to attend his old friend's funeral. He was later told it was a very quiet affair at Lambhill. Jackie and Scott were obviously there, as was Audrey to represent him. There were only one or two other police officers including, Sandy Morton and Jim Kennedy. No top brass, after all Paul Corrigan was supposedly a murderer. Apart from Paul, Moira Clarkson was also dead and poor David O'Neill had also gone through hell. Gerry knew that what the doctors had said was true. He had been through some very dark days.

He was still a long way from being one hundred percent again but he was getting there. From

now on he had to somehow make a fresh start and think more positively about the future.

One thing he would need to do was contact Audrey Jennings. Their relationship was at an end and who could blame her? Certainly not Gerry. He had a lot to thank her for and he intended to do so at the earliest opportunity. He had nothing but praise for her. He was to blame, he had become unmanageable and a changed man. Gerry had to admit he did still have strong feelings for her but also was a little scared about seeing her again.

What he did not realise was that everything that had happened to him in the last couple of years had been transmitted to the Graham family. They had received regular updates. Gerry had a dream to get his own back on them but they felt exactly the same about him. He had been one of the main witness against Frank Jnr. and no matter how long it took, he too would be made to pay.

CHAPTER FOURTEEN

All the time that Gerry was in hospital there were two other people suffering.

When Gerry first had a breakdown and was hospitalised Sandy Morton had to order Audrey to take time off and go away and lay on a beach somewhere, she was exhausted. The effort of trying to work full time, look after Gerry, and also study for a degree was almost too much. She was at the end of her tether.

Reluctantly she had agreed and Aimi McLeod insisted on taking her to South Africa for a month. Isla was improving by the day and her speech was much better. Mary had also persuaded Ami that she too needed a break and she could manage. After all the nurses were still there, if only now part time.

The two women flew to Cape Town for a well deserved rest and some pampering. Aimi had contacted friends and been able to rent a private villa close to the sea with its own swimming pool and stunning views. They spent the days sunbathing, swimming and indulging themselves with the occasional cocktail. Evenings were spent visiting the many marvellous restaurants to sample the diverse cuisine.

***

Back home, what colleagues didn't know was how badly all this had affected Sandy Morton. Why he felt the way he did was deeply embedded in his roots and upbringing in Ayrshire.

Sandy's father Alex had been a coal miner but had moved his wife Margaret and family from Cumnock to Ayr because of the after effects of the Knockshinnoch Pit disaster back in September 1950. Thirteen men had died and one hundred and sixteen were trapped underground. All those trapped were subsequently rescued and two men were awarded the George Medal for their part in the rescue.

Sandy's uncle William had been one of those trapped. He came out physically uninjured but was never the same person again. One day he wandered off and drowned himself in the nearby River Afton. Sandy's grandfather never worked again and died soon afterwards.

After the move to Ayr, Alex had worked for Margaret's parents in the family sweet shop. It was very different from being a coal miner but he took to it like a duck to water. When Margaret's parents retired he had taken over the business.

Margaret had been a school teacher and had insisted that Sandy's education was a priority. He made her more than proud by excelling at school and eventually attending Glasgow University to study English literature. It was there that he met his wife to be, Jean Reid, a chemistry student. They soon became an item and once they both gained their respective degrees they made plans for the future.

Once married they initially moved in with Jean's parents, who lived in Carntyne. This was quite handy as Jean had started work in a chemist shop just along at Baillieston. Sandy took up a teaching post at a school in Easterhouse. They saved hard and the following year put down a deposit on a semi-detached house in Baillieston. It was still their home.

Later that same year their lives were turned upside down when Jean suffered a miscarriage and they learned that it was highly unlikely that they could ever have children of their own. Just as they were coming to terms with this, Alex Morton was killed by a teenage drug addict who had tried to rob the sweet shop.

This started a fire under Sandy who was becoming disillusioned with teaching. He came home one night after a particularly hard day and announced to Jean that he was thinking of joining the police. It was a decision he never regretted.

He loved every minute of his new job. One of his sergeants, early in his career, told him that he was born for it. That was something he never forgot. Not only was he good at his job, particularly enjoying it when attached to the CID but he soon realised that this was more than just any job to him. It was a special vocation.

He was more than sad that he and Jean couldn't have children but his colleagues over the years became his family. He felt it was his responsibility to look after them and keep them out of harm's way, so at the end of the day he could send them home to their own families safe and well.

His potential was quickly spotted and he was promoted to uniform sergeant with just six years service. He progressed steadily through the ranks until today, after nearly thirty years, he was a Detective Chief Inspector, who looked upon all those under his charge as his children.

That was why he had taken things so hard after the Graham court case. Although Paul Corrigan's wife and son had moved away he still wrote to them. He was also in regular contact with Moira Clarkson's family. Even David O'Neill and Kenny Brown who had left the job still got a phone call from Sandy at least once a month, just to see how they were getting on and to let them know they would never be forgotten. What he himself perhaps didn't realise was that every one of his staff loved him like a father and admired him for the cop that he was.

Sandy had known Gerry and Paul from the first day they had joined the police. He was their shift uniform inspector. As they grew into the job he kept a close eye on their progress. It was he who had selected them especially for the 'A' Division plain clothes unit. He had seen something special in the two young men and was expecting great things. They had both passed their sergeant and inspector exams in quick succession. It was only a matter of time before one or both was promoted.

Sandy was devastated by what had happened to them both. Paul dead and Gerry mentally unbalanced, and he felt somehow responsible for them. He was the one who had put them in harm's way by selecting them for the unit. Outwardly Sandy showed no emotions or signs that events had got to him. Only one person knew him well enough to detect that something was wrong and that was his wife Jean. She would help him though it, as she had done for the last thirty years.

Thankfully, after her break Audrey got back to work, very much refreshed. She also knuckled down to her studies and delighted Sandy by managing to obtain a degree in criminology from Glasgow Caledonia university. Hopefully she would soon receive the promotion she deserved.

CHAPTER FIFTEEN

Running a crime family was not an easy job. Aside from the Grahams there were several other families scattered all around Glasgow. Not to mention the Chinese triads, Russian mafia and the Romanians. There was an unwritten code that you never encroached on another family's territory. Invariably this was broken from time to time as one family tried to outdo another, or vied for a bigger slice of the pie. Most families dealt with their problems in the same way. Violence. Do unto others first, before it is done unto you.

Jamie Graham was good at what he did and was definitely not afraid to exert his muscle should anyone get out of line. He wasn't stupid and knew that even within his own group there were those who were looking to fast track their own advancement up the ladder. Even aspiring to take over from Jamie if they could.

Recently things had been good, the business was running smoothly and the money was rolling in. The Grahams' system was easy really. Couriers drove south to Liverpool and Manchester returning with kilos of heroin or cocaine. The drugs were then dropped off at designated locations to be cut into deals. Craig Strachan then arranged for his taxi drivers to uplift various amounts and transport them all over the north side of the city and into Glasgow itself. Should an order be received from farther afield arrangements were made for another courier to deliver it where required.

Aside from the drugs, the family also had the pub, taxi company and a number of other businesses such as garages and a scrap yard to run, all of which were profitable enterprises. Jamie Graham had a busy life keeping everything running smoothly.

Occasionally a situation might arise whereby the family would need to deal with a problem in such a way as to deter others from trying the same thing. They had to show strength in dealing with the matter. One such an occasion had just come to light and Jamie had the matter in hand.

Craig Strachan had earlier been visited by the local constabulary. One of his taxi drivers had been found shot dead in his cab near to the Peoples Palace at Glasgow Green. A rather pale looking Craig had just returned to the Crooked Man from the city mortuary where he had identified his driver or, rather, what was left of him. The police were working on the assumption that a fare must have been responsible. Over a large whisky he had told Jamie all about it.

In fact the driver should've been on his way to Ayrshire to drop off a large quantity of cocaine to a long standing customer. Jamie wanted to know two things: why the driver was at the People's Palace and who was responsible for his murder. He had already ensured that word had been put out right across the city. The other families knew the score. Every source they had that might throw some light on the reason for the drivers death would be seen. All were left in no doubt that those responsible would feel the full force of Jamie's wrath if involved.

On the other hand, anyone giving information would be richly rewarded. Word soon carried and it wasn't too long before several possibilities came to light. In some cases it was just people trying to get even with others trying to settle old scores and they were quickly dismissed.

Over in the Gorbals, however, word had got to the head man, Ally Cranston, that Tam McConnell had been out all day trying to sell cocaine.

Firstly, that was not on. He was no longer a member of the Gorbals' team and therefore treading on their toes in their territory was taboo. Secondly, where had he come by the cocaine? Lastly McConnell had been seen talking to an old crony, Willie McKinley, in a pub recently.

Ally Cranston was shrewd enough to pass this information on to the Grahams. Cranston certainly didn't want the blame for something he hadn't done, nor did he fancy a war with the Graham family. It was Billy Graham who received the information from Cranston. He immediately phoned Jamie for his reaction. Jamie knew Cranston from previous dealings with the Gorbals team.

"Give me five minutes," he told Billy. "I'll phone you back".

Jamie immediately contacted Ally Cranston.

"Ally," he began, "seems that McConnell has been a naughty boy. Are you sure he's not one of yours?"

"Absolutely not, Jamie," Cranston replied, "we cut him loose weeks ago. He's an idiot."

"Do you know where to find him?" Jamie asked.

"I'll personally deliver him to you, Jamie - just say where and when".

"Thanks Ally," Jamie replied. "Give me a bell when you get him and my brothers will come to your pub and pick him up. Oh, and Ally ".

"What, Jamie?"

"I owe you." Jamie hung up and phoned Billy back.

The streets of Springburn were empty as a dark blue Ford Transit van stopped in the front garage forecourt of Meechan Motors. The garage was owned by the Graham family, although you wouldn't find them listed as such anywhere. The place had been used by the family for years to ring stolen vehicles.

Bobby Graham jumped out of the front passenger door, unlocked the roller shutter and began raising the door. Eventually the transit drove into the garage and the door closed again. Tam McConnell lay on the floor of the van. He was bound and gagged with a hood over his head. It was a cold night but he was sweating. He knew what was coming.

The Graham twins opened the rear doors of the vehicle and roughly pulled Tam out. He was told to sit and felt a metal chair below him. His bonds were then removed and he was tied to the chair. It was silent for a moment and then the hood was removed from his head.

It took a few moments for Tam to focus and get used to the light. Then there before him he saw Jamie Graham. He looked down and saw that the chair on which he was seated had a large sheet of plastic on the floor below it.

Jamie spoke.

"Tam, I'm no gonna waste any time here. You know why you're here. We want information and we want it now. Just nod if you understand me." Tam nodded.

"You've got five minutes to tell me all that you know about the hit on my driver at the People's Palace and what happened to the drugs from his car. If you don't tell me what I want to know my two wee brothers here are gonna torture you until you do. I'll no lie to you, there is only one way you are leaving here tonight and that's dead. How that happens, whether quickly or slowly, depends on you. Do you understand?"

Tam nodded again, tears rolling down his cheeks

"Right," Jamie continued, "let's get started. Billy take his gag off."

Billy did as his brother asked and Jamie continued,

"Now Tam, we know you've been trying to sell cocaine in the toon today and we've a good idea where you got it. Tell me, was it you who shot my driver?"

McConnell began to shake and was blubbering like a baby. Jamie nodded to Billy and Bobby. They were both wearing knuckle dusters and both punched Tam several times in the face. Blood and teeth splattered from his mouth.

"Now Tam, you have only two minutes left. Did you shoot my driver?"

Tam McConnell had never enjoyed being beaten up and knew he had to tell Jamie Graham the truth, as God knows what the twins would do to him. Their reputations proceeded them. Despite the fact that his jaw was already broken Tam told Jamie everything he knew, finally whispering.

"It was Willie McKinley done it."

"Willie McKinley eh, good lad," Jamie said. "Do you know where he's hiding?"

Tam replied "Naw" before losing consciousness. Jamie walked over to the office. He didn't sit, because everything was covered in grease. Using his mobile phone he called Ally Cranston. He explained who he was looking for.

"You're not going to believe this, Jamie, but McKinley just walked into my pub ten minutes ago. Where do you want him?"

Jamie went back out into the garage.

"Boys can you return to Cranston's pub? He has a second package for us. Bring it back here and in the meantime me and Tam will wait for you."

Billy and Bobby left in a hurry. When they reached the south side, Ally Cranston and a few of his team were waiting for them. The package was transferred from the boot of their car to the Transit van.

"Thanks Ally," Bobby said, "Jamie will be in touch."

The Gorbals team headed back into the pub safe in the knowledge that they had avoided a possible gang war and would receive payment for their efforts.

The twins drove back to Springburn. When they arrived back Tam McConnell was exactly where they'd left him but was awake again. Jamie had found a box to sit on and he had put some cardboard on top to save getting his suit dirty.

In no time at all the three brothers had Willie McKinley in the same position as his accomplice. Jamie had given him the same warning he had given Tam. Easy way or hard way? Either way he was going to die.

"Fuck you!" had been Willie McKinley's reply. So it was the hard way.

Jamie never blinked, but continued with his interrogation and told McKinley they knew he'd shot the driver. What Jamie wanted to know was why and who had put the two of them up to it?

McKinley wasn't saying a word so Jamie let the twins loose again. They set about him with a vengeance, punching him until their arms hurt.

Between bouts of unconsciousness McKinley told them nothing. Jamie decided it was time for more drastic action. One by one he had the twins cut off some of McKinley's toes with bolt cutters. Still he refused to say anything and when he regained consciousness they began cutting off his fingers. Still he would not talk.

There was only one thing left. Jamie produced his father's cut throat razor and began peeling skin from McKinley's body. How his screams were never heard is hard to understand.

He had met some tough characters in his time but this guy was something else. Jamie almost wished McKinley had been part of his family. How he could withstand such pain was incredible. McKinley fainted yet again and was out cold for some time. The Graham's just left him to come round in his own time. There was no rush.

When McKinley regained his senses again he seemed somehow to have changed. It was as if a calmness or serenity had come over him. He looked at Jamie and it was as if he had thought to himself 'why not just tell him what he wants to hear and get it over with.' He knew he was a dead man either way.

"I'll tell you somethin' Jamie," he croaked, spitting out a mouthful of blood onto the plastic sheet below him. "Your family might love you but Craig Strachan hates your guts. That's why he had me kill your driver and steal the drugs. He wants to be the man. The deal was we killed the driver and kept the drugs as payment. He set it all up."

Just then the side door of the garage opened and two men walked in Cammy Wilson and Craig Strachan.

"Well lads," Jamie directed his remarks to Tam and Willie. "Look who it is, your leader."

Craig, who was already as white as a sheet, made to speak but Jamie cut him off.

"You shut your mouth, not a sound. You're the cause of all this."

Jamie nodded to his two younger brothers. Billy walked behind Tam McConnell's chair and Bobby walked behind Willie McKinley's. Both removed a handgun from inside their jackets and shot their man once in the back of the head. McConnell and McKinley both slumped forward in their chairs dead.

Craig Strachan vomited.

After he had recovered himself Jamie spoke to him again.

"You, you piece of shit. You're responsible for all of this. First of all you are going to clean up that mess. Then you can help the lads put your two pals into the van. You're going to bury them. I'll see you back at the Crooked Man when you've finished."

With that Jamie left the garage, accompanied by Cammy Wilson.

Craig watched as Billy and Bobby put the two corpses into black body bags. At their request he then took a hosepipe from the wall and washed the whole of the garage floor swilling away vomit, blood and brain. Bobby Graham put Willie McKinley's digits into a plastic bag and threw them into the body bag with the rest of him.

Thirty minutes later they were in the woods near what had been Gartloch Hospital, miles from Springburn. Billy threw Craig a shovel and told him to start digging. He dug a large hole and when it was deep enough he helped the twins throw the two bodies in. He then began filling the hole in again.

Suddenly he felt something cold on the back of his neck. As he turned around there was Billy Graham holding his handgun. Without a word he shot Craig Strachan twice in the face. He was dead before he hit the ground. The twins pushed his body into the hole and then filled it in. It was time to head back to the Crooked Man, they both needed a drink.

When they reached the pub it was the early hours of the morning. It was obvious that Jamie had already given Margaret the bad news about Craig. The twins helped themselves to a large whisky each and sat at the bar. Margaret was sitting at the far end of the bar and was in a bit of a state. She had obviously been crying. Jamie got up to leave and in doing so left them all with one last message. "You know what Dad says, nobody messes with the Grahams."

Margaret told her younger brothers what Jamie had told her. He'd apparently suspected for some time that Craig was trying to undermine his authority in the family. With Frank Jnr. out of the picture for a few years, he had obviously thought that now was the time to make his move. What his plan had been they would now never know but it certainly hadn't worked.

Yes, Margaret was upset at losing her boyfriend but at the end of the day, family was family.

The twins had another drink and then drove Margaret home to her empty house.

CHAPTER SIXTEEN

I t was the beginning of August 2005. The day had finally arrived for Gerry Lynch to be discharged from hospital. He thanked all the staff for all that they had done for him. As he walked out of the front door and down the driveway he was full of trepidation.

He only had to wait a few minutes, then found himself stepping onto the early morning bus bound for Glasgow. Almost all he had in the world was contained in the small holdall he was carrying.

It was a gorgeously warm summer morning with not a cloud in the sky. No doubt by mid afternoon half the population in these parts would have been eaten alive by the midges. But Gerry was impervious to the weather. All he had on his mind was getting back to Glasgow.

The journey would take over four hours passing through some of the most beautiful countryside in Scotland. Gerry was to see none of it. He sat on the seat right at the very back of the bus with his eyes closed, trying to relax and figure out his next move but before long he fell asleep. It had nothing to do with the tablets he had been prescribed for anxiety, he just suddenly felt tired and physically totally unfit. In the past two years he hadn't exercised at all and had put on over two stones in weight. Being over six feet tall he still looked okay but somehow he suddenly felt an exhaustion wash over him. Perhaps this is how people felt on being released from prison. A sense of freedom and relief.

When the bus arrived in Glasgow it was midday. Gerry took a taxi to Alexandra Parade. His first task was to retrieve his car. Since his days serving as a beat cop in this area Gerry had always taken his cars to be serviced at Ian Bell's garage on Alexandra Parade. Many of his fellow officers had done the same. Audrey had asked Ian to look after Gerry's BMW whilst he was ill. She had written and told him where to get his car. No one had expected it would be more than three years later before Gerry returned for it.

As Gerry alighted from the taxi outside the garage the weather turned. The sun disappeared. As it began pouring with rain, a rumble of thunder was heard in the distance. 'Welcome to Glasgow,' he thought to himself. He also had the beginnings of a headache which had not been brought on by the oppressive weather. Perhaps he was trying a little too hard on his first day out of hospital in three years. He popped two of his anxiety tablets into his mouth and entered the garage.

Ian Bell was overjoyed to see Gerry and assured him that his car was safe and sound at the back of the garage all covered up under a tarpaulin. He insisted that Gerry allow him to service the car and make sure it was roadworthy before getting it back. As he said if he had known Gerry was coming for it then he would have had it ready.

"You should have phoned," Ian said.

Gerry made a mental note to buy himself a mobile telephone as soon as possible. It was something he didn't have and would without doubt need. He also needed his car but Ian was right; there was little doubt after three years it would need servicing. He agreed to Ian's request and then left to hurry across the street and into the Cross Keys Public House.

By now his head was pounding. The pills the doctor had prescribed were okay but he had another cure. He ordered a glass of single malt whisky and then realised he had not eaten anything since his early morning breakfast in Argyll. After a quick perusal of the pub menu he decided on steak pie and chips. The long road back to fitness could wait until tomorrow.

As the lunchtime trade came and went Gerry found himself sitting at the bar with a wee tank of a man. He was definitely overweight but looked as though in his day he would've been capable of handling himself. Gerry guessed he was about sixty years old. He was only about 5'6" in height with greasy, almost white hair, wearing a shabby looking suit. The man had already been in the pub when Gerry had arrived. He introduced himself as Jimmy Quinn, and told Gerry he was a private investigator with offices just along the street. At first Gerry didn't know whether to believe him or not.

The two men were now matching each other whisky for whisky. In truth drinking far more than was good for either of them. Throughout their wee session Jimmy had continually chain smoked. He went to the machine on the wall to buy more cigarettes and then visited the toilets. Gerry watched him and thought he seemed a decent enough bloke if somewhat down at heel. Everyone in the pub had certainly made a point of speaking to him; he seemed to be popular with the locals. The pub landlord, Alex Stuart, told Gerry that Jimmy was in the pub every day.

"Don't get me wrong, son," he said, "Jimmy 's got a wee drink problem but he's a hard

worker and would give you his last."

Gerry didn't see what was wrong with a wee drink problem. It worked for him.

A couple of hours later Gerry found himself in Jimmy's shabby office. He must have fallen asleep on the lumpy old sofa. He really had to stop the tablets or the drink because taking both was crazy. As he opened his eyes there before him stood a vision of loveliness, holding a mug of coffee. For a moment he thought he had died and gone to heaven. Standing in front of him was a girl in her early twenties with auburn hair and the most fantastic hazel coloured eyes he had ever seen.

"Hi, I'm Jimmy's secretary, Jenny," she said.

Before Gerry could speak the door to the office flew open and there was Jimmy, sweating and breathless. He reached into his trouser pocket and retrieved a handkerchief before wiping the sweat from his forehead. Fumbling in the top drawer of his desk he found some pills and quickly popped a couple into his mouth.

"Hello son, feeling a wee bit better?" he asked, flopping into his chair.

Gerry's head was beginning to clear. He recalled talking at length to Jimmy in the pub and basically telling him everything that had happened to him. That's how it goes when you drink too much.

"Aye, Alex had to throw us out," he laughed. "I brought you here for a wee snooze, son. I don't know if you remember much but we sort of came to an arrangement."

Gerry remembered now. It had something to do with £10,000 and Jimmy offering him a partnership in the business as well as a room at his flat. Perhaps he was being a bit hasty.

"Look," said Jimmy. "I can see how you would need time to think things over and sort yourself out. I don't want you to feel you are under any kind of pressure and if you change your mind then fair enough, there will be no harm done. Why don't you stay at Jenny's tonight and we can discuss it again tomorrow?"

Staying at Jenny's Gerry was all for but, before he got any ideas in that direction, Jenny explained that she lived just around the corner from the office with her mother, Brenda and her six year old daughter Sophie. "Mum sometimes does bed and breakfast to keep the wolf from the door," she explained.

Oh well, thought Gerry, it was still a good idea as he had nowhere else to go. At five o'clock Jenny took Gerry to her mum's flat. It was indeed just around the corner from the office. They were met at the front door by Sophie, who was a mini version of Jenny. Brenda was in the kitchen. She was also a stunner and looked more like Jenny's older sister than her mother.

Over coffee Jenny explained all about Gerry thinking of becoming a partner in Jimmy's business. Brenda thought it sounded like a good idea given his police background, as in many ways the work could be similar. She also had nothing but praise for Jimmy.

"I know he drinks too much but he wasn't always like that. He's been through a lot and was good enough to take my Jenny on when she badly needed a job."

She went on to explain to Gerry how Jenny had fallen pregnant when she was just fifteen and had Sophie. Not unexpectedly the father was nowhere to be seen. Jimmy had not only given Jenny a job but also started Brenda as the office cleaner to help them out.

All this reinforced Gerry's initial thoughts that he might give this partnership idea a go. Jimmy seemed to be a decent bloke and Brenda and Jenny could not speak highly enough about him. Who knows perhaps it might work; stranger things had happened.

They sat talking for some time before Brenda realised that it was past time for making dinner. Gerry announced that he would like to take them all out, on him, as a thank you for their help. They let Sophie choose where they would go. So it was that all four of them found themselves in Mario's Pizza Place on Alexandra Parade. It was Sophie's favourite and letting her choose had made Gerry her friend for life. Straight after the meal though Jenny excused herself and took Sophie home as it was a school day the following morning.

Gerry asked Brenda if she fancied a drink and they ended up back in the Cross Keys. Brenda seemed to know everyone and she introduced Gerry to the barmaid, Babs, and the landlady, Betty Stuart. Gerry asked Betty to apologise to her husband on his behalf if he had caused any trouble with Jimmy earlier. The problem was he couldn't remember. Betty assured him he was okay.

Gerry and Brenda both had two or three glasses of malt whisky before walking home. Jenny and Sophie had both gone to bed long ago. Brenda asked Gerry if he fancied a coffee or a nightcap and he chose the latter. Neither of them could really say how it happened but the next thing they were in Brenda's bedroom naked.

When he awoke late in the morning Gerry took a moment to realise exactly where he was. Then he remembered what had taken place the previous night. He felt guilty but it had felt good to feel a woman's body next to him again. After all it had been more than three years. At first a smug feeling washed over him and then fear and panic.

What would he say to Brenda? Or Jenny for that matter? The house was quiet, not a sound. He quickly got up shaved, showered and dressed. He was hoping to get out before anyone appeared. No chance.

It was just then that the front door opened and in walked Brenda. She had just returned from cleaning Jimmy's office.

"Morning Gerry, ready for some breakfast?" she asked.

"Yes please," he replied weakly.

"Got some nice bacon and eggs," she said, almost, it seemed, laughing at him. "You'll need to keep your strength up," she added.

Gerry was now cringing and his face could not have been redder. It was burning. He didn't know what to say but eventually spluttered,

"Brenda, about last night..."

"That's okay, sweetheart," she cut in. "I know what you are going to say. We had too much to drink, it should never have happened. Well it did and I'm not complaining, so don't beat yourself up. I'm a big girl and know what I'm doing. Oh, and by the way, it's usually £15 for bed and breakfast. We can sort something out once you've seen Jimmy."

"Thanks," was all Gerry could muster by way of a reply.

After giving Gerry his breakfast Brenda set about cleaning the flat.

Gerry walked along to Ian Bell's garage to see how they were getting on with his car. It would be ready late afternoon once Ian had got some parts delivered. Gerry's next stop was the central division headquarters. He needed some advice from his old gaffer. Sandy Morton was delighted to see him. Gerry was amazed to note that he did not recognise a single CID officer in the office. Had there been such a big change in just three years?

Gerry explained Jimmy's offer and asked what Sandy thought. As usual he got a thoughtful, measured reply from a man he admired greatly. It was simple really. Did he trust Jimmy Quinn? At the end of the day, it was only money he was wasting if it didn't work. Sandy knew the work would be no problem as Gerry had been one of the best officers he'd ever worked with.

Inevitably they got around to speaking about Paul Corrigan. Gerry reiterated he didn't think that Paul had done what they said and he had and he was going to find out the truth. All Sandy could say was the case was officially closed and he hoped Gerry would not be opening a can of worms.

They parted on good terms and Gerry took a taxi back to Jimmy's office. On the way back he realised he had not seen Audrey at the police office and had neglected to ask Sandy about her. He felt bad.

When Gerry walked into the office, Jenny was hard at work typing up some reports. There was an awkward silence for a few moments. Gerry thought she was about to give him a rocket about last night. But when she eventually looked up she had a smile on her face.

"Sleep well, did we?" Jenny asked.

His face went bright red like a schoolboy who'd been caught stealing sweeties.

"Yes thanks," he whispered.

"Jimmy's in his office, just go through," she said.

Jimmy was sat at his desk when Gerry went in.

"How are you this morning, son?" he asked "Brenda take good care of you, did she?"

Another red face, just as Jenny walked in carrying two coffees. Jimmy took his mug with a couple more pills.

"Sit down son," Jimmy said. "I'll tell you all about the business."

Over the next hour or so Jimmy did exactly that, explaining it all to Gerry.

The landlords were the solicitors Kane & Bryson whose offices were downstairs. Tom Kane and Sam Bryson had started up their business a few years back straight after leaving university. They were both of the same mind and chose the hard way up rather than entering an established firm and they worked well together. Their secretary, Grace Mitchell, was a lovely lady pushing forty but who didn't look it and they also had an officer junior, seventeen year old Julie Hall.

Jimmy told Gerry his landlords were really good at giving him work, mostly statement gathering, process serving, that kind of thing. He reckoned with their work, plus missing persons and marital problems they had more than enough work to keep them going.

"I'd be a liar if I said we were rushed off our feet, Gerry, but we keep going. My idea of you coming on board is simple son. You're a young man and will bring energy into the business as well as your experience in the police, while I'm the auld heed and can teach you a few tricks of the trade."

He then swallowed two more pills and continued, "Come on son, I'll show you my flat."

The walk to Jimmy's flat was less than ten minutes from the office. En route everyone they passed said hello to Jimmy; he seemed to know all the locals. As they were about to enter Jimmy's flat, which was situated on the ground floor, his neighbour from across the hallway was just leaving his home.

"Gerry," Jimmy said, "this is my neighbour Matty McGowan. Matty this is..."

"Hello Mr Lynch," Matty interrupted, "how are you?"

"I'm fine." Gerry replied.

"Do you two know each other?" Jimmy asked with a bemused look on his face.

"We go way back, eh Matty?" Gerry replied.

"We do that, Mr Lynch," Matty smiled and turned to Jimmy,

"Jimmy I'm just away to the shops, do you want anything".

"No thanks son" Jimmy replied, showing Gerry into his flat. He slipped Matty a £10 note before he left.

"So you know Matty then, Gerry?" Jimmy said.

"Back from my early days on the beat in Springburn," Gerry replied.

"You'll know all about what happened to his girlfriend and their wean then?" Jimmy added.

"Unfortunately, yes," Gerry replied. "Me and my partner Paul Corrigan tried to help him out at the time, he was a sad case."

"Aye he was that," Jimmy said. "just another of the many waifs and strays I've tried to help over the years."

"Well you must have done something right," Gerry said. "He certainly looks a lot healthier than I have ever seen him before. I would swear he's even put some weight on but then," he added, patting his own stomach, "haven't we all?"

As soon as Gerry entered Jimmy's flat he realised that apart from liking the drink he also definitely had another problem. The flat stank and was covered in a brown nicotine layer. Cigarette smoke hung in the air like an impenetrable fog.

Chewing two more tablets Jimmy flopped into a chair.

"Sorry about the mess, son, but if you're moving in I'll get the place tidied up."

The flat was spacious enough with a large living room, kitchen, bathroom and two good sized bedrooms. It probably had been a lovely home at one time but not now. Apart from the smell in the place, all the décor and furnishings were of another time. It seemed that everything was old fashioned. The cooker looked as though it had not been used for years, it certainly had not been cleaned for some time. Gerry could never imagine himself living here but did not want to upset Jimmy.

"Jimmy," he said, "I really should have mentioned this morning but last night I gave the whole thing a great deal of thought and this morning I visited my old gaffer in the police to get his advice. I think we should give it a week or so and see how I go with the business."

He paused for a breath before carrying on,

"As to living with you, I kind of fancy a flat on my own and while I'm looking I'm sure Brenda and Jenny will put me up. Maybe I could look for a flat while you're teaching me the trade. What do you say?"

Jimmy was elated, "That sounds good to me son. This calls for a drink."

On the way to the Cross Keys, Gerry called into Brenda's and gathered the courage to ask if he could stay for a few more days. She was delighted to accept.

CHAPTER SEVENTEEN

For the next few weeks Jimmy led and Gerry followed. There was no doubt that Jimmy knew his job and was good at it. Having Gerry around seemed to give him a new lease of life. At first Gerry was slightly apprehensive. He knew he'd been a good enough cop but did he have what it took to be a private investigator, or would he make a fool of himself?

He'd really no need to worry as it was just a matter of getting back into the swing of things. Like riding a bike. Gerry was a quick learner and before long was taking on jobs alone. The downside of working with Jimmy was that they always ended up in the Cross Keys and whatever tablets Jimmy had, he was eating them like sweeties. All this on top of at least sixty cigarettes a day.

Gradually as the weeks passed and Jimmy headed to the pub Gerry excused himself on the pretence of looking for a flat. He did view a few but didn't fancy living in any of them. In truth he was more than happy staying with Brenda. Gerry had tried to keep things on a professional level, not wanting to upset Jenny or Sophie but had to admit he was finding it hard not to surrender to temptation. So far he had surrendered quite a few times.

The problem was the next day he would think of Audrey. This had the effect of making him feel both sad and guilty because he had, as yet, failed to contact her since returning to Glasgow. He hated himself for this because she deserved better. The more he became involved with Brenda the harder it would be to contact Audrey.

As well as looking for a flat Gerry had decided to throw away his medication and try to lay off the booze. In an effort to lose some weight he had started early morning runs through Alexandra Park before breakfast. He picked up his car from Ian Bell's garage. It was running like new and had only cost him £250. Gerry was delighted to have his wheels back.

One night Jimmy and Gerry went out on a case working for a lady from the Dennistoun area. She suspected that her husband was up to no good. They followed the man down to a bar at the bottom of High Street down next to the River Clyde. They watched as he met a woman in the bar. The couple soon left and headed for a flat just along the street. Jimmy explained to Gerry that he had been following the same guy for the last four weeks and had more than enough evidence to present to his wife, including photographs.

Jimmy also knew the woman. "I've known her for years," he said. "She is the real reason I brought you down here tonight."

Gerry had told Jimmy the full sad tale of how he had met Matty McGowan back in 1994 when he and Paul Corrigan were young cops walking the beat up in Springburn and Matty was just a daft eighteen year old who lived with his girlfriend Shirley, who was in her early twenties, and her wee daughter Cheryl up in a high flat.

Matty was a petty thief back then, who fell in with the Graham family and was a runner for them. He'd not exactly been at the front of the queue when brains had been handed out. He was a bit slow and suffered ridicule because of this. There was, however, no doubt though that he worshipped his girlfriend and her daughter even though she was not his child. Unfortunately both Matty and his girlfriend had a heavy drug habit.

One day Cheryl, who was only six, had waited at school for either her mum or Matty to come to collect her as they usually did, but they both failed to do so. On that particular day Matty had been arrested for shoplifting and was locked up at the local police office. Shirley was unconscious in her flat after accidentally taking an overdose. When Cheryl, who was a bright girl for her age, returned home by herself there was no trace of her mum. She had been found by a friend and taken by ambulance to Glasgow Royal Infirmary. No one thought about collecting Cheryl from school.

Because of his lengthy record, Matty had been detained for court the next day. The young girl made herself a jam sandwich and waited in vain for an adult to come home. Later that night she went to sleep in her mother's bed after eating what she thought were sweets she had found on the bedside table.

The next morning Matty was released on bail. When he got home he learned what had happened to Shirley from a neighbour as he made his way up to his flat. Inside he found Cheryl unconscious.

Despite rushing her to hospital the young girl was dead on arrival.

Neither Matty nor Shirley ever forgave themselves. Matty hit the drink big time and stupidly thought he could steal drugs from the Graham family which he would sell himself to make a new life for himself and Shirley. The Graham family found out and Matty was beaten to within an inch of his life. Some say he received brain damage and that was why, he now appeared to be even slower witted than he had been previously. There was certainly no doubt he was never the same again. The very night Matty was beaten up, Shirley, high on drugs, jumped from the roof of their tower block.

Gerry and especially Paul, who had a young child of his own, felt really sorry for Matty. They tried to help steer him clear of the Grahams but because he owed them for the drugs he had stolen from them he was tied for life.

Jimmy continued his story, "That woman is called Sadie Gleason and she's been a prostitute for more years than she would care to admit. For some reason it seems some men still like to see an older woman. Matty McGowan comes to see her from time to time."

"I wouldn't have thought she was Matty's type," Gerry said, somewhat surprised.

"She's not," Jimmy replied. "Sadie is like a surrogate mother to him. She was his mother's best friend. You think Matty's problems all started in Springburn, well let me tell you this. Matty's mother and Sadie Gleason were the best of friends and both prostitutes. His mother had another son, Thomas, who was a few years older than Matty.

"The story goes that his mum was murdered one night while out working. His father was a drunk who allegedly took great delight in regularly beating both lads. He disappeared shortly after the murder. Some say Thomas, who was a big lad with a short temper, killed him. Whatever happened he was never seen again. Both lads then went into care and Thomas did his best to look after his wee brother who seemed a little slow. Nobody ever thought he might be suffering from all the beatings he had taken from his dad.

"Sadie Gleason remained true to her friend and did what she could for the boys.

"Just before your involvement with Matty, Thomas disappeared and was never seen again. The story goes that he'd apparently been involved in a fight in a nightclub when someone insulted a girlfriend. In the days following the incident she looked everywhere for him, even reported him as a missing person to the police but he had just vanished." Jimmy paused for a moment, lit yet another cigarette, then continued "I just thought you should know. I met Matty a few years back and found him that flat to live in. He'd been sleeping rough and I've tried to help him since to sort himself out. Unfortunately he is bound by his debt to the Grahams, so still has to work for them. Anyway son, let's pack up here. Jenny can type up the report for the lady in the morning. Time we were in the Cross Keys, having a wee dram."

Gerry accompanied Jimmy to the pub but left after just one drink. By that time Jimmy was already sinking his third whisky and looked to be making a night of it.

Walking home Gerry was thinking to himself that he had more or less decided that he was going to go ahead with the partnership. He had enjoyed the last few weeks out and about in the city. It wasn't the same as being a police officer but there were similarities. Hopefully he could take some of the workload off Jimmy and get him some help for his drinking.

Gerry was certainly pleased with his own progress in that regard. He had cut out alcohol as much as possible and had stopped taking the medication he'd been prescribed. Also the running was coming along. He was a long way off being fit but he was enjoying his morning runs. Sometimes he imagined that his old pal Paul was running with him and this in a strange way kept him happy. He knew that his next step was to get back to the boxing and taekwondo. He made a mental note to phone Jim Kennedy at the first opportunity.

CHAPTER EIGHTEEN

Bright and early the next day Gerry completed his run around Alexandra Park. It felt good to be out in the crisp morning air and he was getting used to his new routine.

Back at the house, he was showered and dressed before anyone else had stirred. He thought he would give Brenda the morning off and so made everyone breakfast. After driving Sophie to school he dropped Jenny at the office.

Gerry had an early appointment at his bank. When he got back there was no sign of Jimmy. Jenny was just completing the report on the gentleman from the previous evening.

"His wife won't be a happy bunny when she reads that," she said. "Oh, and by the way, Jimmy's just popped around to his flat, he said he won't be long."

That reminded Gerry he had two more things to do urgently.

First he telephoned Jim Kennedy who was delighted to hear from him. They arranged that Gerry would call out to Kirkintilloch in the near future, with a view to starting classes again. Next Gerry asked Jenny if she could help him find a flat. He loved staying with her and Brenda but needed his own place, plus he knew Jimmy would bring up his moving in with him and that was definitely not on. Jenny promised to help but only if he told her mother. She knew Brenda had become more than a little fond of Gerry.

By then almost two hours had passed and Jimmy had still not returned to the office. Both Gerry and Jenny were beginning to worry about him.

"Come on, Jenny," Gerry said eventually. "Let's go and see what's keeping Jimmy. I'll take you both out to lunch."

It only took a couple of minutes to drive to Jimmy's flat from the office. Jenny had a spare set of keys. She opened both the outer security door and the door to Jimmy's flat. Gerry told her to stay outside while he checked everything was okay.

As soon as he entered the living room Gerry found Jimmy lying on the floor. Just looking at him, Gerry knew he was dead but he still felt obliged to try to find a pulse. There was none and there was nothing anyone could do. Jimmy had passed away. There was a bottle of pills in his hand which had spilled all over the carpet. It looked to Gerry that he had been dead for an hour or so.

He went outside into the hall and spoke to Jenny. There was no way to sugar coat this, "I'm sorry love but Jimmy's dead. It looks as though he's had a heart attack."

Not surprisingly Jenny broke down in tears and Gerry took her back outside to sit in his car. He then telephoned the police and once Jenny had calmed down a little he managed to get the details of Jimmy's doctor's from her. He phoned the surgery which was local.

No more than ten minutes later the doctor attended and pronounced that unfortunately Jimmy had indeed passed away. He told Gerry he would issue a death certificate as he had been treating Jimmy for some time for a serious heart condition.

"If you call round to the surgery later I'll have the certificate for you," the doctor informed them. "I warned him to lay off the drink but that was easier said than done."

Gerry thanked the doctor and as soon as he'd left he phoned to cancel the police as they were no longer required. Jenny had recovered her composure and phoned the local undertakers who attended immediately and removed Jimmy's body to their parlour. There was nothing else to be done at the flat other than to turn off the water, electric and gas.

En route to the doctor's surgery Gerry and Jenny went into as many of the local shops and businesses as possible to let them know the sad news about Jimmy. He had been well liked locally. Having obtained the death certificate, Gerry suggested Jenny just go home and let her mum know about Jimmy. He then went to see Tom Kane and Sam Bryson. They were very deeply shocked and saddened when he gave them the news of Jimmy's death. Gerry went into Tom's office and came straight to the point.

"Well Tom, with Jimmy dying like that, where do I stand regarding the business?" he asked.

"No real change, Gerry," Tom replied. "If there was one thing Jimmy knew about it was people. He asked me to draw up a contract a while ago, which I did and he signed it. Basically if you pay me the agreed sum of £10,000, I deposit it in Jimmy's bank account. That is to say the business account. So in actual fact you would be moving £10,000 from your own account to the business. You would then become a partner in the business or given the circumstances, the owner of the business. Perhaps it may sound a bit unethical but it's perfectly legal. I won't say anything if you don't and it is, I can assure you, exactly what Jimmy wanted. It's a straight forward contract but Jimmy made one stipulation. If anything happened to him, he wanted to ensure that Jenny Galloway's position is secure. You must agree not to let her go within the next five years. If that's okay with you I can arrange for you to be added as a signatory for the company tomorrow and after a reasonable time we can later have Jimmy's name removed."

There was nothing to think about really. No way was he getting rid of Jenny, she was the one who ran the business. Despite the loss of Jimmy, Gerry felt he should give it a go.

"Okay Tom," he said, "let's go ahead."

"Great. I'll set up an appointment at the bank for tomorrow morning," Tom replied.

Gerry then headed back home where he found both Brenda and Jenny red eyed from crying. He quickly explained to Jenny why he was going to be taking her and Jimmy for lunch. He had wanted to celebrate the news he had decided to become a partner. He told her they would sort things in the morning. It was a very quiet house for the rest of the day.

CHAPTER NINETEEN

Although there was a lot to do, early the next morning Gerry was up, more determined than ever to try and get back into some kind of shape. To do so he had to adhere to a strict timetable, therefore he had to go out for his run. If nothing else his runs help him to keep his stress levels down. He also recognised that his runs so far had only really been warm ups. It was time to get serious and step up the pace.

He jogged out onto Alexandra Parade and then into the park. It was still quite breezy and there was not a leaf to be seen on any of the trees. Most of them, as was normal at this time of year, were in the boating pond. As usual at that time of the morning, there was hardly anyone about. He tried to up the pace and maintain it to the end of his run. He was pleased that he managed to do so, although his lungs were on fire as he reached the park gates. He was totally exhausted by the time he got back to Brenda's.

He took a very long hot shower before dressing. He was just sitting down to breakfast when Jenny returned from having walked Sophie to school. Brenda joined them and they all ate together. It was good to see that both women looked much better today after yesterday's initial shock. Gerry reckoned the best way to deal with the situation was to keep busy.

"Right," he said finishing his second cup of tea, "I've got an appointment with Tom Kane and the bank manager this morning. Jenny, I will want a word with you after that. In the meantime can you go and put up a 'closed due to bereavement' sign on the office door? I forgot about it yesterday. Then just come back here and we can catch up later." Jenny told him she would do as he'd asked and see him once his business was complete.

His first stop was at the solicitors to get Tom Kane and then along to the bank. They were shown straight into the manager's office. The manager was expecting them and offered his condolences for their loss. He then got right down to business. Firstly Gerry wrote a cheque for £10,000 made payable to James Quinn Investigations Ltd. He handed it to Tom who in turn passed it to the bank manager. Gerry then signed the contractual documents in relation to the business and the two other men also signed as witnesses.

The bank manager then stood very formally and shook Gerry's hand.

"Congratulations, Mr Lynch," he said, "you are now the owner of James Quinn Investigations Ltd."

Gerry thanked him. There was no real need because there was bad news.

"Now Mr Lynch," the bank manager began, "the balance in the company accounts without your cheque presently stands at £2,517.56. It is also my duty to bring to your attention that Mr Quinn's flat is part of the business and unfortunately the mortgage payments have fallen behind.

Currently £1,446.95 is outstanding. Also, Kane & Bryson, your landlords are owed £1,500 in rent for your office space. In other words, prior to paying in your cheque, the business is in the red."

"Well sir," Gerry joked, "it appears then that the only way is up."

This remark seemed to go right over the bank manager's head.

"Indeed, Mr Lynch," he replied dryly, before continuing,

"Now we come to Mr Quinn's will. There is, as you can imagine, nothing of great consequence in the document. He has left the sum of £1, 000 to Miss Jenny Galloway "in the hope she will buy her beautiful daughter Sophie something nice".

Finally Mr Quinn expressed the wish to be buried alongside his wife and son at Sighthill Cemetery."

Before leaving the bank Gerry withdrew £2400 from the business account. He thanked the bank manager and Tom and went straight back to Brenda's. There was much to discuss. Both women were waiting for him and he wasted no time in announcing that he was now the proud owner of James Quinn Investigations Ltd. He also told them that Jimmy's flat was part of the business. That sort of solved the problem of where he was going to live, although the flat would need to be gutted first. Gerry knew at some point he would need to take the bull by the horns and pluck up the courage to tell Brenda he would be moving out.

"One thing I didn't know is that Jimmy had a wife and son," he said.

"Oh aye," Brenda replied, "that's why Jimmy turned to drink. Jimmy was married to a nurse called Patricia. She was a kind soul. Unfortunately she died of cancer just a couple of years after giving birth to their son. Jimmy was heartbroken and left with a young son to bring up. Eventually Danny worked with his dad. He was a lovely lad. Dan was shot dead in Alexandra Park I think it was back in 2002 .It was the final straw for Jimmy who lost the plot after that Danny was the apple of his eye and he seemed not to care anymore. He'd lost everything."

Gerry knew that feeling.

Brenda continued "Eventually he pulled himself together and continued the business on his own but he was never the same man again."

She then headed for the kitchen to make some lunch while Gerry and Jenny discussed their business.

"I reckon we should keep the office shut until after the funeral as a mark of respect," Gerry suggested, "then we'll have it completely renovated and redecorated".

Jenny could only agree. The office had seen better days and was, to say the least, shabby. Gerry also explained that now the flat came with the business he was also thinking of renovating that as well. He could move in and still be near the office.

"One thing Jimmy insisted on is that I can't sack you for five years. I just thought you should know I have no intention of doing so, in fact. I think you are due a pay rise."

"Why, thank you, kind sir," Jenny joked.

Gerry thought it was nice to see her smile again. He then explained that he knew what Jimmy had been paying her and he proposed to give her £350 per week, paid a month in advance. Then when he told her Jimmy had left her £1,000 in his will, Jenny again burst into tears. So much for the happy face. Gerry handed over £2,400 to Jenny and was straight back to business. He wanted her to obtain quotes for the office and flat for renovating and redecorating both. After lunch he was going to be busy elsewhere.

Over lunch Gerry asked Brenda if it was okay for him to extend his stay with them until he could sort out the flat. He knew the answer before he asked. Brenda said she would be very sad to see him moving out but understood. This was some relief to Gerry as he had been dreading telling her.

In the afternoon Gerry went along to the undertakers to confirm the arrangements for Jimmy's funeral and told them of his request to be buried with his wife Patricia and son Danny in Sighthill Cemetery.

His next call was a visit to see his old boss DCI Sandy Morton. Sandy was delighted to hear Gerry's news about becoming a private investigator and also to see Gerry looking much better physically He was however very sorry to hear of Jimmy's passing.

"I can tell you now you've made your decision," Sandy said. "Jimmy Quinn was one of the best informants I ever had."

It turned out that he had been passing information to Sandy for years. Not only was all of his information spot on but it led to some excellent arrests. Not least of which was Frank Graham Jnr. Jimmy Quinn had been Sandy's registered informant. That led Gerry to think that perhaps Matty McGowan had been feeding information about the Grahams to Jimmy who in turn passed it on to Sandy.

DCI Morton told Gerry that Jimmy had lost it for a wee while back when his wife had died and then again when his son was shot dead. Sandy expressed regret that nobody was ever arrested for the crime.

"You won't remember the case Gerry as that was just after the drug trial, and you had lost your parents and Paul. I just remember Jimmy speaking about his son one day. He'd arranged to meet me to pass on some information on a matter I was investigating. It seems Danny was looking into a number of rapes and serious assaults on ladies which had all taken place in Glasgow. He'd told Jimmy that he'd almost cracked the case and if his theory was correct he was about to open a hornets' nest.

"On the night he was killed Danny told his dad that he was going to meet someone who had all the answers. Unfortunately he didn't tell Jimmy who that person was and didn't document his suspicions.

"Around midnight police officers responded to a call of shots having been fired in Alexandra Park. On arrival they found Danny. He was dead, having been shot twice in the chest. At the time it was believed to be a possible robbery gone wrong, as his wristwatch and wallet had been taken. Despite our best efforts no witnesses or suspects were traced.

Jimmy was adamant that his son was murdered because he was getting too close and someone wanted rid of him. It was really saddening to see Jimmy falling apart. He began drinking heavily and not looking after himself properly. He had always dressed immaculately before then, but just let himself go."

Gerry knew exactly how Jimmy had been feeling. He'd been there but was lucky enough to have Audrey to look after him. He left his old gaffers office promising to let him know when the funeral was to take place.

That evening Jenny told Gerry that she had obtained two quotes for the renovation work to both the flat and the office. One for £10,000 and they could start hopefully in a week or so.

The second, which she was delighted with, was for £6,000 and they could start right away.

Gerry thought about it then said,

"Okay Jenny, phone the first one back and tell him he's got the job and to start as soon as he can. The second might be cheaper but if he can start right away that means he has got no work, so can't be up to much."

Jenny then told him the quote for decorating both places was £3,000. Again Gerry mulled it over. He still had a few thousand in his own bank account but at this rate that would not last forever. Eventually he said, "How do you fancy a bit of painting Jenny?"

"Anything's a change from typing," she replied.

"That's great," Gerry replied. "I'll see if Matty McGowan can give us a hand, because anything we can save just now will be a bonus." Going to the undertakers earlier had reminded Gerry that he would also need to pay for the funeral, as well as new furnishings for both the flat and office once they were renovated. That would make a big hole in his finances.

"By the way," Jenny added "I forgot to say, the lady you and Jimmy did that job for popped into the office when I was phoning the builders. I gave her the result of your findings, plus the photographs and she paid her bill. I wouldn't like to be her old man tonight.

"Anyway, I paid the telephone bill so we have £83.40 left in petty cash."

"Well done you," Gerry thought to himself. He hadn't fancied telling the woman her husband was cheating on her with a near fifty year old prostitute. It was something which he would quickly have to get used to. He smiled when Jenny gave him the amount of petty cash. The business was well and truly at rock bottom financially. Although Gerry still had money in his own account the forthcoming expenditure for Jimmy's funeral and the renovations would make a big dent in that.

The next evening Jimmy's coffin was taken to the local chapel where it remained overnight. The following morning the local priest said mass, the cortège then left for Sighthill Cemetery. As is usual on these occasions it poured from the heavens. Gerry took Brenda and Jenny, Sophie was at school. Under all the umbrellas Gerry could see that the local business community had turned out in force to pay their final respects to a local character. Gerry saw Sandy Morton standing some way back.

Gerry was glad that Jimmy had been laid to rest beside his wife and their son by the people he loved and respected. At the graveside Gerry made a silent promise, to try to make Jimmy proud of him and to continue to help others in the community as he had done. He would be a hard act to follow.

Afterwards everyone returned to the Cross Keys Pub where with the help of Brenda and Jenny, Betty Stuart had laid on a beautiful buffet. The locals gave Jimmy a right royal send off. Alex Stuart had the place in uproar when he remarked,

"Jimmy will be raging, missing a swally like this."

CHAPTER TWENTY

Everyone was up slightly later the next morning, Jenny rushed to get Sophie ready for school. For once Gerry missed out on his morning run, having relented the previous evening and been back on the booze to celebrate Jimmy's life.

After a hot shower, coffee and toast, Gerry and Jenny headed for the office. The first job for Gerry was to call into the funeral parlour and pay the bill for Jimmy's funeral.

Gerry had decided just to leave the old office closed until the renovations were completed. The builder was due to start any day. In the meantime. Tom and Sam were good enough to agree to rent Gerry some office space in their premises downstairs, whilst the refurbishment was going on upstairs.

As it turned out that was a very handy arrangement as they had a lot on, which kept Gerry busy. So much so he had to take Jenny out of the office to help him on more than one occasion. She loved it. The only thing was work Jimmy had generated was running out. Just a couple of days later Tom let Gerry know that his cheque had cleared at the bank, all the business debts were paid and the mortgage for the flat was back on track but there wasn't much left.

The builder was as good as his word and the renovations began a couple of weeks later.

During that period Gerry went to bed each night absolutely shattered but in some ways elated. With Jenny's help he was making a fist of the business and not once had he touched, let alone thought about, alcohol or medication. Despite working hard he stuck to his training and ran every morning in Alexandra Park. Each day every muscle ached. Sometimes he wondered if it was worth it but he had to have a positive mindset if he was to make a full recovery. It wasn't just him. He was now an employer with others to think about. Anyway the saying was, 'No pain, no gain.'

The builder made a magnificent job of the offices and as promised completed the work before

Christmas. He would be starting on the flat early in the new year. Having been busy in the last few weeks Gerry was able to put money aside to furnish his beautiful new offices. He and Jenny planned to hit the city centre and get everything required. First the whole premises needed to be decorated. Matty McGowan was enlisted to lend a hand, and was only too happy to help. In no time at all the office was ready for reopening and looked completely different. It now looked like a modern office, painted in soothing pastel colours. A much better environment in which to work. Gerry made sure Matty and Jenny were well paid for their efforts. They had both worked really hard and done a fantastic job.

Next came the visit to the city centre and some serious shopping. They had to buy absolutely everything for the office, new furniture, computers, the list was endless. Gerry knew how much he could spend but the pot was emptying at an alarming rate. He and Jenny spent hours in the city getting all that they needed and by the time they got home both were shattered.

The next morning it was two very tired people, who reluctantly headed to Jimmy's old flat. Gerry gave his run a miss as he was just about to give himself a workout clearing out the flat. This was hardly a task that either was looking forward to. As arranged a large skip had arrived. It was going to take some time to sort through Jimmy's possessions but Gerry reckoned most of it would end up in the skip. He had previously asked Matty McGowan to give him a hand with some of the heavier stuff and he was happy to oblige.

Gerry felt a strange responsibility towards Matty, as though Jimmy was looking down on him expecting that he should now take on his mantel and care for all the waifs and strays who came his way. It wasn't long before both men had worked up a sweat. The skip was indeed filling up with most of the heavy stuff, cooker, fridge, washing machine, three piece suite, bed sideboard and chest of drawers.

Gerry was glad of the help, slipped Matty a £50 note and thanked him for his assistance. Matty was over the moon and wandered back into his flat muttering his thanks.

After a break for coffee and a bacon sandwich from the local cafe, Gerry and Jenny then set about tackling all of Jimmy's clothing, bedding, ornaments and curtains. Like the suit Jimmy had always worn, most of it was past it's best. Between them they filled numerous black bin bags which would all end up in the skip as well. It was strange but they both had the same feeling, as though Jimmy's life had been for nothing and was now being discarded into a skip.

Jenny came across an album of photographs which showed Jimmy in his younger days. He had been slim then and was pictured with a beautiful, tallish woman with, what looked like, long blonde hair. They were accompanied by a young boy also with fair hair. Obviously Jimmy, his wife and Danny, their son. He was his mother's double.

In one cupboard Gerry came across a number of old case files and a briefcase. On opening the briefcase, amongst the usual birth, marriage and medical certificates, he was surprised to find some medals and a citation. The medals related to Jimmy's army service in Germany, Northern Ireland and the Falklands War. In a box he found the Military Medal with a citation which read:-

'Presented to Private James McGrory Quinn, No3 Commando, for outstanding bravery in the face of enemy fire during the Battle for Mount Kent, Falkland Islands May 1983'

There was also a newspaper cutting account of Jimmy's actions which told of his great bravery under enemy fire and how he helped to save the lives of several of his comrades, despite having been severely wounded himself. The article went on to say Jimmy had to be medically discharged from the army due to injuries to his right leg and abdomen.

Bloody hell, Gerry thought, the man was a war hero. Gerry also found what looked like a bayonet, probably from an Argentine weapon. It gave him an idea for the office.

From the paperwork Gerry was able to find out that James McGrory Quinn had been named after a famous legend of Glasgow Celtic Football Club. He was born on 2 February 1955 in Bridgeton, Glasgow and became a boy soldier. In 1980 Jimmy had married Patricia Fallon, a nurse. Two years later their son Daniel McGrain Quinn was born, named after Jimmy's favourite Celtic footballer. Just two years after the lad was born Gerry saw that his mother had died from breast cancer.

This must have been a devastating blow, not only would Jimmy be still suffering with his injuries, his wife had died and left him to bring up a two year old boy on his own. No wonder he liked a drink and no wonder he seemed so old. He'd only been fifty years old when he died but looked worn out by life itself.

That night Gerry lay awake into the wee small hours thinking of Jimmy and reading the old case files. They made for interesting reading. When he had the time he would look into some of the unsolved cases. He was particularly drawn to the file regarding the three woman who had been attacked in Glasgow city centre. This was the file Danny Quinn had been looking into when he was murdered. Gerry found startling similarities in the cases to the attack on Isla Buchanan, although they were separated by a number of years.

At 10am the next day, just a couple of days before the Christmas holidays began, after his morning run and breakfast, Gerry and Jenny opened up their newly refurbished office for the first time. Things got even better when the builder contacted Gerry to let him know he would be starting the renovations to the flat earlier than anticipated. They would start straight after the holidays. This was good news.

With all that had happened recently no one seemed to have given much of a thought to Christmas, Gerry certainly hadn't. It was only when Brenda asked what he was doing for his Christmas dinner that he realised that the holidays had sneaked up on him. He graciously accepted an invitation from Brenda to have dinner with her and the family. That afternoon he left the office telling Jenny he had private business to attend to and he could be contacted on his mobile if she needed him. He then went Christmas shopping in the city centre. It was just as well.

On Christmas morning he was awakened early by Sophie. She was so excited she had the whole house up. As Gerry entered the living room, still half asleep, she was attacking yet another parcel. The floor was strewn with presents and brightly coloured wrapping paper. Gerry had to smile, he recalled when he was Sophie's age being so excited on Christmas morning. The only difference back then was you got one big present and a few smaller ones. It seemed that now the kids got so many more presents.

Brenda and Jenny sat watching Sophie, just happy to be a family. It made Gerry think of his father and mother and brought a tear to his eye.

Gerry was more than a little surprised when he received presents from Brenda and from Jenny and Sophie. Brenda had bought him some expensive after shave and he got a very stylish new shirt from Jenny and Sophie.

He, in turn, had bought both ladies perfume and vouchers to shop at a top end ladies store in Glasgow. As he explained, he'd never been very good when it came to presents. He certainly could have fooled Brenda and Jenny as they were both delighted. Gerry gave Sophie a new doll that could do just about everything. It too had been very expensive. Finally, there was a box of Belgium chocolates each.

Everyone had been working so hard recently that after an excellent Christmas dinner, they

settled down to watch television. It wasn't long before all could be found asleep in easy chairs. All except Sophie who sat on the floor playing with her new doll.

They had a quiet time at Hogmanay. After a few drinks in the Cross Keys they all retired early. Just like everyone else around the country, they eagerly anticipated the arrival of a new year and all they hoped it would bring.

CHAPTER TWENTY-ONE

Gerry told Jenny to take an extra couple of days holiday. He had a lot of thinking and planning to do. The new office looked fantastic and had all been paid for. This had left the bank account low, once more.

Despite it being New Year's day, Gerry still went for his morning run. The air was crisp and cold and his breath billowed in front of him as he jogged around the park. If he were honest, he had probably eaten more than his fair share of mince pies over the past week.

Later in the office Gerry took a look at what enquiries they had on the books. That didn't take too long, because there were very few. He knew that with Jimmy's passing he would need to build his own reputation in the community to gain peoples trust and confidence. Thankfully he knew that Tom and Sam would probably have work for him to keep the firm ticking over but he would also need to generate some of his own.

As lunchtime approached Gerry decided, that he needed something to eat. Anything but turkey. The problem was, where would be open? He already knew the answer to that question - the Dragon Palace Chinese restaurant in Alexandra Parade.

Five minutes later Gerry was just about to cross the road when he saw the owner of the Dragon Palace, Sammy Chen, staggering out of the front door of his premises. He was bleeding from a nasty head wound and collapsed on the pavement. Gerry ran over to help him just as Sammy's daughter Soo Li came out of the premises. Gerry saw that her dress had been ripped.

"I'll phone for the police and an ambulance," Gerry offered.

"No, please no police," Soo Li replied, "my father will be okay."

Gerry helped her to lift the old man back inside the building. The interior of the restaurant had been trashed. Tables and chairs had been upturned and dishes were lying smashed upon the floor.

"What happened here?" Gerry asked.

"It's okay," Soo Li replied "everything is okay now."

Soo Li insisted that Gerry could leave and she would look after her father. She would not take no for an answer. Reluctantly Gerry returned to his office. He had a feeling that there was more to the situation than met the eye. No doubt he would hear more about it in due course.

As soon as everyone was back to work, after the holidays, Gerry went downstairs to see if his landlords required his services. He was not disappointed. Sam gave him the job of looking into an incident which had occurred locally and a young lad, now Sam's client, had been charged with serious assault. Gerry was right on it. The incident had occurred outside a club, which Gerry knew well. It had a bit of a reputation for trouble and so his first thought was to speak to someone in the police force to see if he could get any information on the case.

He phoned a friend at Baird Street Police Office to pick his brains about the incident. Gerry also took the opportunity to let his former colleague know that he was now a private investigator and if he or any fellow officer felt the need of his services just to give him a call. His former colleague promised to put up a notice with Gerry's address and telephone number on the notice board in the office for all to see Gerry was also able to glean from the officer information which led to him tracing two witnesses to the incident he was investigating. That evening Gerry met the couple in a local cafe and took statements from both which proved Sam's client to be completely innocent of the charge against him. Gerry went back to his office and typed out the statements himself. The next morning he handed them to Sam Bryson who was more than impressed.

Just as he had promised, the builder took just over three weeks to renovate the flat. The transformation was incredible. A brand new state of the art kitchen and new bathroom complete with power shower. New wooden flooring and rewiring throughout. All that was required now was redecoration of the whole flat and then new furniture. Gerry was now too busy trying to build up the business to contemplate doing any of the redecorating himself and Jenny was also tied up with plenty of work at the office. The answer lay close by. Gerry had been more than impressed by the way Matty had helped during the office decorating, so he asked his new neighbour if he fancied doing the flat. Matty was only too delighted to take on the extra work. Gerry knew he still worked for the Grahams helping out at the taxi office on an evening but the wages they paid were pitiful, barely enough to get by on. It had been funny bumping into Matty again after all these years, now he found himself about to be his next door neighbour.

The new year seemed to have started very well for the rookie private investigator but things may be about to take a turn.

On Saturday 28 January 2006, the day before Chinese New Year, things livened up. Sammy Chen had chosen to close the Dragon Palace early. He would be back in just a few short hours to prepare the premises for the forthcoming celebrations. Sammy had invited many family and friends to his restaurant to welcome in the year of the Dog. It would be a lavish feast and the Chinese community all over Glasgow looked forward to the festivities.

There was much to be done and despite feeling less than well Sammy had a certain standing in his community which he had to maintain. He had hardly recovered from the injury he had received just a few short weeks before, when Gerry Lynch had come to his aid. Although the stitches had been removed Sammy still suffered from severe headaches. Something he kept to himself as he did not want his family worrying. He just told himself it was what he could expect, no longer being a young man.

Around midnight Sammy left his restaurant and walked to his car. He was unable to open it as someone had put something in the locks. While he was distracted with this problem, he was suddenly set upon by two men, who struck him from behind several times with what later, given his injuries, were believed to be either machetes or swords. He sustained very serious injuries and was rushed to hospital. Thankfully Glasgow Royal Infirmary was close by and he was quickly admitted to the intensive care unit. He had a fractured skull and sustained numerous deep lacerations to his neck, back, legs and arms. Sammy had lost a lot of blood and was lucky to be alive.

The Police were called but could not interview him that night. No one from the restaurant or in the nearby vicinity had seen or heard anything.

On Monday morning Gerry's first visitor was Sammy Chen's daughter, Soo Li. She had come to see Gerry for his help. She looked completely worn out. Since the attack on her father she had spent the last two days at the hospital sat at his bedside, only being able to speak to him briefly. She was now here to see Gerry at her father's request.

"How is your father?" Gerry asked,

"He is still very poorly," Soo Li replied. "It will take him a long time to recover. That is why I have come to you. I know the police are involved but I fear they will only come up against a wall of silence. The Chinese community tend to keep their problems to themselves but I have spoken to my father and he has given me permission to speak frankly with you and to ask for your help. I have been able to persuade him that we need help to stop these evil people from exploiting us any longer. My father said that Jimmy Quinn was a good man who would have helped us and if he chose you as business partner then you must be a good man too." Gerry realised straight away that he was being paid a great compliment. For a Chinaman to place his trust in him was an honour. Sammy Chen must believe that he and his community were in real trouble if he was prepared to do such a thing and break with age old traditions.

Soo Li gave Gerry some of her family history. She explained that Sammy Chen had come to Britain from Hong Kong just after the Second World War. Even back in the 1950s her father paid protection money or blood money to the Wo Sing Wo Triad. Everybody did, it was just part of life for the Chinese community trying to make their businesses work.

Back then the amount paid was tiny compared to today. Recently they had been visited at the restaurant on several occasions by three or four men, all Chinese, who said they were members of the Tai Huen Chair Triad or Big Circle Gang. They demanded payment of £10,000 for protection, saying they had taken over. Her father had told them that he paid the Wo Sing Wo and, anyway, could not afford such an amount.

"That was when the attacks started," Soo Li went on. "At first they just came in annoying customers and making threats and then as you saw recently, Mr Lynch, they attacked my father and I in the restaurant and damaged a lot of the furniture. I am terrified for my father. He will not speak to the police but even if he did we don't believe there is much they can do.

"We live in a small Chinese community not far from Hogganfield Loch. All the other Chinese there have their own businesses, either restaurants or takeaways . They look upon my father as the leader of our community as our family has been in Scotland the longest. I don't want him to end up like Philip Wong did back in the 1980s. I will speak to the members of our community on behalf of my father and if I can get any information from them, will you help us?"

Gerry could hardly refuse. He was more than honoured that Sammy Chen would place his trust in him. Also it seemed that the local community were already taking him to their hearts, just like Jimmy before him. He wasn't yet sure how he could help but he would try to find a way.

Once Soo Li had left Gerry knew exactly who to call for advice. He spoke to Sandy Morton and outlined his problem. Sandy told him to leave it with him. He would contact someone that could help and get back to him.

While waiting for Sandy to get back to him Gerry had another matter to look into. Remarkably his free advertising through the police had already paid dividends.

One of the cops working in the support unit had contacted him. The officer was suspicious that his wife might be having an affair. She was in the habit of going out every Sunday night, according to her, to play bingo. But the officer had heard whispers that she was going elsewhere. For the next three Sunday nights Gerry followed the lady from her home. It didn't take long to establish that she wasn't going to bingo. She wasn't having an affair either.

Each Sunday she was attending the local old folks home and entertaining the residents with a few songs. She had been asked just before Christmas, when someone had let them down and had enjoyed it so much, she continued in the new year.

Afraid that her husband might ridicule her she had told him she was going to bingo. It turned out that, apparently, in her younger days the woman had been quite a good singer but her husband had never given her any credit or the support she deserved, so when she had got the chance to sing again, she had kept it from him.

His lack of support for his wife cost him £300 plus expenses, as well as a red face.

CHAPTER TWENTY-TWO

When Gerry had phoned Sandy with his problem regarding the Chinese community, he had known exactly who to contact. Denis Mitchell was an inspector at Her Majesty's Revenue and Customs. He and Sandy had been involved in several enquiries together over the years. Nobody knew more about the Chinese communities in Scotland than Denis.

When he phoned, Sandy knew exactly how to get him on board.

"Hello Denis," Sandy said, "can I buy you lunch?"

Sandy took Gerry with him, firstly to introduce him to Denis Mitchell and secondly, so he didn't have to repeat the conversation later. He knew Denis of old, he liked his food and could talk for Britain. They met in a restaurant overlooking the River Clyde. Denis drove into the city from his office in Paisley. After the usual introductions and having ordered from the menu they settled down to business.

Gerry told Denis about the incidents involving Sammy Chen and his daughter, Soo Li, and asked what he knew about the triads in the UK and more especially Glasgow.

Denis laughed and said, "I hope you are both sitting comfortably, this could take a while."

Over a fine lunch Denis explained to Sandy and Gerry all that he could.

The triads or secret societies had been in existence for centuries. They were involved in all types of crime, contract killings, drug trafficking, human trafficking, extortion, murder money laundering, arms trafficking, importation of illegal tobacco as well as forged documentation, passports and the like. You name it, they did it. When the Communist Party came to power in China in 1949 there was a crackdown on organised crime on the mainland. This forced the triads to move elsewhere and they went to Hong Kong which of course at that time was a British ruled territory.

It is thought that most triad societies were formed between 1914 and 1939 and there were once more than 300. Numbers had fluctuated over the years. In the1950s it's thought there were 300,000 triad members. In 1956, after riots, the Hong Kong Government introduced much stricter law enforcement to the colony and the triads became less active. It is around this time they are thought to have spread their wings all over the globe to places such as New Zealand and Canada as well as Britain.

"There are, of course, various triads. The Sui Fong, Wo an Lak and Tai Huen Chair or Big Circle Gang are amongst them and known to be active in the United Kingdom and are involved in all the crimes I mentioned earlier. They are believed to divide land or areas between them. Each has their own region. The trade in illegal tobacco in Scotland alone is worth more than ten million pounds a year. It mainly involves rolling tobacco which the authorities know is very bad for the health of those using it. The tobacco contains high tar, nicotine and carbon monoxide. It really is amazing how they get so much of the stuff into the country. We've had some great results lately but, to be honest, we are just scratching the surface."

The sale of illegal cigarette was a massive industry and quite simple to run.

"How do they get the tobacco into this country?" Gerry asked.

"Easier than you think," Denis replied. " Packages weighing less than two kilos are posted to various people or companies in the UK. The triad accomplices are paid between 50 pence and £2 for each package. A member of the triad then collects it and takes it to a factory to be packaged into 50 gram pouches. The favourite brand to copy was Golden Virginia which sold for £6.50 compared to around £15 for the genuine article. It was estimated that in the region of £3 to £3.50 profit was made per pouch. It seems incredible the lengths they go to but the profits outweigh the risk."

Denis paused for a moment, to attack another piece of the rather large steak he had ordered and then went on,

"Things in the UK quietened down back in the 1970s and 80s especially after the murder of Philip Wong. It may be that the Big Circle Gang are now trying to muscle in and expand their territory at the expense of another triad. Things could get really nasty. I'll keep my ear to the ground and let you know if I hear anything and if you could do the same I'd be obliged."

Three hours after the soup had arrived they parted after a very nice, informative and expensive lunch. Denis and Sandy were quite happy as Gerry footed the bill. Gerry drove Sandy back to Stewart Street Police Office to pick up his car. En route he asked Sandy what he knew about the Philip Wong murder.

"It was a murder that occurred back in October 1985, I think it was," Sandy began. "Philip Wong, or to give him his real name Kwong Wong, was a 49 year old businessman who was hacked to death by, it is believed, three men outside the Tin Tin bookshop in Rose Street, in Garnethill, Glasgow. The bookshop was used as a Mahjong gambling school. Wong, like Mr Chen, went to open his car and someone had stuffed something in the locks. He was then attacked and killed.

"Wong owned the Lucky Star Chinese restaurant in Sauchiehall Street, as well as other eating establishments in Stirling, Perth and Edinburgh. He was described as a man of integrity and responsibility in the Scottish Chinese community. His first restaurant had been the Mandarin in Sauchiehall Street, which back in the late 1970s was allegedly the hub of a widespread extortion ring. There was a High Court trial and some Chinese criminals were imprisoned. Mr Wong was apparently a great help to the police during the enquiry.

"It's really guess work as to why he was killed. It may have been drug related and that might possibly lay the blame on the Manchester based Wo Sing Wo. Some say Wong was an advisor or 'white paper' to the triad, others that he was their leader in Scotland and Northern England. His family have always strongly denied this. Whatever the reason nobody has ever been charged with his murder."

As Gerry dropped his old gaffer off he realised that it was a dangerous game he had got involved in. He was still determined to get to the bottom of the matter though and help the Chen family any way he could. No doubt it would be a tough nut to crack.

CHAPTER TWENTY-THREE

It was almost the end of February and already time to move into his new flat. Matty had once again done a fantastic job of decorating the place.

Gerry was sorry to be moving out of Brenda's. He would miss Jenny and Sophie as well; he had started referring to them as his girls. But he needed to be in a place of his own. Brenda had agreed to continue doing his laundry and clean his new flat, so everyone was happy. Gerry was just looking forward to Saturday nights, lying on his new leather settee with a takeaway meal and a few beers watching Match of the Day. It didn't get any better than that.

Since Jimmy's death, Gerry and Matty had become very close. Each knew the others story but they never spoke about the past. They didn't need to, as both knew the other hated the Grahams and would do whatever they could to avenge the loved ones they had lost because of that family. Gerry had been very open with Matty and had asked if he ever heard anything while working at the taxi office which might be of use if he could pass it on. He was willing to pay for the information. He wasn't asking Matty to become a 'grass', just to keep him in the loop.

If their hatred of the family wasn't enough there was further bad news to come. Frank Graham Jnr had been imprisoned in January 2002 for a period of ten years. Everyone knew he would do half that time and be out in 2007. What they didn't know was that the Graham family's legal team, under Maurice Henshaw QC, had continued to work very hard on behalf of their client and had succeeded in getting the sentence reduced. Frank would be released in June 2006, in a matter of just over four months.

Gerry just knew that even now, almost four years after the court case, he wasn't safe from their clutches. At some point the Grahams might still come looking for him and it was better to be ready. He really wanted to do something about the whole Graham family but he was too busy building his business and rebuilding his life to pay them much attention. So it was that when they came Gerry was caught slightly off guard.

It was a Saturday night in early March and as was now his habit, Gerry was in the Cross Keys. He'd limited himself to having a couple of beers before grabbing a takeaway and heading for his flat. Despite being very busy at work Gerry had started going to boxing again and to Jim Kennedy's Taekwondo classes in Kirkintilloch once a week. He was now much fitter than he had been for some time although he knew he would never get back to the level he and Paul had achieved together. Jim Kennedy had cheered him up by entering him into a forthcoming competition.

"Just so you can gauge where you are on the comeback trail," he had laughed. "Oh and, by the way, you'll be up against a southpaw."

It had been a long week and Gerry had enjoyed a laugh with the punters in the pub but it was home time. His only decision now was what type of takeaway to buy: Chinese, Indian or a pizza from Mario's. He settled on a sweet and sour chicken from the Dragon Palace. Fifteen minutes later Gerry was just letting himself into his building when he became aware of several large figures suddenly appearing out of the shadows.

He dropped his takeaway leaving his hands free to defend himself. Gerry aimed a kick at the first man and as he did so a second man struck him on the left arm, with what appeared to be an iron bar. He felt the bone in his forearm snap. However it didn't stop him carrying the fight to his attackers. They all ended up in the street and Gerry saw that there were in fact four of them. One was carrying a knife. A thought immediately flashed through his mind. "Were these the ones who had carried out the cowardly attack on young David O'Neill?"

By now Gerry's adrenaline levels were through the roof as the battle continued. His opponents were strong and didn't seem as though they would be giving up any time soon. In a strange way Gerry welcomed the confrontation. He was using all the moves that Jim Kennedy had taught him to fend them off, as well as the hatred he had stored up for the Graham family over the past few years. There was no way he was going to be defeated by this lot.

The fight continued for several more minutes and Gerry sustained damage to his face and rib cage. The guy wielding the knife slashed him on the face. Remarkably Gerry managed to overpower and disarm him. Another lay on the roadway semi conscious. At one point Gerry found himself rolling about on the road held by one of his attackers in a vice like grip around the neck. Only a well aimed blow to a certain part of the male anatomy extricated him from his opponents grasp. Not a move he had been taught at Taekwondo class,

After what seemed like an age, despite his injures, Gerry got the upper hand and his attackers made off into the night, nursing their own wounds. The altercation had not lasted very long but had been a violent, brutal and bloody encounter.

With some difficulty Gerry retrieved his takeaway meal from the pavement before managing to reach his flat. He knew he had a broken forearm and his ribs hurt like hell, so he was certain they were also broken. Apart from feeling sore all over his face was bleeding where he had been slashed and would need stitching. Gerry had no idea who the four guys were but he was fairly sure that they worked for the Grahams. However he couldn't really worry about that now, he needed to get to the hospital. He phoned a taxi and twenty minutes later found himself in the accident and emergency of the Royal Infirmary. Because it was Saturday night the place was heaving. What else could he expect on a weekend in the centre of one of Britain's biggest cities?

Having been sat for about an hour almost bored to distraction and trying to breath whilst in agony, Gerry was amazed when Matty walked into the reception and saw him. He quickly told Matty what had happened . Matty said that he was there to pick up Sadie Gleason, who it seemed had been given a 'kicking' by a punter, whose wallet she had tried to steal. A few minutes later Sadie was brought to the front desk in a wheel chair. Gerry hardly recognised her, she had been given such a beating. Matty said he would take her home and come back for him but Gerry insisted he would get a taxi, as he said he didn't know how much longer he would have to wait. So Matty left with the sorry looking Sadie.

Eventually Gerry was examined by an exhausted doctor who after an x-ray confirmed his own earlier prognosis. Gerry had to have a plaster cast fitted to his left forearm right up to the elbow. He was supposed to keep it there for six weeks, then return for further examination. He also had, at least, four fractured ribs. His facial wounds were cleaned up and twenty stitches inserted where he had been slashed.

The doctor also gave him some painkillers to allow him to get a sleep once he got home. No way was he going to take any tablets and thought he wouldn't be able to sleep because of his ribs anyway.

Apart from that how was he going to carry on his business with a 'stookie' on his arm? It was a very tired, and depressed Gerry who alighted from his taxi and entered his flat around four o'clock in the morning. He sagged down onto his settee and remarkably fell asleep almost immediately. The takeaway he had purchased earlier remained uneaten on the coffee table.

The next morning Gerry was awakened by Matty McGowan knocking at the door. He had come to make sure Gerry was alright. Over a cup of coffee Gerry explained how he'd come to have been assaulted. He described his assailants and Matty thought he knew them. Just as Gerry feared, they did work for the Graham's.

"Well there's one thing for sure, Matty," Gerry said. "There's not much I can do with this thing on my arm. I can't even drive my bloody car, so how am I gonna work? "

"I'll drive you if you want, Mr Lynch," Matty offered.

So Gerry agreed to employ Matty as his driver for at least the next six weeks or until he got the all clear from the hospital. He arranged that Matty would start on Monday morning by driving him to his office and then they would take it from there.

Whilst he was incapacitated Gerry also made the decision to look more closely at some of Danny Quinn's old outstanding cases. That one regarding the three women in particular had caught his eye and he kept coming back to it. Similarities to the attack on Isla Buchanan could not be ignored and there must have been something about it that had got Danny Quinn killed.

On the Monday morning, bright and early Matty appeared at Gerry's door to take him to work. He found a bedraggled Gerry fighting to get into his clothing. He was still wet from the shower and hadn't even combed his hair. Matty smiled at Gerry which was the wrong thing to do.

"Are you laughing at me, McGowan," Gerry growled. "you want to try sleeping with bloody broken ribs and a stookie on. Never mind trying to go to the toilet and get a bloody shower."

Matty said nothing but helped Gerry into his chinos and then held his shirt while he put his arms into the sleeves.

"Thanks," Gerry said begrudgingly, as he started coughing and holding his ribs.

Once they arrived at the office Gerry asked Jenny to bring him a coffee. She asked what had happened to him, as he did look as though he had been involved in a car crash. When Gerry explained what had happened she asked why he hadn't phoned the police. He just replied he would deal with it and went into his office, taking Danny Quinn's files with him. He was already exhausted and this was only day one with his 'stookie'. When Jenny brought his coffee he asked if they had any ice. Eventually he sat reading the files with ice wrapped in a tea towel icing his ribs. It eased the pain for a while until he coughed again. Breathing was still difficult.

When Matty came back to drive him home at the end of the day Gerry apologised to him. He realised he'd been frustrated and out of order earlier. He shouldn't have taken it out on him. If

anyone knew what it felt like to take a beating it was Matty.

"That's alright, Mr Lynch," was all Matty said.

CHAPTER TWENTY-FOUR

Every Monday evening in life, about seven o'clock, Frank Graham senior and his wife Agnes were picked up from their home by one of the families taxis and deposited at the Crooked Man public house. Frank then stayed in the pub playing dominoes and holding court with his pals, whilst the lovely Maggie accompanied her mother across the road to the Willow Centre bingo hall. Around ten o'clock the two 'ladies' returned to the pub. Usually about midnight the lovely couple were poured into a taxi and driven home.

Frank and Agnes had moved from their old home to their spacious new ground floor flat only three weeks before this particular Monday. The new complex in which they lived had state of the art CCTV surveillance covering the front of the building. They were delighted with their new home.

It was around two in the morning and not a thing was stirring. Least of all Frank and Agnes Graham who had both been more than a little tipsy by the time they reached their new flat that evening. It was just two days after Gerry Lynch had been attacked outside his home.

No one saw the figure dressed in all black with a balaclava covering his head flitting between the shadows and moving towards the back door of the building. The man had watched these premises being built and noted that for all the CCTV coverage of the front, they had neglected the rear doors. Perhaps this was because all the back doors had a unique key which only a tenant and the local housing office possessed. But it hadn't been difficult to obtain a key while it was being fitted and have a copy made.

Silently the figure approached the front door of the ground floor flat and listened. There was no sound from within. The figure opened the letter box and poured a quantity of flammable liquid down the door and into the hallway. He then ignited the liquid with a lighter before escaping through the back door which he locked again. It seemed only moments before the fire took hold and soon the flat was an inferno. There was no escape for anyone within.

Frank Graham Senior and his wife Agnes Graham were burnt to death just as Gerry Lynch's parents had been.... and so it began.

The newspapers the next day were full of it. *'COUPLE DIE IN BLAZE'*, *'GANG WAR DECLARED'*, *'PARENTS OF CRIME FAMILY SLAIN'*

Gerry had slept well, sat up in a reclining chair, despite the stookie and his sore ribs. He was about to get a rude awakening. Someone was banging on his front door and at first he thought it was Matty. A look at his alarm clock revealed it was only six o'clock in the morning. He struggled to the front door while wrestling on his dressing gown . Upon answering the door he was confronted with half a dozen uniformed police officers in riot gear and a couple of suits from the CID. One of whom produced a warrant card and identified himself as Detective Inspector Samson from Baird Street Police Office. Gerry had heard of him but they had never met. He was known for obvious reasons by the nickname 'Delilah' and had the reputation of being a bit of a bastard. You had to laugh though, the police did like a nickname. Samson's fitted perfectly not only because of his surname, but also he was as bald as a coot.

DI Samson was however not in a jovial mood. He was in possession of a search warrant. Before Gerry knew what had hit him he was being detained, handcuffed and conveyed in his boxer shorts and dressing gown to Baird Street Police Office whilst the police began searching his flat.

About an hour later he was sat in an interview room, in a paper suit which the police had provided for him. On the opposite side of the table were DI Samson and Detective Sergeant Bob Lorimer. Still half asleep, Gerry had gleaned they wished to speak to him regarding the murder of Frank Graham Snr. and his wife Agnes Graham who had been burnt to death in their home in identical circumstances to Gerry's parents. Having searched Gerry's flat they'd found a jacket with petrol staining on the left sleeve and in their minds Gerry was as guilty as sin. There was only one problem, they couldn't prove it.

Samson and Lorimer grilled Gerry for over an hour. He was then required to allow the police to take swabs from his hands and arms. They were obviously looking for residue of petrol or some other flammable liquid on him. Over the piece Gerry had learned one thing. Samson was indeed a bastard. Eventually he could take no more.

"Listen, Detective Inspector," he wheezed, struggling for breath. "I've answered all your questions and told you how I got petrol on my jacket. I was assaulted on Saturday night and you can see the result. Just in case you haven't noticed, the petrol is on the left hand sleeve of my jacket, which I can't wear whilst I have this stookie on my arm. Neither can I drive my car. So please tell me how I got to Springburn, carried out this crime and how I came to be wearing a jacket which at present does not fit me?"

Samson knew he was beaten but found it hard to give in.

"You must admit Lynch, you're not sorry these people have died?"

"No Inspector, I'll give you that," Gerry replied holding his ribs. "I'm only sorry the rest of them weren't inside as well."

Samson knew the history of what had happened to 'A' Division crime squad.

"Lynch, you just listen to me now, I'm warning you. We all know what happened to your family and colleagues but we can't have a vigilante on the streets. I'm releasing you without charge at the moment but we'll be watching you, Lynch."

Half an hour later Matty arrived in response to Gerry's phone call and picked him up from the police station and took him home. The flat was a right mess.

"Polis bastards!" Matty exclaimed. "Oh sorry, Mr Lynch, I forgot."

"Naw, you're alright, Matty," Gerry replied. "what a bloody mess. Can you go and get Brenda and ask if she can come and clean up?"

Matty collected Brenda and she had the place shipshape in no time. She wanted to stay and look after him but Gerry said he had to get to work. Once he had taken a shower and managed to find some clothes to wear, he eventually had Matty drive him to the office but couldn't work.

He found it impossible to concentrate. He had no idea who had brought about the deaths of Frank and Agnes Graham but he would love to shake them by the hand. If Gerry thought that his troubles were over though he was mistaken, as they had only just begun. Matty excused himself to take Sadie Gleason for a check up. Gerry didn't mind as he wasn't going anywhere anytime soon. Jenny went to the local cafe to pick up some sandwiches for lunch.

Along in Springburn, Jamie Graham was in a rage. He was obviously distraught at having lost his parents. What he wanted to know was who was responsible. He had called an urgent family meeting at the Crooked Man.

In recent weeks the Chinese triads had been encroaching on the Graham's territory trying to off load a huge amount of cannabis, as well as flooding all the pubs and shops with illicit, cheap tobacco. The family had reacted and more than a few beatings and woundings had been handed out on both sides. Jamie believed the Chinese were the favourites for killing his parents. He admitted it did appear to have been carried out in the same way as they had killed Gerry Lynch's family but he knew Lynch was not responsible. Bobby and Billy had seen to that. Lynch had a broken arm and other injuries after a fight with four of their associates. Jamie was disappointed he had only been injured but strangely had a certain respect for Lynch, because being able to fight off four men took some bottle. Next time hopefully there would be a different result.

No, Jamie was convinced that the circumstances of his parents death were just a coincidence. It was down to the Chinese. He gave orders to wreak retribution on everyone and everywhere that had anything to do with the triads. At the end of the meeting Jamie left the pub and was following his driver over to his Mercedes Benz. Although it was Tuesday morning the street was very quiet, and there were only a few people about.

The driver got behind the wheel as Margaret came to the door of the pub and shouted to Jamie. He went back to speak to her while the driver turned the ignition of the vehicle on.

There was a huge explosion and Jamie was thrown into the doorway where he and Margaret landed in a tangle. Both were uninjured which was more than could be said for Jamie's driver. The Mercedes was on fire and had been totally destroyed. The driver had been blown to bits. Jamie scanned the street looking to see if he could see anyone who might be responsible. He saw no one but knew he'd had a very lucky escape. That would not happen again.

Within minutes the police and fire brigade attended. The fire was extinguished and arrangements made to have the car removed for forensic examination. All the Graham family were interviewed and for once told the truth. They had seen nothing and had no idea who had carried out this atrocity. Jamie had his own thoughts on the matter and someone would suffer for having the temerity to try to kill him. As his dad had always said, nobody messes with the Grahams.

In the next few days the streets of Glasgow were like a war zone. The casualty departments of several hospitals were inundated with members of both rival gangs, the Graham's and triad members, seeking medical attention. Mostly for stab or cutting injuries. There were worryingly, also a couple of gunshot wounds. Par for the course, the police received not one complaint and amazingly none of the victims were able to describe or identify their attacker. By the weekend, thankfully, everything seemed to have calmed down again.

On the Saturday night a group of Chinese businessmen were entering their favourite casino in the city centre. As they walked up the steps towards the front door a car came around the corner, tyres screeching. The driver slammed on the brakes and the vehicle came to a halt right at the front door of the casino. The rear passenger door of the vehicle opened and a holdall was thrown into the doorway. The car made of again at speed and disappeared into the night.

Everyone froze for a moment trying to take in what was happening, then the bomb exploded. Four people were killed and two received life threatening injuries.

When the incident occurred every member of the Graham family was within the Crooked Man. Each giving an alibi to the other. Detective Chief Inspector Sandy Morton knew that this was only the start. Things would get much worse before they got better.

CHAPTER TWENTY-FIVE

The day had arrived for the funeral of Frank Graham Snr. and Agnes. The church in Springburn was packed to capacity. It seemed as though every criminal in Glasgow and beyond were present to give Frank and Agnes a proper send off or, in some cases, to ensure that they were in fact deceased. No one could really believe what had happened and like the remainder of the family they were at a loss as to who the culprit was. As was usual on these occasions the weather played its part. It was cold and icy rain fell the whole day.

Detective Chief Inspector Morton told Gerry to keep well away and he did exactly that. But that did not stop Strathclyde Police Serious Crime Squad from mounting a special intelligence gathering surveillance operation. They filmed the whole thing, noting all those in attendance as well as associates and their vehicles.

Even those who would be classed as sworn enemies of the Graham's were there to offer their condolences. After the service the huge cortège made its way firstly to Daldowie Crematorium where Frank and Agnes were cremated. Afterwards they all went back to the Crooked Man to drink to the departed. Matty McGowan tagged along and mingled with the mourners picking up any information he could.

Later he reported back to Gerry Lynch. He believed that two of the men who had attacked him were a couple of lowlifes from Partick called Willie Collins and Pat Reilly. Both had a string of convictions involving violence. They were known associates of the Graham twins and had done quite a few jobs for them in the past. It also appeared that Gerry had laid a few good blows on them as they were still carrying some nasty looking bruises. Matty was still working on the identity of the other two assailants.

Matty had also overheard Cammy Wilson saying the remaining members of the family were to hold a meeting in the Crooked Man the following week to work out what was to happen next, as regards the family business. Jamie knew Frank Jnr. would be released from prison shortly and they needed to look to the future. He knew given the large attendance at the funeral that the vultures were circling only too ready to step in and take over. They had to remain strong.

Gerry had spent the day trying, without much success, to get some work done. He was just about to think about going home, when Jenny popped her head around his office door.

"Gerry," she whispered, "I know we are just about ready to close but there is a man in reception who says he knows you. He is in a bit of a state and wants your help."

"What's his name?" Gerry asked.

"Robert Leishman, says he knows you from Easterhouse."

"Show him in please Jenny" Gerry said.

Gerry remembered Robert Leishman well. A big strong strapping lad who had lived just a couple of doors down the road. They had gone to the same schools and although Robert was a couple of years older than Gerry, they had been friends and ,as lads did, got into a few scrapes together as they were growing up. Robert's younger brother Alan was the same age as Gerry and he made up the trio of wee terrors.

Robert Leishman entered Gerry's office. He looked twenty years older than his thirty-eight years. He was a broken man, stooped, with a gaunt look on his face. Quite simply he looked ill.

Gerry asked him to take a seat and he slumped into a chair. It took a couple of strong whiskies before Robert could compose himself sufficiently to tell Gerry his problem.

When he eventually related his story Robert explained that he and his wife Kathy had lived in Cumbernauld for the last few years. They ran a distribution business. They had a daughter Chloe who was 18 years old. As soon as he mentioned his daughter Robert began sobbing.

After a few minutes he settled again and continued his story.

Chloe had done really well at school gaining four 'A' passes and three 'B' passes in her examinations. This allowed her to fulfil her dream of attending Glasgow School of Art to study textiles and jewellery design. She had started her first course in September the previous year and had settled in right away. She loved it.

Just before Christmas Chloe and her friends had gone into Glasgow for a night out. Chloe did not come home. She had died after digesting tablets in a night club.

"Nobody has got the jail for supplying her Gerry". Robert began sobbing again, "It has broken Kathy and me. I just want justice, Gerry, can you help?"

Gerry saw his old friend down onto Alexandra Parade and watched as he left in a taxi. He had promised to look into the matter for his old pal, once his sore ribs and broken arm had mended. What else could he do?

The only problem was he would need to speak to the investigating officer looking into the case. That meant he had to see Detective Constable Audrey Jennings again. Something he was afraid to do after failing to contact her even once since his release from hospital several months before. Now it seemed he had no choice. A friend had asked for his help. He would need to man up.

CHAPTER TWENTY-SIX

All through the night Gerry couldn't sleep. Apart from his injuries, something was eating at him, and he mulled things over and over in his mind. At first he thought about how the Graham parents had been murdered and then it was Danny Quinn's outstanding cases. He had become obsessed with the files. He tossed and turned and when eventually he got up, he felt awful.

Still no question of going for a run but at least his ribs felt better and he had taken to walking to the office in the morning. Gerry headed straight to the shower. Again he had to wrestle himself into his clothes, not the best mood to start a new day.

Once he had arrived at work Gerry once again shut himself in his office and told Jenny he was not to be disturbed. He sat with a large mug of coffee, yet again reading Danny's files and jotting down notes on a large pad.

He realised what had been troubling him all night. Someone was dealing with the Graham family and he really wanted to be that person. To do that he had to rid himself of the buzzing in his head which was caused by the Danny Quinn files. Once he had dealt with that he would be free to turn his attention to the Graham's.

By lunchtime he gave Matty a call. He would only need him to drive over to Drumchapel in the afternoon and make another call in Haghill on the way home. Matty was to pick him up at 3pm.

Gerry decided that some fresh air was in order and he offered to go to the nearby cafe to pick up some lunch for Jenny and himself. He felt strangely lethargic walking along the footpath. The broken arm was hampering his exercise regime and the lack of sleep wasn't helping either.

Perhaps all the incidents involving the Grahams and the assault upon him were indeed beginning to take their toll. Maybe Gerry wasn't as well as he thought he was. He was full of doubts.

There was no doubt DI Samson had taken a dislike towards him and felt he was somehow involved in the murders. The ironic thing was that Gerry did wish he had been involved. Someone was doing his work for him. He decided to try to put the Graham's out of his mind and concentrate on Danny's outstanding files.

The usually reliable Matty was half-an-hour late in picking Gerry up at the office. Gerry thought he was looking pale and asked if he was alright. Matty said he was fine and apologised for being late. He had forgotten he had promised to take Sadie Gleason for another check up at the hospital and it had taken longer than he had expected.

It was no big deal. Gerry had arranged his first appointment in Drumchapel for 4.15pm.

Matty drove Gerry over to Drumchapel. As they travelled into Glasgow Gerry explained that he was looking into outstanding enquiries which had been started a few years before by Jimmy's son, Danny.

Basically it was the case that three women had been raped and badly beaten in very similar circumstances. As far as Gerry could tell, from statements they had made at the time, all three women had more or less given the same description of their attacker but nobody was ever arrested as a result of police enquiries at the time.

"I want you to come in with me when I interview these women, Matty. If you think of anything, let me know."

Okay, Mr Lynch," Matty replied, pulling the BMW into the kerb. "That's us at the first address now."

Carol Duffy had been the second victim but Gerry had decided to visit her first and then work their way back into town. Carol still lived in a flat in Kinfauns Drive with her three now teenage children. The flat was in a bit of a state but Gerry thought nothing of it. Who could keep three wild kids under control and do the housework as well?

She was expecting them as Gerry had telephoned earlier in the day. From Danny's files he already knew that Carol had come to live in Drumchapel when she had married her late husband Bernard Duffy. The three children came along in quick succession before Bernard had died of a drugs over-dose. It was an all too familiar story, Carol Duffy was still quite an attractive woman if a little thin. She was hardly at her best when Gerry and Matty called, despite knowing they were coming. She wore no makeup and was still wearing her nightdress and dressing gown.

According to the file Danny had collated Carol had been attacked in late November 1993. Back then she had been an eighteen year old prostitute.

Gerry read out the statement she had given to Danny Quinn. She had been picked up by a good looking man in the lounge bar of a pub down by the River Clyde. They had a drink together and he had led her outside to his car.

"I just thought we would do it and I'd be back in the bar in no time." Carol. said.

Gerry continued to read her statement to her.

She had stated she remembered feeling drowsy and recalls the same man who had picked her up having intercourse with her but his face was somehow disfigured. The next thing she knew she had been dumped in Blythswood Street in Glasgow city centre where two other prostitutes found her. She had been badly beaten and raped. The matter was reported to the police but nothing happened. They just said it was an occupational hazard. Both Gerry and Matty felt sorry for the woman.

Just to clear up a few points Gerry had questions.

"Carol, you said the guy was good looking. Can you describe him to me?"

"Sure" she replied "he was in his mid twenties, I would say, not very tall but well built.

I remember he had a beautiful suit on. He said it was Italian and it looked really expensive".

"Can you recall what type of car he had?" Gerry asked

"I think it was a Mercedes," Carol replied.

"What happened to you once you recovered and went back on the street?" Gerry inquired.

"Well it took me weeks to recover from the beating. My mum persuaded me to get back out on the street again but I just couldn't face it. That's when I took an overdose. Then I met my Bernie and got married."

Gerry checked Danny's notes and they confirmed exactly what Carol had said. She had met Bernard Duffy in rehab, got married and had their kids before Bernie had died of an overdose.

"Funny," Carol added "they never got anyone for attacking me but just over 9 years later, I got a phone call from my brother to say he had found out who was responsible. He was coming to tell me everything the next day but he never got here. He was shot dead the next day by a polis in his flat in Dundasvale Court."

Gerry felt sick, he had just had a terrible thought.

"What was your brother's name, Carol?" he asked.

"Joseph Patterson," she replied. "Patterson was my own name before I got married."

He thanked her for her time and headed for the door.

Gerry sat silently in the car for a few minutes trying to regain his composure and make some sense of what he had just heard. It was Matty who broke the silence.

"I don't know that lassie, Mr Lynch, but I did know her brother. He was a drug dealer working for the Graham family. I remember being sent to drop drugs off at his flat a few times."

Gerry knew that he was indeed opening a can of worms just as Sandy Morton had said he would, but it was time to get to the truth.

The next stop was Haghill, Glasgow to interview Ann Marie Docherty. She had been the first victim. She lived in a two bedroom, top flat, just off Duke Street with her current waste of time boyfriend. When Gerry and Matty called he was stretched out on the settee in the living room, watching *Sky Sports* on a huge wall mounted television. He was drinking a can of strong cider and smoking what appeared to be a joint. He never even acknowledged the presence of the two men.

Ann Marie showed them through to the kitchenette, which contained a sink full of unwashed plates, cups and cutlery.

"Sorry about the mess," Ann Marie apologised, "he's a lazy bastard."

Gerry had again read Danny's file and agreed with everything he had written, apart from one thing. Danny had described Ann Marie as a plump lassie with large breasts. All these years later she had lost her puppy fat and now had a voluptuous figure.

Her story was almost identical to that of Carol Duffy. She had been a seventeen year old prostitute back in October 1993 and had been the first of the three women to be attacked. On the night it happened she too had been in a bar in the city centre and been propositioned by a good looking man. She had a couple of drinks with him before going to his car. Ann Marie also mentioned feeling strange and remembered having sex. She said it was like a horror film, one minute the guy looked okay the next his face seemed deformed. Just like Carol Duffy she remembered nothing more until she found herself sat on the pavement in West Nile Street. She too had been raped and badly beaten.

Despite the attack Ann Marie had continued on the game probably, Gerry thought, just to keep her pain in the arse boyfriend in the manner to which he had definitely become accustomed.

"What happened with the investigation, did the police not arrest anyone?" Gerry asked.

"Nothing happened," Ann Marie replied. "The officer in charge told me it was just something that happened to prostitutes. He still did nothing when I told him who did it."

"What do you mean?" Gerry inquired.

Ann Marie went on to relate a story which stopped both Gerry and Matty in their tracks. She told them of a night at the beginning of August 1993, several weeks before she was raped. She and a few pals had gone to a popular club at the time, 'The Carousel', in town. Ann Marie had met a nice tall lad called Tommy and they were getting on great.

Towards the end of the night she and Tommy were about to leave when this man at the bar said something about Ann Marie's breasts and had tried to grab her. Tommy took exception and a fight developed. It was a proper set to and there was broken glass everywhere. Tommy had got the better of it as the other man had a horrible slash down his face. Ann Marie and Tommy had then left and taken a taxi home. They had arranged to meet the next night but he didn't turn up. Despite Ann Marie making enquiries about him all over town and even reporting him as a missing person she never saw Tommy again.

"The night I was raped I had been working all day and, like every other tart in Glasgow, had taken a little something to help me through the day. I was already a bit out of it when the guy hit on me in the bar. I thought I recognised him but couldn't place him. Anyway after I was raped the penny dropped. The guy was identical to the fella Tommy had fought with but his face was okay. I guessed the guy Tommy fought with would have had to have a huge amount of stitches in his face."

Ann Marie went on to say she had told the police this information but nothing happened. It was Matty who spoke next.

"Ann Marie, can you remember Tommy's second name?" he asked.

"Oh aye, Jardine. Tommy Jardine was his name, he was a lovely fella."

Matty bolted for the front door, threw it open and bounded down the stairs. Gerry apologised and followed him down to the street. Matty was sat on the pavement, he had vomited into the road and tears were streaming down his face. Both of them had now had a massive shock today.

Gerry managed to bundle Matty into his car and despite the stookie he drove him home. Matty said he would be okay and they arranged to talk about what they had learned later. Gerry decided that he would visit the third victim himself on foot. She lived locally.

Whilst walking to the last address Gerry tried to process all he had learned that evening.

Neither Carol nor Ann Marie were strangers to drugs. They were quite open about the fact that at the time nearly all the prostitutes were using large amounts of temazepam capsules, or 'jellies' as they were known, to get them through the day.

They were both adamant that they had been drugged by the man who attacked them. Carol's brother, who was a dealer for the Graham's, had been shot dead, allegedly by his partner Paul Corrigan. That incident needed revisiting. Then the revelation from Ann Marie. Matty's brother goes missing, never to be seen again, after a fight with a man whom she later believes raped her, or at least someone who strongly resembled him. The description fit the Graham twins. Who else could it be?

Yet another thought entered Gerry's mind. Although it was six years later, he recalled that there were definite similarities to the attack on Isla Buchanan. The drugs, the beating, the physical abuse. Even being dumped on the street like so much rubbish. He wondered if anyone had ever been apprehended for that crime? It also reminded him that perhaps he should also pay Ami McLeod a visit to find out about her sister, also to thank her for all her help when he was ill.

The third and last girl attacked was a Sarah McCarty. She lived in Roebank Street, Dennistoun which Gerry could see from his office window.

Gerry was expecting to see a woman in her early thirties. On ringing the doorbell what looked like at best a middle aged woman opened the door.

"I'm looking for a Sarah McCarty," Gerry said.

"You found her," the women replied, "come in".

On entering the flat Gerry was shocked. It was like its occupant, a right royal mess, a far worse state than even Jimmy's place had been. There were empty cans and bottles strewn across the floor and furniture. Ashtrays piled high with discarded cigarette ends. The place stank.

Sarah McCarty wasn't much better. Her clothes looked as though they had never seen a washing machine or ever been ironed. Her hair was lank and greasy and her face bloated and red.

Also her right eye was missing.

"I take it you're Gerry Lynch?" she smiled through rotten teeth.

"Yes, I'm the very man," Gerry replied.

"I thought so, I can see your office from here and I've seen you about." Gerry took out the notebook from his pocket and began the interview.

"Right then Sarah, you were seventeen back in December 1993. Can you tell me what happened to you?" he asked

Sarah slumped into a chair, lit a cigarette and began. She related her story to Gerry and it was word for word exactly as she had told it to Danny Quinn. She explained how she had gone to Clancy's Bar with a work colleague and once her friend had left with her boyfriend, how she was approached by a good looking young man who asked if he could buy her another drink.

As Sarah said herself, "I thought well, it's nearly Christmas what harm can it do?"

They had the drink and Sarah complained of feeling drowsy. The man had taken her outside, supposedly for some fresh air. She recalled being in a car and the next thing she remembered was a young couple coming to her assistance. She had been dumped in Blythswood Square, her clothing was torn and whilst she had been apparently unconscious, she had been brutally raped and beaten. To such an extent that she lost the sight in her right eye which had to be removed.

Sarah went on.

"I was in a right state when I came out of hospital, I didn't want to go out looking like this and I couldn't work. I turned to drink and drugs just to get through the day. Now look at the state of me."

"Tell me Sarah," Gerry asked, "how come Danny Quinn was looking into your case?"

"Well one day a while back I was watching the evening news and I saw the guy who did this to me on television. It was a report from the high court, some big case or other and I saw the guy outside the court. The reporter mentioned the surname Graham. Come to think of it, I think you were interviewed as well. Anyway I contacted the policeman in charge of my case but he did nothing about it.

I decided to ask for Jimmy Quinn's help. I phoned your office and Danny came to see me. He was lovely and told me he would look into it for me. I heard a wee while later that Danny had been shot dead and his old man really hit the bottle so I just gave it up."

"Can you remember the name of the police officer who was in charge of your case Sarah?" Gerry quizzed.

"Oh yes, how could I forget him? I was lying in a hospital bed with the curtains around the bed and the police were just leaving. I heard him say 'Just my luck, another tart raped and I get lumbered with it.'"

He thought I was a prostitute. I'll never forget the bastard's name as long as I live, Detective Constable William Robertson. Once I got out of hospital he used to call here and harass me. I think he really did think I was a prostitute. Sometimes he even sold me drugs."

Gerry closed his notebook and thanked Sarah for her time. As he got to the door he turned to see her reaching for a bottle of cheap vodka. Who could blame her? Someone else suffering dark days.

Gerry walked home and retrieved the other two case files from his car. He made two phone calls. One to Carol Duffy and the other to Ann Marie Docherty. He asked both the same thing, which he had neglected to earlier.

"Can you remember the name of the police officer investigating your case?"

Both gave the expected reply.

"Detective Constable William Robertson" and, yes, he had harassed them looking for sex and offering to sell them drugs. He was well known to all the girls.

Independently, both threw another spanner in the works. They mentioned that it was common knowledge amongst all the working girls that Robertson was suspected of being responsible for the death of one of their own back in the 1980's.

Having spoken to the two women again Gerry knew one thing. He would not be getting any sleep again. He

had statements to prepare before visiting his old gaffer
Sandy Morton.

CHAPTER TWENTY-SEVEN

Gerry had fallen asleep at his desk. He was awakened by the sun streaming through his office window. He had worked late into the night putting together the statements, both old and new, made by Carol Duffy, Anne Marie Docherty and Sarah McCarty. If nothing else, they needed looking at again. All three attacks were similar, the description of the assailant or assailants were similar and there was also the fact that Detective Constable William Robertson had acted appallingly towards all three women victims and had not taken their cases seriously. And the last time Gerry had looked it was illegal for anyone to sell controlled drugs, let alone a serving police officer.

Gerry left his office and walked home. Despite feeling weary he went for his morning run into the park. Although still hampered by the stookie on his arm he just about managed to jog around.

After a shower he dressed and ate breakfast before calling on Matty to run him into town. Both men agreed to speak about yesterday's events back at the office once Gerry had seen his old boss. He hoped by that time to have some news for him. Gerry noticed that Matty was not his cheerful self.

Perhaps hearing about his brother had upset him more than he'd let on. Then again he may just have had a drop of the hard stuff the previous night and was a little off colour.

At 8.45am Gerry was sat in the front reception room awaiting the arrival of Detective Chief Inspector Sandy Morton. He didn't have to wait long. Morton was a creature of habit and always at his desk at 9am sharp.

Gerry wasted no time in getting right to the point. He showed the statements to Morton who agreed they required to be investigated thoroughly. The bad news was that Detective Constable Robertson was not available as he had just started three weeks leave in Spain and wasn't due back until the end of the month. It was very frustrating but Morton promised that he would look into the matter personally and Gerry believed him.

They also spoke about the recent deaths to members of the Graham family. Gerry told Morton about his encounters with Mr Samson who seemed to think he had in some way been responsible.

"As I told you months ago boss," Gerry explained, "I would love to get back at those bastards but you were right, I've been too busy and the broken arm doesn't help."

Morton was sympathetic,

"All I can say Gerry is if 'Delilah' gives you any more hassle give me a call and I'll have a word."

Once again Gerry left his old boss on good terms. He knew two things. Morton would be as good as his word and Robertson was in deep shit. Gerry was half way to his next appointment when he realised that once again he had failed to pop in to see Audrey. What was wrong with him?

Gerry had called Aimi McLeod earlier, and asked to see her. She told him to come to over to her apartment. When he arrived Gerry realised that Isla and her mother were still living with Aimi. In fact all three were in the process of packing.

Isla wasn't sure at first who Gerry was but her mother and Aimi reassured her that Gerry was a friend. Aimi explained that she was in the throes of changing jobs. She was moving back to Edinburgh to take up a post in the city. Her mum and Isla were also moving back there. Mary was looking forward to getting her teeth back into the property game and Isla was to join her in the business. Although she had now regained her speech Isla walked with a limp and was easily frightened. No longer the bright young thing, she was very timid and withdrawn.

Gerry asked if he could have a word in private with Aimi and they went into her bedroom. Firstly he thanked her for all the help she had given him and Audrey during the time of his illness. He apologised for taking so long to come and see her and her family. He then asked if anyone had been charged with the attack on Isla. Aimi told him that nobody had been, but wondered why he asked.

"Well" Gerry began "it's a long story but I am now a private investigator and I have been looking into three attacks which took place back in 1993. All three are similar in many ways to the attack on Isla. I know who I believe is responsible for my three attacks but was wondering if the culprits had anything to do with Isla or if she knew them or had even heard of them?"

Aimi said there was only one way to find out and that was to ask her. So Gerry asked Isla, but unfortunately the names

Billy and Bobby Graham meant nothing to her. They meant something to Mary though.

"Tell me Gerry," she asked, "the case you had just before you were ill, who was that again?"

"Do you mean Frank Graham Jnr.?" Gerry replied.

"That's the one," said Mary. "Was the QC defending him not Maurice Henshaw, the 5th Lord Dunbeth?"

"Yes it was," Gerry said, "why do you ask?"

"I bet the Graham family retain him as their QC so he will be involved with them all. He's not a nice man at all. Not only that but he has a certain reputation when it comes to women. You should speak to my brother about him".

"Perhaps that would be a good idea" Aimi added, "I'll phone and ask when he can see you if you like". So it was arranged Gerry would drive up to Perthshire the next day with Ami to interview her uncle Archie.

Matty had waited for Gerry in his office in Dennistoun. The two of them sat in a corner of Gerry's office for almost two hours discussing what they had learned yesterday.

There was definitely something fishy about Paul Corrigan's death, Gerry could not put his finger on it, but there were things that were just not right. The police had gone to search a known drug dealers house and come up empty. Someone had been tipped off. Patterson worked for the Graham family. It didn't take a Sherlock Holmes to work out that it had been a set up. But why?

Matty's brother Tommy's disappearance was connected to the Graham twins. They were also the favourites for raping the three women in Glasgow and could also have been involved in some way with the attack on Isla Buchanan. Gerry updated Matty on the fact that DCI Morton was going to look into DC Robertson.

"I don't know who killed the Graham's parents," Gerry said " but fair play to them. I wish it had been me, but I'm not finished with these bastards yet."

Matty agreed with him, now that he knew the Grahams were without doubt responsible for his brother's disappearance. Gerry eventually got Matty to agree on taking a more cautious approach so as to gather as much evidence as possible to bury the family forever. And Matty was certainly all for that.

CHAPTER TWENTY-EIGHT

Even although he now had a lightweight plaster cast on his arm, Gerry played the old soldier when Ami had volunteered to drive him up to Perthshire in her Audi. She picked him up at midday the following day at his office. They headed straight up the motorway and were at their destination in just under an hour. Aimi left the motorway at Glenfarg and drove right through Auchtermuchty. Five miles farther along the road Gerry saw the sign:

WOODCROFT HOUSE PRIVATE SCHOOL FOR BOYS

Aimi turned into the tree lined gravel driveway which was several hundred metres in length. After parking at the front doors of the school building she and Gerry entered the foyer. They informed the secretary, Miss Carmichael, that they had an appointment to see Mr Buchanan.

"Mr Lynch and Miss McLeod, is it? The headmaster is expecting you."

She directed them to Archie's office.

As usual Aimi greeted her uncle with a big hug and a kiss. She apologised for not phoning enough to updated him more often on Isla's progress. He, for his part, was just delighted to see his niece.

"I'm so sorry, Mr Lynch, we Buchanan's are a sloppy lot. We have a need for affection."

Aimi blushed.

"From your phone call Mr Lynch, I understand you wish to interview me, as it were, to get the full picture regarding Woodcroft House and some of its former pupils?"

"Yes Mr Buchanan that is correct, and please call me Gerry."

"Very well Gerry, but I'm afraid my tale is not for the ears of my niece. Aimi dear, why don't you go for a walk in the grounds or visit our library. I rather think we may be some time."

Aimi fully understood, gave her uncle a kiss and left. It was a beautiful day for a stroll in the school grounds and she knew Miss Carmichael would sort her out with tea and biscuits when she returned.

"Right, Mr Lynch, I beg your pardon, Gerry, where shall we begin?"

Gerry sat with pen and notebook at the ready.

"If you don't mind starting with the history of the school and we'll take it from there." Gerry said.

Archie Buchanan began as though delivering a history lecture to his students.

"The school was founded in 1856 by Edward Woodcroft. He was an importer and exported based in Edinburgh with warehouses down at the docks at Leith. He made a fortune from his business, and some say from slavery but this was never proven.

The land on which the school is built once formed part of the Balmuir Estate. Woodcroft purchased the land from the 1st Lord Dunbeth who, as many like him at the time, suffered from a lack of funds due to their excesses in life.

Initially twenty boys attended the school and paid £2 per term. Over the years the number and indeed the fees have risen steadily. An extension built between the world wars means we now have twelve hundred pupils aged eight to eighteen who each pay £8,000 per term. The extension was funded by the 3rd Lord Dunbeth hence it was named Dunbeth Wing after him. The Dunbeths have been Governors at the school for many years."

Gerry was scribbling notes trying to keep up and asked,

"Can you tell me a little about your early life here at the school and how you came to be a teacher here?"

"Goodness where to begin. My sister Mary and I are twins, I am ten minutes older. Our father worked in banking and was a very strict man who, in all honesty, had little time for either of us children. He was a little too pompous. My dear mama was quite different, she was a loving, caring person and I loved her dearly. I still miss her although she died 40 years ago.

"When I was eight years old my father sent me to Woodcroft House. I loved the place from the minute I arrived. I cannot say the same for some of the pupils. What I am about to tell you must go no further Gerry. I must have your word on it."

"I give you my word," Gerry said.

"Very well," Archie continued. "I arrived here in 1948 aged eight. I knew quite early in life that I was different. I am, Mr Lynch, a homosexual. None of my family knows any of this and I have never spoken of it before. Here at Woodcroft House I met a kindred spirit in Calum McCall."

Gerry noted tears in Archie's eyes.

"Simply, I loved him from the first time we met, and I still love him today. You must, of course, remember that back then it was illegal to be gay in Britain.

"In the same year as Calum and myself were, amongst others, Maurice Henshaw, Reginald McLeod and friends. They made many pupils' lives hell, but seemed to take greater delight in annoying Calum and I. We were the butt of all their jokes, bullying and assaults. It was bad enough when we they young, but as theye got older it got worse. Henshaw was always the leader and the rest followed like sheep.

"Unfortunately as they got older and their behaviour worsened they turned their attention to young ladies in the nearby village. Many were groped or worse by these morons. They always seemed to get away with it, probably because Lord Dunbeth intervened on their

behalf. It was more obvious back in 1956. I won't go into it but the yobs almost wrecked the Centenary celebrations here at the school. The then headmaster, Mr Farquarson, resigned over the affair.

"In my last year as a pupil here was a summer fete here at the school. My sister Mary attended and that pig Reginald McLeod took a shine to her. He had banking connections which seemed to impress our father and as soon as he left Woodcroft House, McLeod set out to marry my sister. My mama saw right through him and forbade it. Unfortunately she died and immediately Father agreed to the union. I suppose Mary told you the hell she was put through with him. Always womanising, never at home, and yet he fathered beautiful Aimi, although he had little time for her either.

"Anyway back to the school. At the end of our last year they were to hold a grand ball. The night before I was taken ill with mumps and the school doctor had me placed in quarantine. I sincerely believe to this day that saved me from the same fate as befell Calum. Henshaw and his gang got hold of him. He was stripped naked, beaten and tied to a tree directly outside the main terrace with a sign around his neck that read 'QUEER'. As you can imagine, there were rather a lot of young ladies at the function and during the course of events some came out onto the terrace for fresh air, to be confronted by the sight of poor Calum. The embarrassment on both sides must have been horrendous.

"Eventually Calum was freed. He apparently never spoke to anyone and just marched off in the direction of the dormitories. The next morning he was found dead, hanging from the roof beam in his room by a rope. He had left a note in the typewriter which read:

JUST CAN'T STAND ANY MORE

He also wrote this."

Archie reached into the top drawer of his desk and produced a letter. He handed it to Gerry.

"Please Gerry, read that," he said.

Gerry noted that Archie again had tears in his eyes. These were indeed painful memories he was recalling.

DEAR ARCHIE

I AM SORRY TO LEAVE YOU LIKE THIS BUT I JUST WANT OUT

I WILL LOVE YOU ALWAYS

CALLUM

"I can see he really loved you, Mr Buchanan," Gerry remarked.

"Can you Gerry? Yes, I suppose that is what I was meant to believe. There is just one problem. It never came to me at first, I was grief stricken when Calum died. I have read the letter over and over many times for all these years. Then one day it hit me. In a moment of clarity, I realised what had been eating away at me every time I read it. Calum didn't write it, nor probably the note left in the typewriter. You see, Calum never typed me a note or letter in his life. He wrote everything long hand similar to yourself with your notebook.

"Also, he never referred to me as Archie. When he was trying to make a point or was angry with me he always called me Archibald. The rest of the time he called me AB and I always referred to him as CMc. Finally, you will see that the note is signed Callum.

"That is what was shouting at me for all these years. His name was Calum with one 'l' so why would he not spell his own name correctly unless, of course, someone else did in fact write it. This being the case, I don't believe Calum committed suicide. I think somebody murdered him and I know who my money is on."

Gerry could see that even after all the years Archie Buchanan was greatly affected by what had taken place.

Archie continued, "Unfortunately all these years have passed and I have no other evidence to support my theory. A week or so after the incident we all left Woodcroft House. It was 1958. I went to university and got my degree. I wanted to be a teacher and when I got my chance to return here in1982, I jumped at it. In 1990 I was given the great honour of becoming headmaster.

"Obviously you know Henshaw went into the law and is now a Queen's Counsel and the present Lord Dunbeth. Also regretfully he is one of the school governors. Worse still he is the MSP for East Perthshire and was Isla's employer. I must say, I was very annoyed with her going behind Mary's back and going to work for that man. I was so angry but couldn't tell her my reasons."

"Well, Mr Buchanan, I can only thank you once again for all your help. It has been most enlightening and I think may help no end," Gerry said, ending the interview.

As if on cue, Aimi put her head round the door.

"Have you two finished yet?" she asked. "You're like a pair of old fish wives."

"I'm so sorry dear," Archie said, "you can have him back but only if you promise to return for Founders Day in August. It's the 150th Anniversary, you know."

"A party, me! Oh well, okay Uncle, I promise," she joked.

Whilst Aimi gave her uncle a full update on Isla, Gerry headed back to the car. The headmaster had given him a lot of food for thought.

The visit now over Gerry and Aimi were on their way again. They stopped at a quaint little pub for lunch and Aimi tried to interrogate Gerry about his meeting with her uncle. He had promised not to divulge what they had said and kept to that. He simply told her that her uncle had given him a few leads which he could work on.

After lunch Aimi drove Gerry back to his office. As she dropped him off she invited him to come along to her apartment that night for a farewell drink. Gerry told her he would try and be there. She slipped in the fact that Audrey would be there. Knowing that he couldn't refuse. He did pop along for an hour, but on arrival was disappointed to learn that Audrey had been held up at work. The gods were conspiring against him and so he decided he needed to do something about it and take the bull by the horns.

CHAPTER TWENTY-NINE

Gerry had been really busy of late. He had not forgotten about the promise he'd made to his old friend Robert Leishman. His very next job would be looking into the circumstances of his daughter Chloe's death.

Before he set off he had one task to perform. He removed the stookie from his arm. It had been driving him crazy for days, itching in places he couldn't reach. He had done all that they asked of him and after six weeks was due to have his arm checked out again. Now was just not the time to do that as he was far too busy to waste his time going back to hospital. As long as he paid Matty for his time everything would be good. Trouble was, he hadn't seen Matty for a couple of days and he had not been answering Gerry's calls.

Gerry drove himself up to Cumbernauld and interviewed the friends who had been out with Chloe on the night she died. All of them said basically the same. They all agreed that Chloe was almost like their leader. When they were at school she was the dominant, flamboyant one in the group. Not bossy but more self assured than her pals. All the girls left school at the same time at the age of eighteen.

Chloe, as Gerry already knew, went to the famous Glasgow College of Art to study textiles and jewellery design. He had learned from her tutor there that she was a very talented, popular girl who got on with everyone. Her death had come as a huge shock to staff and students alike. Catherine Stevenson was attending Aberdeen University and studying history. Jenny Stark, who by her own admission was the serious one of the group, was studying politics at Edinburgh University. Chloe's best friend Nicola Meek who lived right across the road from her had taken up a position with a large insurance company in Cumbernauld.

It had been Chloe who, just before Christmas, had arranged for them all to go out together one last time, before they went to find their own way in the world.

On a typically crisp, Scottish, December evening the girls boarded the train in Cumbernauld to travel into Glasgow. They were all looking forward to a great evening. Also on the train that night were Mark McCabe and Chris Irvine. Both were nineteen years old, and worked in the dispatch department of Robert Leishman's company. The boys had met Chloe and Nicola when the girls had been working in summer jobs at the factory, to earn some spending money.

They got chatting on the train and when it reached Glasgow thirty five minutes later all six went into a nearby pub just off George Square for a drink. Eventually they made their way down Hope Street to a night club called 'Chaos'.

When they got inside the place was cram packed with people, a heaving mass of humanity all it seemed with the same intention, to party. Whilst Mark and Chris went to the bar to buy a round of drinks the girls managed to find a table. During the course of the next hour, they all took it in turns to guard the table, for fear of losing it, whilst the rest of the group were up dancing.

About an hour after they arrived, Chris recalled Mark speaking to a man just inside the front door of the club. He seemed totally out of place. Chris described the man as being late forties or early fifties, fairly tall and skinny, with dark hair going thin on top and wearing a suit, shirt, tie and despite the heat inside the club, an overcoat. Chris had no idea who the man was but Mark seemed to know him.

After this all the friends agreed that Mark and Chloe were as thick as thieves. They all knew Chloe was a bit of a flirt and Mark really fancied himself with the ladies. From the group's recollections it seemed everyone was drinking vodka and coke, dancing and having a great time.

About two hours in Chloe complained of being hot but no one really took any notice, as everyone in the club was hot. Shortly afterwards Chloe became distressed and the girls helped her to the toilets. It was much cooler and the air conditioning was on. Nicola made Chloe drink some cold water and splashed some on her face in an attempt to cool her down. It did not work. Chloe suddenly screamed that she was on fire. Nicola immediately telephoned for an ambulance and the friends literally carried Chloe out of the club and into the fresh night air.

Once outside she collapsed. When the ambulance arrived Nicola went with her to Glasgow Royal Infirmary while Jenny and Catherine attended in a taxi. Chloe was found to be dead on arrival at hospital. There was absolutely nothing anyone could do.

The hospital staff must have contacted the police as the girls were required to give statements before somehow making their way home to Cumbernauld. It was as they gave statements that the girls realised they had been so intent on helping their friend, that they had been separated from Mark and Chris.

When they got home to Cumbernauld the police had already been to see Chloe's parents and given them the sad news. Nicola was just thankful she had not had to do it.

The police managed to speak to Chris Irvine later the same day but Mark McCabe could not be found. He wasn't at his home and never appeared for work on the Monday morning. Nobody knew where he was but it was obviously a priority to find him. It appeared that he perhaps knew more about the incident than the others. Even now, several months later, he had not emerged into society again and he still remained a priority for the investigating officer DC Audrey Jennings.

There was one thing that Gerry did glean from his interviews. Although they worked together Mark McCabe and Chris Irvine were not particularly close friends. It appeared that Mark was quite a good looking lad who was popular with the ladies, or at least he thought so. Chris was a tall gangly lad who wore glasses and was more of a geek. He even said himself, Mark probably just took him out with him to make himself appear more attractive to the girls.

Having left Cumbernauld, Gerry made his way back to Glasgow. He had already explained that he was now a private investigator who had been asked by the family to look into the incident. Whether he wanted to or not, he now had an appointment to see Audrey in her official capacity at their old office. It was a weird feeling. He had really loved her and she him, but he doubted she would feel the same now. After all he had really put her through the ringer. It would be nice if they could remain friends but that would be down to Audrey. Gerry knew he couldn't push it. What he was sure of was the night he had gone to Aimi's farewell party, he'd be devastated when she didn't turn up.

As Gerry entered the foyer, Audrey was waiting and seemed delighted to see him again. Perhaps he had worried about nothing, maybe she did still fancy him. Whatever her feeling towards him, today was about all business. They shook hands and Gerry followed her through to the main CID office. They sat opposite each other at her desk. Gerry felt the eyes of all the other detectives upon him. Audrey, efficient as ever, had the relevant files to hand.

What interested Gerry were three things. Had the police had any luck identifying the older mystery man? Were they any nearer tracking down Mark McCabe? What were the findings of the post mortem? The simple answer to questions one and two was the same. No. They had not been able to identify the mystery man. If anybody in and around the club knew who the older man was they weren't telling. The CCTV at the night club was worse than useless. Probably on purpose, so as not to show the drug dealers selling in and around the premises.

They had not traced Mark McCabe and Audrey was at a loss regarding his whereabouts. She had exhausted every avenue, even circulating his description via Interpol. The police had expected that he would have surfaced somewhere by now so there were now genuine concerns for his wellbeing. With regard to the third question, Audrey was able to give Gerry more information. Chloe Leishman had died due to organ failure having digested what was believed to be rogue ecstasy tablets. Audrey explained that the pathologist had been most helpful in explaining the problem having, only a month or so prior to Chloe's death, attended a conference in England on that very subject.

Around the time of Chloe's death there had been two other deaths in Scotland. A sixteen year old girl in Ayr and a twenty two year old man in Kirkcaldy. In all cases the subjects had displayed similar symptoms. They had complained of feeling very hot as though their bodies were on fire, before collapsing and suffering organ failure. The pathologist had learned that, around the time of the deaths, rogue ecstasy tablets were flooding Britain. There had also been a number of deaths in England, Wales and Northern Ireland.

Tablets called 'Red Dragon' and 'Mortal Combat' were the main culprits. They were being manufactured abroad and smuggled illegally into the United Kingdom. They were identified by a dragon embossed on each tablet. It was believed, and the toxicology results seem to bear this out, that the tablets contained deadly levels of a super strength amphetamine. Other similar tablets doing the rounds include green coloured tablets called 'Speckled Rolex' and heart shaped fake ecstasy called 'Dr Death' or 'PMA'. These varied in colour and could be yellow, pink, purple or blue.

As the doctor had said it would have been nice to get their hands on some of the tablets, to see exactly what they contained. At least it might give medical staff half a chance to try and treat victims instead of them dying so horribly.

Gerry thanked Audrey for her time. He just kept things professional. It was hardly the time or place to ask her out on a date, when she was surrounded by a number of her colleagues, who were no doubt earwigging everything they said. Gerry said his goodbyes and popped along to see his old gaffer Sandy Morton before leaving the building.

CHAPTER THIRTY

In the following week came a twist which nobody could have predicted.

Jamie Graham had always been security conscious, that was how he had stayed alive. He always carried a handgun for protection and wore a Kevlar bullet proof vest. His home was covered by state of the art CCTV and he had bought the house facing straight down the street. This afforded the best view just in case uninvited visitors decided to call.

After the incident outside the Crooked Man when his car had been blown up and his driver killed, he decided that further measures needed to be taken. He had not been surprised that the police forensic examination of his Mercedes and fragments of the bomb led to no arrests, Jamie had his own theories on who was responsible and that was why the casino had been bombed.

Jamie didn't do things in half measures. He was now the proud owner of an Audi A6 which had been specially modified for him at the factory in Germany. The vehicle was bullet and bomb proof and had cost mega bucks. He didn't care, as his own safety was paramount. He couldn't put a price on that.

He had promoted one of the gang, whom he trusted the most, Roddy McVey, to be his new driver and enforcer. Jamie had Roddy drive him into Glasgow on a regular basis. He liked to pop into different establishments which were part of the Graham empire, just a wee surprise visit now and then to keep everyone on their toes. Anyone he caught trying to swindle the family, suffered the consequences. Like his father before him Jamie ruled with an iron fist. Jamie called these wee runs out 'taking care of business'. It was something he did and no Chinese Triad was going to interfere with that. So as not to be different from his boss, Roddy McVey also carried a handgun and wore a Kevlar vest.

Jamie made sure that Roddy always varied their route but invariably they ended up heading home down Balmuildy Road. They would enter Bishopbriggs passing the council cleansing yard and over the bridge which crossed the canal at the bottom of the hill near to the sports centre. Tonight it had turned cold and was quite misty early on. Typical of a Scottish summer, when you never knew what to expect next.

Having completed their visits, Jamie instructed Roddy to drive him home. They followed the usual route down Balmuildy Road. It was very quiet with hardly any traffic. It was just turning dark despite being around 10.30pm

As they approached the bridge over the canal, as if from nowhere, a black coloured SUV appeared at speed from the tow path and rammed right into the side of Jamie's car. Roddy McVey was taken by surprise but tried to steer away from the other vehicle. The driver of the SUV kept their foot on the accelerator forcing the Audi off the road and into the canal. The Audi may have been bullet proof but this made the car much heavier than a normal vehicle. The Audi landed in the water upside down on its roof. In no time at all it sank like a stone. There was nothing Jamie Graham or Roddy McVey could do. Neither of them survived.

The SUV, although badly damaged, made off and was later found burnt out a few miles away. It was no surprise when it turned out that the vehicle had been stolen earlier the same day from the grounds of Stobhill Hospital.

That evening Gerry was sat watching some crap documentary about trying to save the planet. There was a knock at the door. He was more than surprised to see Audrey Jennings standing there as lovely as ever. Gerry invited her in and then wondered how she knew where he lived.

"I am a Detective, you know," she said. "I heard about your run in with 'Delilah' and that you had apparently been assaulted, so thought I would come and see how you are. Oh, and I got your address off the system at Baird Street."

"Of course you did," Gerry replied. "Clever you. Well as you can see after recovering from a broken arm and having several fractured ribs, I'm just fine."

He knew Audrey was driving so didn't even bother to offer her an alcoholic drink, and made her a coffee instead.

Despite his fling with Brenda, Gerry could not help having special feelings for Audrey. He knew that he had missed her more than he could say and, it seemed, she had missed him too. They sat chatting for quite some time, just like the old friends they were. If Gerry apologised once for not having contacted her he apologised a dozen times.

Eventually they both realised it was getting late and time for Audrey to make a move. Gerry saw her to the door and promised faithfully that he would keep in touch. He was just about to open the door when somebody knocked on it. He opened it immediately and there again stood DI Samson with his lap dog DS Lorimer. They had returned just like a bad smell. What now?

Before he could say anything, Samson said "A word," and pushed past Gerry and Audrey into the flat. Once in the living room Gerry wanted to know what Samson wanted.

"Where were you this evening about 10.30pm? Samson asked

"That's easy," Gerry replied, "I was right here."

"Can anyone corroborate that?"

"I can," Audrey interrupted.

"And you are?" Samson asked.

"Detective Constable Audrey Jennings, 'A' Division, Sir," Audrey replied, producing her warrant card at the same time.

"What is your connection to Lynch?"

"My connection to *Mr* Lynch," Audrey corrected him, " is that we are former colleagues and also friends." She thought it best not to complicate things by letting him know that they had also been lovers.

Samson was grudgingly satisfied with Gerry's alibi and told him why he had needed one.

"At about 10.30pm tonight Jamie Graham's Audi was forced off the road by another vehicle in Bishopbriggs. Graham and his driver, Roddy McVey, were both killed."

"Just the same as Moira Clarkson," Gerry commented with a note of almost glee in his voice. "It looks like you do have a vigilante on your hands Detective Inspector. I wish you luck with that. Are you sure it's not gang related? I mean Jamie Graham is a big scalp. He was after all the family's top man, hence his nickname, 'The Man'."

"I'm leaving my options open at the moment, Lynch, and I've still got my eye on you." Samson said as he headed for the front door.

Gerry and Audrey were both stunned. Another Graham family member murdered. They stood silently facing each other.

"Thank God you were here to back me up, Audrey, or that idiot would have had me down at the station again," Gerry finally said. Then he closed the gap between them and kissed her cheek.

Audrey blushed.

"Yes, that was lucky," she said as she too headed for the front door. "I really do have to get off Gerry. I'll keep in touch."

He was alone once more and his head was reeling. Seeing Audrey again had been a pleasant surprise. Finding out Jamie Graham was dead was even more of a surprise. Who was responsible? It had been three years since he had lost his parents and colleagues, so why suddenly was someone apparently taking revenge on the Graham family? Gerry had, of course, heard of the trouble the Grahams were having with the Chinese Triad from Matty. Could they be responsible and was it just coincidental that the deaths had occurred in similar fashion? He found that hard to believe.

CHAPTER THIRTY-ONE

The following week Frank Graham Jnr. was released from prison. What a homecoming; first his parents and now Jamie dead. The very next day, after a small celebration to welcome him home, the family held a meeting within the Crooked Man at which he was voted the new head of the family. There wasn't much choice really. It would be business as usual. Frank, however, insisted on running things from his regular haunt, the lounge bar of the Railway Inn.

It seemed that the bomb at the casino had quietened things down for a time. However Frank knew that because the Chinese Triad were involved it may not remain so for long. He had always been less belligerent than Jamie, so he would have preferred to look at ways to end the violence by negotiation if he could. Bobby and Billy insisted on continuing with Jamie's plan.

They had discovered that the Triad had a factory in a smallholding on the road between Bishopbriggs and Lenzie. As far as they were concerned that was Graham turf. It was their intention to destroy the factory and anyone involved with it. Frank reluctantly gave his blessing to the plan in deference to Jamie. He left all the arrangements to the twins.

Later he would need to come up with a plan to try to kerb the twins and their tendency towards violence. Frank knew that sometimes it was the only way to get things done, but not all the time. This was something that they must learn.

The first order of business for the family was Jamie's funeral. Two days later the church in Springburn was again full to capacity. Thereafter Jamie Graham was laid to rest in Cadder Cemetery, Bishopbriggs. As with his parents' funeral, all the great and the good attended. It really was time for the family to pull together and prepare for attacks on their business that were expected any day now. They were still strong but Jamie was a massive loss. In that regard Frank realised that perhaps the twins were right, that a show of force against the Chinese may well help to secure the family's standing in the criminal fraternity. They would find out shortly. For now it was back to the Crooked Man to drink to Jamie 'The Man'. Frank knew that it was now he who was 'The Man' but, he wondered, "For how long. How long would he reign as head of the family before he was murdered by whoever it was, responsible for the deaths of his parents and Jamie?" The question was about to be answered much sooner than he had expected.

The following Monday morning Frank Graham Jnr. was back sat in the lounge bar of the Railway Inn accompanied, as usual, by his minder Cammy Watson. He assumed there would be no problems as only those known to him got into his inner sanctum. Cammy Watson made sure of that.

Just before noon there was a knock at the lounge door. Cammy answered it and admitted the lone male who he knew. As he walked to the centre of the room Frank also recognised the man and said,

"What the fuck do you want, you halfwit?"

Much to his amazement the man produced a Glock 9mm handgun from inside his jacket and replied, "Just this."

Before anyone could move he had shot Cammy Watson twice in the chest before walking calmly over to Frank, who was frozen to the spot with fear. Nothing more was said. The man simply placed the gun to Frank's right temple and fired once, blowing his brains across the bar. Another member of the Graham family had been slain. The man then left the building as quietly as he had entered, unobserved.

Gerry Lynch was working at his desk when DI Samson and DS Lorimer arrived at his office. He was requested to voluntarily accompany them once more to Baird Street Police Office.

"Who am I supposed to have killed this time?" he joked.

Several hours later after once again having been grilled about his whereabouts by an increasingly annoying Samson and Lorimer it had all become far from a joke. The questioning had been fierce from the start. It had now descended into a slagging match and Gerry snapped.

"Okay Samson, enough is enough," he said, "I want my lawyer right now."

Samson knew that yet again he had failed to deliver the main suspect and he was bloody angry.

"Alright Lynch, you'll get your lawyer but it doesn't detract from the fact that for a third time we have another copycat killing. First the fire, same as your parents, then the car crash, same as your DS and now a shooting same as your pal Corrigan."

"Don't you dare mention Paul's name, you bastard!" Gerry screamed.

"What's wrong Lynch, can't you take it?

"The fact is somebody walked into the Railway Inn today shot Cammy Watson in the chest twice, just as your pal did with Joseph Patterson, and then shot Frank Graham in the right temple, just as your pal did to himself, and you're telling me you know nothing at all about any of it. YOU'RE A LIAR LYNCH!" Samson roared.

Suddenly, Gerry went very quiet. Samson and Lorimer braced themselves thinking he was about to leap out of his seat at any second and perhaps resort to violence. They were well aware that he could handle himself.

But far from it. Gerry was calmer now than he had ever been before in his life. The penny had just dropped.

"Forget about my lawyer," he said. "I want you to give DCI Sandy Morton a phone and ask him if he could come up here and tell him to bring all the files on the Paul Corrigan case with him".

"What are you up to now, Lynch?" Samson replied. "Your old gaffer can't save you."

"We'll see," Gerry said, "we'll see."

Fortunately Sandy Morton was on duty and only fifteen minutes later he attended as requested with the necessary case files at Baird Street.

DI Samson had already informed him of the latest murder. The two detectives entered the interview room. Gerry was sat quietly opposite a very nervous looking DS Lorimer.

"Okay Lynch," Samson said. "As you can see DCI Morton has attended as you requested and with the case files on Paul Corrigan. So what is all this about?"

Gerry ignored Samson and turned his attention to his old boss. "Thank you for coming, Sir, and for bringing the

189

files with you. Hopefully now we can bring this nonsense to an end once and for all."

Gerry asked if DCI Morton could read aloud from the file the account by DC Robertson on the incident. Morton did so. Robertson had stated that on the conclusion of the search the two younger officers were returning documents and other sundries to the police vehicle. At that time for no apparent reason and without warning DC Corrigan drew his weapon and shot the householder Joseph Patterson twice in the chest before putting the gun against his own temple and firing.

"There you are," Samson interrupted, "just the same as today's shooting."

"Just a minute," Gerry said. "Please, DCI Morton, can you now read what the two young CID officers said when they went back into the house."

Once again DCI Morton obliged. Both stated that DC Robertson was seated on the floor in a state of shock. Joseph Patterson was lying partly on the settee and partly on the floor. He had two bullet wounds in his chest and appeared to be dead. DC Corrigan was lying on the floor, bleeding from a single bullet wound to his right temple. He too appeared to be dead. They noted that his firearm was still in his right hand.

"And the post mortem report on Paul's body, as to the cause of death?" Gerry asked.

"Cause of death was a single bullet wound to the right temple which entered the brain and...."

"Thank you, Chief Inspector," Gerry interjected, "that is enough."

"WELL?" Samson asked. "Just the same as today, what's different?"

"What is different, Detective Inspector? I'll tell you what is different. I recently went back to Jim Kennedy's Taekwondo classes which Paul and I used to attend regularly. Jim told me he was going to put me in a competition to see at what standard I was and what work required to be done."

"What the hell has that got to do with anything?" Samson barked.

"If you'll shut up, I said I'll tell you" Gerry continued, "Jim always had Paul and I fight each other because he knew how competitive we were and that I had difficulty fighting southpaws. You see Paul Corrigan was left handed. He did everything left handed including using a firearm. And it is impossible to shoot yourself through the right temple whilst holding a gun in your left hand. That's not to say whoever shot Frank Graham wasn't left handed. All I'm saying is that Paul Corrigan did not shoot himself and as only one weapon was fired in the room back then he didn't kill himself or the guy Patterson either."

"Who did then?" Samson asked.

Gerry and DCI Morton answered in unison "DC Robertson."

Just to confirm the point that Gerry had made, Sandy showed his colleagues the photographs of the murder scene. He pointed to the body of Paul Corrigan. He was wearing the harness and holster for his weapon on the right side of his body. Thus confirming he was left handed.

Gerry was once again released without charge. He had no idea who was killing the members of the Graham family but he still wished it had been him. Sandy Morton insisted on running Gerry home. They sat in Gerry's kitchen and spoke over coffee.

"You know Gerry, I've just realised something else that compounds Robertson's guilt," Morton said. "He signed out both firearms on that day, which was against procedure. That's something everyone missed, including me. He must have shot Patterson and then Paul and swapped guns, but why?"

"You can ask him when you meet him off the flight from Alicante next week" Gerry said "but I have a feeling it has something to do with keeping Patterson quiet about the attack on his sister Carol Duffy. Patterson worked for the Grahams and I'd put my house on the twins being responsible for the attack on the lassie Duffy, if not all three lassies, given the descriptions of the assailants. It looks to me that the Grahams had Robertson in their pocket. He's probably been passing them information and doing their dirty work for years".

"Do you think it was him let them know where the Squad were celebrating that night after the trial?" Sandy asked.

"Without a doubt," Gerry replied.

Both men sat very quietly for a few minutes lost in their thoughts. Morton then left with Gerry's thanks once more ringing in his ears. As he drove home Sandy Morton knew he was thinking exactly the same as Gerry. He was elated that hopefully Paul Corrigan's name would be cleared after all these years and also that there was nothing worse than a bent copper. He couldn't wait for Robertson to fly back to Britain.

CHAPTER THIRTY-TWO

Willie Robertson could not wait. Only three more months and he would be done with the bloody police force forever. Thirty years and in all that time not one single promotion. They just didn't have a clue. No idea how brilliant he was. What a waste of his talents.

But he didn't care. Here he was now in the sun looking for a detached villa to buy as his retirement home in paradise. He was halfway through his stay and had narrowed down his search to two properties just minutes from the beach and even nearer his favourite bar. Both properties had spacious living accommodation as well as their own private swimming pool.

Money was not a problem; he had a large bank account in Spain, as well as any police pension he had coming his way. Over the years he had also been well provided for by the Graham family for services rendered. He had no love for any of the Grahams but they paid well.

Robertson was however glad that once he had retired he would no longer be beholden to the family. He enjoyed taking their money but doing their bidding had become tedious. Because he was superior to most of his work colleagues he'd had no problem in covering his tracks, and over the many years he had been of great use to the Graham clan.

This was the life, plenty to eat and drink, lovely warm weather and best of all at night, and at a price, his choice of the local tarts who frequented the many nightclubs and casinos in town.

He would make his mind up about his new property in the morning. The only thing that had put a damper on his mood was earlier in the day he had been in his local bar and seen the television news from Scotland. There was a report that a fourth member of the Graham family, Frank Jnr., had been murdered. As soon as he returned home he would need to speak urgently with Billy or Bobby to see what was going on.

But that was for later. Tonight he would turned his attention to the young naked Eastern European girl presently sleeping in his bed.

CHAPTER THIRTY-THREE

Clive Ellis had been a thirty-five year old, former insurance salesman when he broke free of his shackles back in the 1980s. He had adopted a hippy lifestyle, travelling all over Britain, until he finally arrived at a commune in the highlands of Scotland near Findhorn.

This was where he'd met Nancy Baumann, an American lady of German-Jewish origins from Boston. They became a couple and travelled to different parts of the world together. Money was not a problem, as although they had been disappointed with their daughter dropping out of school, Nancy's parents still sent her a monthly allowance. This enabled them to purchase a Volkswagen camper van, which being pink in colour, would not have been out of place at any music festival and it suited their hippy persona.

Eventually the couple were drawn back to Scotland and when Nancy's father passed away, they purchased a small holding with the money she inherited. It was situated off a quiet back road between the towns of Bishopbriggs and Lenzie, just outside Glasgow. They called it 'The Homestead' to remind them of their time together in America. They settled down there and kept a few chickens and grew vegetables, but mainly they reared pigs. Life at their small holding was hard but they enjoyed it. They soon built up a good clientele of local shops willing to buy produce from them.

Towards the end of 2005 Clive, just short of his sixty-first birthday, was beginning to suffer from memory loss and was exhibiting the early signs of dementia. His brain was addled, probably due in no small measure to the large amount of weed he had smoked over the years. It was his one vice.

Nancy was just a couple of years younger than Clive and it was hard trying to run the business on her own as Clive's health deteriorated. She was also running short of cash as she no longer received an allowance from America. The solution seemed to be simple. Nancy advertised the barn and other outbuildings on the property for rent. She was delighted when a short time later, two very smartly dressed Chinese gentlemen, offered her a large cash deposit up front. It was a godsend and she accepted immediately.

The following week numerous vehicles brought in lots of equipment. Thereafter every morning, very early, about twenty workers, who all looked to be Chinese, were delivered to the smallholding. They worked inside the barn and outbuildings until late at night. Sometimes as long as sixteen or seventeen hours per day.

Nancy soon realised that they had set up a large hydroponics unit in the barn and were cultivating a huge amount of cannabis. Although she knew it was illegal, Nancy was quite happy to leave the Chinese to their business and collect rent from them each month. She was getting on with her life and with the little help she received from Clive was trying hard to keep the smallholding going. There were chickens and pigs to feed as well as vegetables to grow.

She and Clive were totally unaware that the unit in the barn was just a small part of a much larger operation that was ongoing over the central belt of Scotland. It was run by the Chinese triad gang, Tai Huen Chai or Big Circle. Also what they had failed to realise was that the Chinese had set up an illegal cigarette factory in the other outbuilding.

The factories which were set up were invariably staffed by slave labour. The illegal activities at the smallholding would eventually come to light. Sooner or later the Graham family would get to hear of it and that would mean only one thing. Trouble.

Friday was Nancy's day to go to speak to the local shops and deliver produce. She left Clive sitting quietly by the fireside smoking yet another reefer. Nancy smiled to herself as she pulled the old Volkswagen, laden with goods, out of the driveway heading for Lenzie. Clive's dementia was getting worse. He was a harmless soul who wandered about the property, sometimes being of use but more and more becoming a burden. However there was no way Nancy would leave him or place him in a care home. She would make sure he had everything he needed as over the years he had cared so much for her.

It was a shame to leave him on his own while she went out but she could get things done much quicker by herself. And it was a time Nancy looked forward to just for a bit of peace and quiet. Also that was when the Chinese moved their week's 'produce' . The less she knew about it the better she liked it.

Over the last few months, Gerry had been looking into the problems Sammy Chen and his family had been experiencing. At first he didn't get too far but later some people, probably due to Sammy Chen's influence, opened up to Gerry. What he found wouldn't please Sammy or his family. It seemed that Lee Zhu, Soo Lin's husband, had a problem. He was a gambler and, it appeared, a bad one at that. He owed the triad £70,000 and the interest was growing by the day. They wanted payment. This was probably why not only Sammy but also Lee Zhu's father, who also owned a business, had also been attacked.

As a way of trying to make amends, Lee Zhu had become a 'Blue Lantern', or uninitiated member of the Big Circle Gang. He naively thought that he could work the debt off. He became heavily involved in the distribution of cannabis to various locations. Part of his job entailed uplifting the cannabis and also large quantities of illegal cigarettes from various 'factories', one of which was The Homestead.

Just ten minutes after Nancy had left, a van drove into the smallholdings yard. Lee Zhu was driving. He reversed up to the barn doors and stopped. The passenger, a huge man, went inside the barn. Moments later the barn doors opened and a procession of workers carried out several boxes packed with rolling tobacco. This shipment was then to be driven to a warehouse in Glasgow which was the base of operations.

As the workers were loading the vehicle Clive appeared from the cottage and made his way towards the pig stys. The Chinese just carried on with what they were doing. They knew that Clive was harmless and just wandered about the place. They laughed at him as he passed in his warm overcoat and carpet slippers.

Suddenly several cars screeched into the yard and a number of men jumped out. They were all carrying firearms and immediately began firing at the Chinese. Lee Zhu never made it out of his van. He died where he sat behind the wheel, shot through the head. Several workers were also killed, whilst others ran for cover. Those inside the barn and others in the out buildings were alerted and a violent battle ensued. Firearms, machetes and knives were used with impunity.

It all stopped as quickly as it had begun about fifteen minutes later.

There were numerous casualties on both sides. Ten Chinese and three of the Graham gang had died. Included in these were Pat Reilly and Willie Collins, two of the men who had previously attacked Gerry Lynch. Several others required hospital treatment. Someone had phoned the emergency services when they saw smoke rising from the barn.

Billy and Bobby Graham had already made good their escape with the remnants of their gang. They had been successful in damaging the triad operations and setting fire to the barn. Both sides had paid a heavy price.

When Nancy got back from Lenzie, 'The Homestead' resembled a battleground. The police, ambulance and fire service were all in attendance dealing with the fire, the dead and the wounded. Her first thought was for Clive. She ran from her van, which she had to abandon on the roadside, towards the cottage. There was no sign of Clive. She looked everywhere and after some minutes found him lying inside the pig sty. He had been shot in the back and had fallen into the pen. The pigs had eaten away his face. Such a sad and horrible ending for such a gentle man.

Nancy had to identify his remains for the police. Arrangements were also made to have the pigs put down. When she was later interviewed Nancy Baumann admitted renting her premises to Chinese business men. She denied knowing anything about cannabis or illegal tobacco. The authorities had no real evidence against her, so she was not charged with any crimes or offences.

In the weeks that followed Nancy arranged Clive's funeral. It had been his wish to be cremated. Thereafter she travelled north in her pink Volkswagen van to the Findhorn community. There she scattered Clive's ashes on the hillside. It had been a special place for both of them. On her return down south Nancy put the smallholding up for sale and flew home to Boston. She left a solicitor in Lenzie with the job of winding up her affairs in Britain.

Nancy and Clive had lived the dream but now the dream was over for both of them.

Given the circumstances Gerry did not feel it would be right to tell Sammy Chen about Lee Zhu's gambling debt. The problem with the triad had ended.

CHAPTER THIRTY-FOUR

It was 5.35pm and just three weeks since Willie Robertson had left for a break in the Spanish sun. As he descended the stairs from the plane he was greeted by typical Scottish weather, a light drizzle fell from a leaden sky. This had the effect of immediately depressing him. Great to be back, not. He wasn't pleased to be home and couldn't wait until he was back in Spain and a lovely warm climate permanently.

Having crossed the tarmac at Glasgow Airport he made his way into the terminal building to reclaim his luggage. As he came to the passport check desk he recognised Detective Chief Inspector Sandy Morton standing there waiting. He then noted two or three other faces who also seemed familiar.

Before he could even think, Sandy Morton had cautioned him and informed him that he was under arrest. Something to do with drugs and being a disgrace to the force were words he recalled being used but which he could not seem to process. What was happening? How could he be arrested? They had nothing on him.

He was taken not to Stewart Street but to London Road police office. At the charge bar he had sufficiently composed himself to request that his solicitor James McCandlish be informed. He was then searched before being placed in a cell. Sandy thought it was an interesting choice of solicitor, the same one as used by the Graham family. A very interesting start to what was probably going to be a very long night.

DCI Morton and his team left Robertson to stew, whilst they went to his home in Uddingston. They were in possession of a warrant to search the premises. No one realised the Pandora's box that they were about to open.

Robertson lived alone in a very neat, semi detached, three bedroom house, in a quiet cul de sac in the leafy park of the town. Sandy Morton opened the front door with the key taken from Robertson's possessions, with his knowledge and permission. No need to knock down doors, all very civilised. What bothered DCI Morton was that Robertson seemed quite happy to allow them to have the key. He seemed very confident that they would find nothing.

Sandy and his team set about searching through the premises with a fine tooth comb and came up totally empty. Perhaps there was nothing to be found, hence Robertson's attitude back at London Road. They had been in every room, including the attic and garage, but had found nothing of a criminal nature. The last thing Sandy needed was to go back to London Road with his tail between his legs to listen to some jumped up overpaid lawyer spouting off about his clients rights and police harassment. He needed evidence.

Robertson was a disgrace to the force. There was no doubt in Morton's mind that he had been, at the very least involved in the sale and supply of controlled drugs and had been the Grahams' man on the inside for years, feeding them information. Never mind that he may well have also murdered people in cold blood. One of them being one of Sandy's own detective constables.

He gathered his group together and let them know his feelings in no uncertain terms. They would find something before they left this place even if they had to demolish it brick by brick. Sandy's men had never seen him so animated before. They redoubled their efforts and once again searched every nook and cranny. Still no joy.

Eventually, as is so often the case in these instances, it all came down to a bit of blind luck.

The team were just about to pack up and head back to Glasgow with heavy hearts. Nobody had done anything wrong, they had all done their jobs, everything by the book, but each one of them felt the same. In some way in finding no incriminating evidence they had let down not only their detective chief inspector and force but every police officer in Scotland.

It was by pure chance that on the way out one of the younger detectives had to visit the toilet in the downstairs cloakroom. He had spent most of the search in the attic, being one of the younger, fitter, members of the team. As the officer stood at the toilet, he noticed that there were a lot of toiletries on the shelf behind the cistern, shaving foam and such like. It was the silliest thing though, there was shaving equipment but no mirror. He carefully removed all the various items and found that the shelf was actually hinged and opened up. He looked into the void and hit pay dirt.

Detective Chief Inspector Sandy Morton was later to admit that throughout his whole police career he had never had the urge to kiss another police officer, female or male. But without doubt he definitely had the urge that night.

At 11.40pm Sandy and his team wearily returned to London Road police office. They were met by the duty officer who informed DCI Morton that a very irate solicitor had been waiting in the foyer for some considerable time demanding to see his client.

Sandy realised that what had been retrieved from Robertson's house would require careful examination. He, for one would get no sleep tonight. Just before midnight DCI Morton allowed McCandlish access to his client. He and a detective sergeant then joined them in the interview room, to give them the good news. Robertson was charged with offences under the Misuse of Drugs Act and informed that he was being detained in custody pending further enquiries into more serious crimes. McCandlish demanded to be informed what these crimes were. Politely Morton told him he would be informed in the fullness of time but in the interest of the safety of his client he was not prepared to discuss them at present.

Sandy was playing a very clever game. He was letting McCandlish and Robertson know that he knew the Graham family were involved and as such had placed a very large target on Robertson's back. He had done this for two reasons: so McCandlish would let the Grahams know and, hopefully, Robertson may, fearing for his life, come across with some information about the crime family. Robertson refused to say another word and McCandlish left in a hurry.

Sandy Morton returned to his own office at Stewart Street police office. Although it was very late, he phoned Gerry Lynch on his mobile just to let him know Robertson was in custody and that the search of his home had been fruitful. He now had to stay up all night just to see how fruitful.

The following afternoon William Robertson appeared in private at Glasgow Sheriff Court. He made no plea or declaration and was remanded in custody. Sandy Morton could now go home for a very well earned sleep.

It took many hours to put together the case against William Robertson. He could forget retirement in Spain or any police pension as he would soon be sacked from the force in disgrace. Eventually, in total he was indicted for the murders of five people, Josephine Jardine, Daniel Quinn, Joseph Patterson, Detective Constable Paul Corrigan and Mark McCabe.

Who was the main witness against him? Himself.

Under the shelf in his cloakroom he had kept several items. All of an incriminating nature. Something from each of his victims.

He had in his possession a small ladies powder compact which had been owned by Josie Jardine. It had been a present from Sadie Gleason and she was later able to identify it. He had Danny Quinn's wallet and wristwatch. A silly wee ornament from Joseph Patterson's home which his sister Carol Duffy was able to identify. It had been her mother's. Paul Corrigan's warrant card and a pay slip in the name of Mark McCabe.

Being the egotist that he was Robertson had also kept a journal of all his activities. In his mind he was so clever nobody would ever suspect he was involved in criminal activity. Entries outlined who he had murdered and how, complete with what he had taken from them. If that wasn't bad enough he had listed all the times he had passed information to the Graham family. Even which member of the family he had told. There was also a column showing the cash payments he had received for services rendered.

It also indicated, that for many years, he had been heavily involved in the sale and supply of controlled drugs, totally independent of the Graham family. If they had known he may have been dealt with years ago. As if that was not in itself a catalogue of shame, there were other entries which Sandy and his team still had to look into. There were names which referred to yet more killings. Some had occurred abroad and these would need to be investigated. There were also many entries written in code, describing drugs deals, and other crimes such as rapes. Sandy knew Gerry Lynch would be interested in these entries, never mind the police.

The enquiry gathered momentum and soon more evidence piled up against Robertson. Apart from identifying her friend's compact Sadie Gleason also identified Robertson as the young beat cop who had sexually harassed the working girls all those years before. There was a growing list of prostitutes, young and old, coming forward to complain of being sexually assaulted by Robertson.

Carol Duffy, Ann Marie Docherty and Sadie McCarty all identified him as the officer who had not taken their complaints of rape and serious assault seriously and had demanded sexual favours from them in exchange for drugs. The entry regarding Danny Quinn simply stated, 'getting too close, eliminate'. Even Chris Irvine was able to identify Robertson as the man who had sold drugs to Mark McCabe at the Chaos nightclub.

From the entry in his own journal Robertson had told how McCabe had been looking for a date rape drug at the Chaos night club. Robertson had sold him some rogue ecstasy and when the girl died McCabe had lost the plot.

He had come looking for Robertson's help and had threatened to expose him. A bullet in the head and the River Clyde had solved that problem. Fortunately during the search in Robertson's home, officers had found a number of the rogue ecstasy tablets. They were now under forensic examination and in the future it was hoped that medical staff would know what they were dealing with.

Robertson was going to jail for a very long time, probably the rest of his life.

On top of losing out on his police pension, the financial investigation people were looking into his bank accounts both in the United Kingdom and abroad. They had already learned that he had an account with over £400,000 deposited, as well as a similar amount in Euros, in a Spanish bank. There was also his house in Uddingston to be taken into account. Hopefully all these assets could be seized under the Proceeds of Crime Act.

Of all the entries made in Robertson's journal one stood out to Sandy Morton. When he read it, it made his blood boil. 'January 2002 - Phoned Billy Graham to let him know the plain clothes unit were all meeting at their usual pub to celebrate putting Frank Jnr. behind bars. (Usual fee).'

CHAPTER THIRTY-FIVE

I t was the day of Frank Graham Jnr.'s funeral. Notable by their absence were the twins, Billy and Bobby. They were being sought after for interview by the police in relation to a number of matters including the serious assault and rape of three women, who according to sources, had identified them as being responsible for the crimes. They were also wanted for questioning regarding the carnage at 'The Homestead' smallholding near Lenzie. As a result they had been hiding out in a farmhouse owned by the family. It was situated out Eaglesham way, near Fenwick Moor.

Despite their non attendance, once again the great and the good of the criminal fraternity gathered to pay their respects. The Graham family were fast running out of options. Once more the serious crime squad were there filming all those in attendance. For once the weather did not interfere. It was a lovely summer's day. Frank was buried with his brother Jamie in Cadder Cemetery.

Again afterwards everyone who was anyone went back to the Crooked Man for a drink. At closing time Margaret simply locked the door and what remained of the family and their close associates continued drinking into the small hours. Billy and Bobby had been smuggled in after insisting on attending the party, despite warnings to the contrary. They should have heeded their friends.

Nobody had a clue as to how it started, or what it was about, but Billy Graham suddenly became engaged in a heated argument with a family associate, Tony McGuire, who was in fact one of his own closest friends. Since having sustained his facial injury everyone knew Billy was definitely the more unstable of the twins, although Bobby was not far behind. After the funeral both had been hitting the bottle hard and had partaken in more than their fair share of cocaine.

Things got so bad that Margaret told them to take it outside. She let Billy and Tony out. Bobby and Tony's younger brother Kevin also went outside to try to calm things down. It didn't work. Fuelled by drink and drugs Billy was unmanageable. Without warning he reached into his jacket, pulled out an automatic pistol and shot Tony McGuire in the head, killing him instantly. Bobby and Kevin McGuire just stood in disbelief. Then all hell broke loose.

Before the police arrived Kevin McGuire was whisked away. Although it was his own brother he knew better than to grass on the Graham's. If he kept quiet he would be looked after. Billy and Bobby were poured into a car and driven away from the scene, firstly to their flat in Glasgow, where they picked up a couple of bags of fresh clothing, money and some food before once more disappeared into the night back to the farm at Eaglesham.

To all intents and purposes Billy and Bobby Graham had disappeared off the face of the earth. Only their sister Margaret and one or two close associates knew of their whereabouts.

In the meantime the Graham family empire was slowly eroding.

Jamie's widow Michelle had sold her business and house and was moving to the Ayrshire coast for a quiet life. Frank Jnr.'s widow Shirley was doing likewise and heading for America to live with her daughter Annette, who now had a job in New York. Even the Crooked Man was up for sale.

Sandy Morton had to smile to himself when he heard this news. Whoever did the books would need to be a magician to make the place seem like a viable proposition. The word was that Margaret would be heading to Spain to open a bar. Obviously nobody trusted the twins to run the business as they were loose cannons.

Already some criminal firms from other areas of Glasgow were reportedly moving in slowly and taking over Graham turf. Margaret was also in the process of selling the taxi business to a team from Possil. They would be running the drugs trade from now on and the triad would then become their problem.

CHAPTER THIRTY-SIX

I t was now early July and Gerry sat in his office contemplating that it would soon be a year since he had left hospital. What a year it had been. He and Jenny were now working at full tilt, perhaps it was time he thought about taking on more staff. One good thing was that he was back in touch with Audrey. He knew he had to take things slowly with her as he didn't want to blow his chances. He would have a chance this weekend as Sandy Morton was holding his retirement party. What great memories he had of working with Sandy.

There was a soft knocking on his door which brought him back to the present.

"Just the mail," Jenny said. "I have a very posh looking envelope here for you".

It certainly was a very nicely embossed envelope, none of the usual rubbish. Gerry opened it puzzled as to what it contained. He was delighted to see that it was an invitation. Archibald Buchanan had, as the invitation said, requested the pleasure of the company of Mr Gerald Lynch and partner to the 150th Anniversary of Founders Day dinner at Woodcroft House School, Auchtermuchty on Saturday 26 August 2006.

That's great, Gerry thought, then looked at his desk calendar. It was in just a few weeks time. What would he wear? Who would he invite? Then he read the invitation again. He had never had such a posh invite in his life. He hoped Audrey would go with him, he assumed she would. It was then that he also noted a short handwritten message from Archie Buchanan himself.

'The trip may help your investigation into our friend, A.B'

Reading the note somehow suddenly triggered something in Gerry's brain. Firstly he thought he had better ask Audrey, he was afraid she might turn him down. As it was she told him she had known about the forthcoming event for weeks. Aimi McLeod had told her and yes, of course she would be delighted to go with him. What a relief.

Next he contacted Aimi who was now back in Edinburgh. She put him wise as what to wear and was what required. She would arrange a shopping day in Edinburgh for the girls to get outfits and include Audrey in that.

When he came off the phone after speaking to Aimi, Gerry felt better. He read the invitation again. That was when he spotted that the cost was £500 a plate. The business was doing okay but not that well. Still, he wouldn't be going to a party like this one every day and Audrey was going with him.

Perhaps he could learn more about Lord Dunbeth when he was there. The more he had gone over all the case notes the more he felt Dunbeth had questions to answer. Particularly since getting the invitation from Archie Buchanan. He had given Gerry the key to hopefully getting to the truth of a few matters which still needed to be resolved.

He would need to see Audrey right away, even though he had just spoken to her. He had forgotten about Dunbeth because he had been more worried about whether she would go to the party with him.

He phoned her back and arranged to meet her in ten minutes at her office. He arrived breathless at Stewart Street. It seemed strange to know Sandy Morton wasn't inside. Gerry was shown into the CID room where Audrey was waiting for him.

"Well you madman, what is so urgent that you needed to see me in person only half an hour

after speaking to me on the phone?"

"Robertson's journal," Gerry gasped.

"What about it?" Audrey replied, exasperated.

"I think I can work out some of the coded entries," he exclaimed.

Audrey went to speak to her DI. Ten minutes later Audrey and Gerry were in his office pouring over the journal which William Robertson had written, which was a catalogue of crime. Some of the entries had been deciphered but many still remained a mystery.

Archie Buchanan had confided in him regarding his love for a fellow student and how they had communicated using initials. Gerry recalled that Sandy Morton was stumped by some of the journals entries. Gerry explained his theory to Audrey and her Detective Inspector.

"Look at these entries," he began. "*301093AMD = BGBG*. I think that reads 30 October 1993, Ann Marie Docherty, equals Billy Graham and Bobby Graham. That was the date when she was raped and Robertson is telling you who did it. Look at the next, *261193CP= BGBG*. Carol Patterson raped on 26 November 1993 by Billy and Bobby Graham, and the next, *24121993SMCC= BGBG*. Sarah McCarty raped on that date by Billy and Bobby Graham.

"Once you work out the code all the other entries become easier. Some go back over a few years but I believe that they may have been committed by the same person.

"Look at the initials MH, LD, QC and MSP, all could refer to Maurice Henshaw, Lord Dunbeth, Queen's Counsel and Member of the Scottish Parliament, at different times throughout his life. If for instance you look at this entry which is of particular interest to both me and DC Jennings. 270401IB=QCBGBG. That is the date Isla Buchanan was raped and I would suggest that Maurice Henshaw QC and the Graham twins were the culprits. All my research tells me that Henshaw has been a predator all his life, at school, at university and with a reputation of being a bit of a brute with women. He has managed to escape justice because of his father, criminal associates and downright luck. He is a known associate of the Graham family and also William Robertson. We just need to somehow get him to admit it."

"What if we were to get a warrant to plant a listening device in his study at the country pile when we are up there for the party?" Audrey asked.

Both men thought it was a brilliant idea and the DI stepped out of the office to start making the arrangements.

Before leaving, Gerry whispered in Audrey's ear, "I love you," and kissed her on the lips.

While he was in the city centre Gerry decided to go see about hiring his outfit for the party. He was looking for and, indeed, found a Lynch tartan kilt with Prince Charlie jacket and everything else that went to complete the outfit. He tried the outfit on and looked at his reflection in the mirror. He had to admit he looked impressive.

CHAPTER THIRTY-SEVEN

The next thing on everyone's agenda was Sandy Morton's retirement party. Sandy had mentioned to Gerry some time ago that he was retiring from the police force. Every time he had brought it up at work, people seemed to change the subject. Nobody could believe that the great man was actually going. When the day eventually came there was a sadness descended over the office. Now he was gone and they all had was an open invitation to come along to his leaving party which was to be held in the same pub in town where the old squad had held it's celebration when Frank Graham Jnr. had been jailed. It was were the police held all their nights out.

Gerry and Audrey had been seeing a bit more of each other lately so he phoned to ask her if she was going to Sandy's retirement party.

"Are you asking me out on a date, Lynch?" she had replied.

He had managed to stutter back "Yes."

"Okay then," had been her reply. Gerry was over the moon.

That whole day at work he couldn't concentrate. His thoughts just turned to the evening ahead. Brenda had been good enough to press his suit and he had been out and bought a new shirt and tie. He aimed to impress.

The party was due to start at 7.30pm and Gerry was travelling into the city by taxi. Audrey had arranged to meet him in a little cafe not too far from the pub, just so they could make an entrance together. If nothing else it would start the tongues wagging. Gerry hoped it did mean they were a couple but didn't want to blow it.

The taxi had been pre booked and so he had plenty of time to shower and get dressed. He had thought of buying Audrey something to mark the occasion but again the thought of being too presumptuous put him off the idea. His inner voice spoke to him again, "Just get there and enjoy yourself. " '

When Gerry arrived at the cafe around 7.30pm, it was empty apart from two students who were lingering over coffee. He ordered a latte and sat at a table, for what seemed like forever. He was behaving like a frightened schoolboy on his first date. He kept staring at the door. A few minutes later Audrey arrived. She looked gorgeous in a plain cream fitted dress which stopped just at the knee. For once she was wearing high heels. Gerry went to kiss her but she shied away and he thought he'd made a huge mistake.

"I'm not kissing you with froth all over your face," she laughed.

Gerry looked over at the two students and turned red as he wiped his mouth with a napkin. Audrey then leaned forward and kissed him tenderly on the lips.

"That's better" she smiled. He was dumbstruck.

She didn't want a coffee so Gerry left his, they made their way along the street to the pub.

As they walked Gerry told Audrey she looked beautiful and she replied that he wasn't looking too shabby himself.

Soon they were in the pub, which was already quite full with lots of faces they both recognised. From the Chief Constable to CID clerks, past and present, all of who had worked with Sandy. Jean Morton was also there but only for a time. She had organised and helped prepare a beautiful buffet, but as she said herself,

"This lot are always the same. They get drunk and tell the same old stories that you've heard a thousand times."

By 10pm she excused herself to let her husband and his cronies get on with it. As expected Sandy received many gifts, from his favourite whisky to new golf clubs. He had been well liked and respected throughout the force and beyond. There was no doubt that the criminal element of Glasgow would be breathing a collective sigh of relief tonight.

At the start of the party the current chief constable had said a few words and presented Sandy with a shield bearing the coat of arms of Strathclyde Police. Having fulfilled his obligation he quietly slipped away.

It was good to see Kenny Brown, Rona McLean and David O'Neill again. Rona was now a uniform inspector in Edinburgh and had obviously been selected for greater things. Kenny was doing well, still selling cars and now had two children. David had gone into property development in Edinburgh and was earning a fortune. Did Kenny and David wish that they were still part of the force? Gerry could answer that one for them, all day long.

Towards the end of the evening Sandy got up to rapturous applause. He silenced the crowd and joked.

"Don't clap yet, you don't know what I'm going to say."

In the end he thanked all those who'd attended the party and those whom he'd had the pleasure of working with in his thirty years in the job. He had enjoyed every single minute of it whether good or bad days. He also had a special mention for his long suffering wife, who he noted had disappeared early, not only for the work she had put into the evening but also for all the support she had given him over the years.

Before closing he raised his glass and asked for a toast. He looked directly across to his old

unit who were stood together.

"To all those not here tonight, absent friends."

The crowd stood and cheered and clapped his remarks and sentiments for several minutes. Sandy stood and took it all in with a tear in his eye. Gerry and Audrey were the same. They were thinking of their colleagues and friends that had been lost back in 2002.

Before leaving Gerry asked Sandy if he could fit in time to visit his office in Alexandra Parade soon. Sandy said he could be there tomorrow afternoon, which was fine with Gerry.

Gerry and Audrey grabbed a taxi which headed as directed to Audrey's flat. When they arrived Audrey asked Gerry if he wanted to come in. He wanted nothing more but couldn't. He needed to be ready for Sandy's visit. He promised to call her once Sandy had left and insisted that she come out with him for dinner the following week. She smiled and immediately agreed. They kissed and then she was gone. As Gerry sat in the back of the taxi as it made its way to Dennistoun, he was blissfully happy.

CHAPTER THIRTY-EIGHT

Today was going to be busy. After his daily run and breakfast Gerry went to the office. As usual he had lots of administration to do and wanted to be completely clear when Sandy arrived. He had thought long and hard about what he wanted to say. Normally he gave up after an hour, but today he stuck to his task and by lunchtime his desk was clear.

Gerry went to reception and asked Jenny what she fancied for lunch. He needed to go out and get some fresh air. Jenny wasn't about to look a gift horse in the mouth and asked if he could pick up a chicken salad sandwich for her. That sounded good, so he made it two. He insisted she shut up shop and join him. They also picked up two takeaway coffees and headed towards the park. It was good to get out of the office once in a while.

Once back at the office Jenny got back to her work load. It was almost time for Sandy to arrive. At exactly 2pm he walked into the office and was shown straight into Gerry's office. He was always punctual but then he did only live ten minutes away in Baillieston, just along Edinburgh Road.

Sandy told Gerry how much he had enjoyed his party the previous night. It had been so good to see so many old friends. Yes, he would miss the job but everything comes to an end.

That was what Gerry wanted to speak to him about.

"What are you going to do now Sandy?" he asked.

"Well Gerry, me and Jean are off on a cruise at the end of the week. I promised her several weeks sailing around the Mediterranean. After that I don't know. As you know Jean has also retired from the chemist shop and she has warned me, I'd better find something as she does not want me under her feet. I've had a few offers, two from superstores and one from a university wanting me to become head of security but to be honest I don't really fancy any of them."

"How would you fancy working with me?" Gerry said.

"Interesting," was all Sandy said in reply.

"We would be equal partners and you could work as many days per week as you liked. It's maybe not as silly as it sounds. I have been doing this for just about a year now and need help. I can't think of anyone who I'd rather work with and I know in a way Jimmy Quinn would be tickled pink to think you would be part of his business. Let's face it Sandy, it's handy for you, just living along the road and you are the best detective I have ever met".

Gerry also knew that having Sandy Morton on board would bring in a mountain of work as his reputation was second to none.

"I'll tell you what I'll do, Gerry," Sandy replied, "I'm very flattered by your offer. I will speak to Jean and once I come back from our cruise, I'll have an answer for you."

"That's brilliant" Gerry replied.

They shook hands and Sandy departed.

Gerry was straight on the phone to Audrey. She was delighted to hear his news about Sandy and also said how much she had enjoyed herself at his party. They arranged to have dinner that night in a little out of the way Italian restaurant they both liked. Gerry would pick her up at around 7pm.

The rest of the day passed in a flash. If you had asked Gerry what he had done during the time he wouldn't have been able to tell you, other than gone into town and bought some more new shirts and ties.

At exactly 7pm Gerry rang the doorbell to Audrey's flat. She let him in and he gave her a bunch of flowers he had bought for her. Audrey was delighted and put them straight into a vase of water. Once again she looked stunning in a figure hugging black dress. They had a wonderful meal washed down with plenty of wine. All Gerry could have told you was that they had some kind of pasta followed by tiramisu. He had it bad. He only had eyes for Audrey.

After a lovely evening he took her back to her flat. This time he didn't go straight home. They did not speak but the front door had hardly closed behind them before they were stripping one another. They made love into the early hours.

Later Gerry lay in bed, wide awake, watching Audrey breathing next to him. His mind was racing. How could he have treated her the way that he had? Yes, he had suffered a breakdown and been somewhat fragile on his release from hospital. But that was still no excuse for being so selfish. Audrey should have been his first port of call, He should have got down on his knees and begged her forgiveness. Would they ever get back to where they had been? Tonight had been amazing and certainly a step in the right direction. As he lay there his mind turned to thoughts of Sandy Morton, what would his answer be, it could change his life.

Gerry hoped that he and Audrey could progress with their relationship. At breakfast that morning he definitely got a boost. Audrey said,

"That was lovely last night, the meal, everything."

"I'm glad," he replied and then was taken aback with what she said next.

"Making love was magical. I've been wanting you to do that for ages. That night I came to your flat, the night Samson was there, I wanted you so badly."

She had an impish look in her eyes.

"Oh did you indeed," Gerry said as he lifted her up into his arms and carried her back to the bedroom.

It was noon before he arrived at work. He could get nothing past Jenny.

"I see you had a good night last night then," she remarked.

"Yes thanks," he smiled, heading into his office.

CHAPTER THIRTY-NINE

I t was Friday 25 August 2006, and he was ready to go. Gerry had stayed overnight at Audrey's again. They were taking his BMW and needed to stop at the police office in Perth on the way. They had an appointment with the local detective inspector.

Gerry knew Audrey had bought a new dress for the occasion, but she refused point blank to let him see it until tomorrow night. She had been over to Edinburgh the previous weekend shopping with Mary and Aimi for hours, including a rather leisurely lunch. The consensus was that they were all going to look stunning.

Isla was still not fully fit and so would miss the trip. Aimi drove her mother straight to Woodcroft House School, as Mary would be staying there to assist her brother with any last minute problems and be at his side basically to support him. This was to be a big day in the school's history and had been many months in the planning. Hopefully everything would pass without a hitch.

Aimi would be staying in the same nearby hotel as Gerry and Audrey. She had a surprise guest who was due to arrive from New York in time for dinner. The guest would be a surprise to everyone but her mother. Then she had an announcement to make over the weekend.

One thing none of them were especially looking forward to was lunch on Saturday. They had all been invited to Balmuir by Lord and Lady Dunbeth. This was because he was the Chairman of the Governors for the school, and it went against tradition to decline. Gerry was looking forward to the event as it would hopefully give Audrey the chance to plant a listening device in Henshaw's study.

The drive up to Perth was lovely as for once the weather was kind. Gerry and Audrey popped into the police office to ensure everything was in place. The local police had nothing on Henshaw, there had been plenty of rumours but never any actual evidence of wrong doing. He had never even been issued with a parking ticket, let alone sexual offences libelled against him.

Having stopped in Perth for coffee, Gerry and Audrey arrived at their hotel where they were met by Aimi. That evening at the hotel prior to having dinner Gerry and Audrey were sitting having a drink at the bar. Aimi walked in with a handsome man on her arm. He was tall with blonde haired, just like Aimi. Gerry noticed straight away that although dressed in casual clothes they looked very expensive. He was immaculate.

Aimi introduced her mystery guest,

"Hi guys," she said. "This is Richard Jonson and he's my fiancé."

"Well you kept that very quiet, Miss McLeod, how could you do this to me?" Gerry joked.

They all laughed and Aimi explained how she and Gerry had a running joke about her finding a boyfriend as good as him. She had met Richard who was an American, several months before at a medical conference in England. He worked for a leading pharmaceutical company. The fact was they were getting married at Christmas in Richard's home state of Hawaii.

Gerry and Audrey were delighted for the couple and insisted on celebrating with champagne. Richard had an easy way about him and soon the four were laughing together and enjoying each other's company over more champagne and an excellent dinner. Later that night Audrey told Gerry that Aimi had asked her to be a bridesmaid at her wedding, and she was thrilled. Gerry just wondered how much this was all going to cost him.

The next morning Gerry was up early as usual for his morning run before breakfast. It was going to be a long day and he had to make room for all the food he was likely to consume. Richard Jonson must have had the same idea for he too was out ready to run. They ran together side by side and after a good three miles were approaching the hotel. No words passed between them but suddenly both picked up the pace until they were sprinting neck and neck back into the car park. It appeared to be a dead heat and both men were soaked in sweat. It was obvious that they were both fierce competitors.

Thirty minutes later after having showered and dressed both men joined the ladies for a light breakfast. It was plain to see that both men were getting on really well. Aimi took the opportunity to tell her friends that she was three months pregnant. "Only my mum knows at present," she said. "so if you could keep it under your hat for now." Gerry and Audrey were sworn to secrecy.

As midday approached unfortunately there was no putting it off. It was time for lunch at Balmuir. All four piled into Gerry's BMW and they drove over to the Henshaws' house. As they turned into a long driveway it took Gerry's breath away. He had only seen places like this in films. It was a beautiful house, and although building had begun in Victorian times the house had a Georgian facade. There were perfectly manicured gardens, complete with a fountain in front of the house. It really was a delight. Gerry wondered how many staff it took to keep the place is such pristine condition.

They parked with the rest of the cars at the side of the house and made their way to the front door. Just inside the main entrance they came upon the butler who informed them that lunch would be in one hour. They noted that there was a notice board in the foyer which indicated that the premises comprised of nine suites. They noted the names of those in residence. Aimi noted that one of those names was her father. She had no idea who his companion was.

The four friends decided on a walk before lunch, and as they went back towards the cars, Archie and Mary were parking. Aimi lost no time in letting them know her father was there. Exactly one hour later the butler announced lunch in the dining room. They all filtered through and the necessary introductions were made. There were, in total, fourteen for lunch. Archie and Mary went nowhere near Reginald McLeod to whom the years had not been kind. The once handsome man was now bald with a rather large paunch. His partner, many years his junior, was a South African who was drop dead gorgeous. She purred when she spoke about the fact her family had a diamond mine.

Maurice Henshaw was similar in many ways to Reginald. He had obviously been a good looking man in his younger years, indeed his two sons William and

James were testament to that. Lady Henshaw was quite a bit younger than her husband and seemed to Gerry and Audrey to be a pleasant sort. She was slim and very attractive. William's wife Karen was a quiet, pretty thing and James' girlfriend for the weekend was called Christine and didn't have much to say. Aimi only spoke briefly to her father to introduce Richard to him. To be fair to the Henshaws, the spread which had been prepared was lovely. It was just nobody really wanted to be there. At one point in proceedings Audrey gave Gerry a dig in the ribs and alerted him to the time. As if by magic the telephone in the hallway rang. Moments later the butler announced there was a call for Audrey. She asked if she could take it somewhere more private as it was police business. The butler directed her into Maurice Henshaw's study.

Audrey wasted no time in planting the listening device and quickly returned to the dining room. Not long after that the lunch ended and everyone went to prepare themselves for the evening party.

CHAPTER FORTY

They had all been under orders to be ready by 6.45pm as limousines had been ordered to uplift all the guests at the hotel. They gathered in the foyer.

At Balmuir, Lord and Lady Dunbeth were to leave in the family Rolls Royce. Dunbeth wore a dinner suit. His family had originally come from England and had by tradition never worn kilts. Lady Dunbeth wore a designer dress in dark green lace and she looked wonderful. They were to be accompanied by Reginald McLeod who wore a kilt, in the Dress McLeod tartan. His partner Miss Van Groot looked like a Hollywood star, bedecked in diamonds, wearing a white figure hugging sequinned full length dress with a slit up one side. It left little to the imagination. Maurice Henshaw could not take his eyes off her.

William Henshaw, his wife Karen, brother James and his girlfriend, Christine Montgomery, followed in a limousine. The Henshaw brothers both wore dinner suits, like their father. The ladies wore simple cocktail dresses.

Back at the hotel a limousine duly arrived for Gerry, Audrey, Richard and Aimi. Gerry had not seen Audrey's dress until just a few minutes earlier. It was a simple cream coloured knee length dress with shoulder straps. Quite simply, Gerry had never seen her look more beautiful. Ami wore a very similar dress which was a deep blue colour. Richard wore a very expensive looking dinner suit, every inch the rich American. Gerry was of course resplendent in his Lynch tartan kilt.

The hotel foyer was a mass of people awaiting a limousine to convey them to the party. In honesty Gerry had never seen so many beautiful women all together in one place and they hadn't even reached the party yet. Eventually they boarded their transport and arrived at the school. Above the front door a huge banner read,

FOUNDER'S DAY 150TH ANNIVERSARY

The day had finally arrived. Everyone was escorted to the main hall where the headmaster made a short speech welcoming them all to the school. Archie wore a kilt and looked magnificent in his family tartan. Mary was beside him wearing a lovely plain black dress which she said would be set off by her mother's pearl necklace. She had been right.

They all then made their way to the dining hall. Lots of work had been put in here to decorate the room which now contained two hundred circular tables, each to seat ten guests. The senior pupils undertook the task of escorting guests to their tables.

During the meal the assembled company were to be serenaded by a string ensemble taken from the Scottish Philharmonic Orchestra who under the direction of Sir Ralph McMillan were to perform later.

Gerry and Audrey were seated at their table. They did not know any of the other guests. They were an eclectic mix, a grandmother and grandson plus three couples. All they had in common was the fact that all the men, with the exception of Gerry, were or had been pupils at the school. The meal itself was delicious, worthy of a Michelin star chef. In between each course was either a toast or speech. Archie, as headmaster spoke again, as did Maurice Henshaw in his capacity as the Chair of Governors.

At the conclusion of the meal, there was a short interval, whilst pupils to moved all the tables to the sides of the room to allow dancing. Many people took the opportunity to wander out into the garden or onto the terrace to prepare for the start of the concert. Some remained inside to dance.

It was a lovely summer evening and for the next hour or so the Orchestra played everything from Lennon and McCartney to Mozart. Everyone was thoroughly enjoying the music. At the conclusion of the concert the majority of people came back into the hall. Some of the younger ones and their partners disappeared into the gardens. Whilst most were finding a seat and getting refills for their drinks, Gerry noticed that Lord Dunbeth had commandeered the table nearest to the bar. He was holding court, surrounded by his cronies included in which were Reginald McLeod and Julie Van Groot.

Lord Dunbeth must have said something untoward as Miss Van Groot stood up, slapped him hard across the face and stormed off. Aimi's father didn't even seem to notice, he was blind drunk. The rest of the table thought it was hilarious and the whole table, including Lord Dunbeth were laughing. He really was an odious creature, Gerry thought to himself. He also noticed that Lady Dunbeth was conspicuous by her absence. She was in fact seated as far away from her husband as possible with her sons and their partners.

Gerry and Audrey were having a drink with Aimi and Richard just as the final entertainment for the evening struck up. A ceildh band. A loud cheer went up and it was as though the whole gathering had suddenly become animated. Aimi grabbed Richard and said "Come on let's dance." Gerry and Audrey followed them onto the floor. As the band struck up for their first tune the whole place was a sea of swirling tartan, and it really was a sight to behold. For the next hour the band played tune after tune and the crowd danced themselves into a frenzy. By the end everyone was exhausted but happy and many a glass had been drunk. It had truly been a wonderful evening.

Reluctantly the crowd got into their cars and headed home. Some of the younger ones taking the opportunity of the beautiful clear night to walk home, Gerry and Audrey among them.

Just before they left the school grounds, Gerry looked about him and saw he and Audrey were alone. They stopped for a moment and she leant against a tree.

"Do you know something Audrey Jennings, I love you," Gerry said and they kissed.

"I love you too," Audrey replied.

"Remember last weekend, you went shopping for dresses in Edinburgh with Aimi and her

mum?" Gerry asked.

"Of course I do," Audrey replied.

"Well, you were not the only one went shopping" he said. Producing from his sporran a box small which he opened to reveal a diamond ring. "Audrey Jennings, will you marry me?"

"About time, Lynch, I thought you'd never ask."

They almost ran back to the hotel to tell Aimi and Richard their news and celebrate.

CHAPTER FORTY-ONE

As usual the next morning Gerry was up early but nothing like as bright as he normally was. He and Audrey had celebrated into the small hours and eventually he'd had to put Audrey to bed. After waiting all these years for him to pop the question, no doubt she was exhausted. Mind you, getting up at his usual time was a bit of a surprise to Gerry, given all the energy he had expended dancing last night. It was going to be a lovely sunny day and he was glad to be alive. If this was what it felt like to be engaged to be married, then bring it on.

He went for his usual run and was not surprised that he worked up quite a sweat courtesy of the alcohol he had drunk at the party and then the celebration back at the hotel. There was no sign of Richard.

Back at the hotel Audrey was still sleeping soundly. He showered and dressed in a polo shirt and cords. As usual he found that he was the first person down for breakfast again. Once more there was a mountain of fried food to tempt him, but he stuck to coffee, muesli and toast. Gerry was sat for some time, even indulging himself with a second cup of coffee before anyone else surfaced.

People eventually started to appear in the dining room in dribs and drabs. Everyone was quiet, no doubt nursing a few sore heads. Even Audrey was looking a bit rough, if that were possible. She just grabbed a coffee and a slice of toast before sitting next to Gerry. He gave her a cheeky grin. She groaned and looked at him as though it was his fault.

"Don't you go blaming me, Audrey Jennings," he laughed. " It's not my fault you fancied a brandy, or was it two? And after all the champagne you drank at the party."

All Audrey could manage was "Shut it, Lynch."

She went for a second coffee and as she did so her mobile rang. It was Aimi. After ending the call Audrey had a concerned look on her face and asked Gerry to follow her outside.

"That was Aimi on the phone. We'll have to go to the school. Something is wrong with Archie and her mum's in an awful state".

They left straight away and minutes later Aimi and Richard met them at the front doors of the school, and they were shown through to Archie's private quarters. Both were surprised to see that Archie was still dressed as he had been the previous evening , in his kilt. He looked terrible, gaunt and old. He had obviously been crying.

Mary said, "He's been up all night, never slept a wink, pacing up and down mumbling to himself."

Gerry spoke to him, "Archie, calm yourself down and let's try and sort out whatever the problem is. Come and sit near the fire and tell me what's wrong."

"You know what's wrong," Archie cried, "it's that bastard Dunbeth."

Mary was shocked, as she had never heard her brother swear before. After some minutes of cajoling, Gerry managed to get Archie settled in a seat by the fire and poured him a whisky. He noticed that the decanter on the table was almost empty. Archie automatically took the whisky from Gerry, had a sip, then slowly began to relate the story.

"As you all know, last night was a marvellous success. So much hard work had been put into making it so. It was a tremendous evening spoiled by just one person, Dunbeth. What is it that makes him always act in such an evil manner when he is within the walls of this school?

"Last night you may or may not have seen Reginald's young lady slap Dunbeth in the face. He had obviously made some lewd remark to her. The more he drank throughout the evening the worse his conduct became. Thankfully by then almost everyone was up dancing and may not have noticed his outrageous behaviour. But I had numerous complaints from several women regarding his conduct during the course of the evening."

Archie paused for a moment and took a sip of his whisky, before continuing." In the end I had no choice but to ask him to come to my office at the conclusion of the party. I rebuked him and for want of a better word an argument ensued. Some of the things he said to me, I could not possibly repeat in the company of ladies. The man has hurt me in the past but he has done it for the last time."

"What did he say to you?" Mary pleaded with her brother. "What has made you so upset?"

Archie cracked and began crying uncontrollably. After several minutes and a few more sips of whisky he was able to continue. "He admitted killing the only person I ever loved. He killed Calum." Suddenly he realised what he had said and burst into tears again.

"Why are you crying Archie?" Mary asked calmly. "Is it for Calum or because you have finally admitted your sexuality? I've known you were gay for years, you silly man," she said stroking his head.

Archie sobbed uncontrollably in her arms.

Gerry suggested that the rest of them go for a short walk and let Mary help Archie to compose himself, so he could finish his story. Once outside Gerry explained to the others what Archie had told him the day he had visited with Aimi and interviewed him regarding Lord Dunbeth.

"He swore me to secrecy, Aimi, that's why I couldn't tell you. I'm sorry."

When they went back inside Archie was much better. Aimi gave him a kiss and a cuddle and told him she loved him. He smiled weakly at her and then continued with his story. He explained how Dunbeth had called him a queer and a poof and taunted him about Calum. Eventually Dunbeth was in full flow and admitted going to Calum's room the night he died.

"He said he typed the letter and the note after he had hung Calum. His exact words were 'the spineless gay boy couldn't do the deed himself, so I put the rope around his neck and made him stand on a chair. He just cried like the baby queer he was. I got fed up listening to his whining and kicked the chair away. He squirmed for a while until he choked himself to death.'

"I have been marching up and down all night unable to sleep, thinking about what he said and what to do about it. I have almost devoured a full decanter of whisky. You know what I have told you in the past Gerry, It's alright him admitting things in private but can we ever prove it? I just want to kill him."

Everyone was quiet for a time trying to digest what Archie had said. It was Gerry who broke the silence.

"Archie, you must get yourself off to bed and leave this to me. I've got an idea things will change quite quickly with a bit of luck."

Gerry and Audrey left the school promising to return later. Whilst heading back to the hotel Gerry said he was going to speak to Maurice Henshaw and try to get him to admit guilt for some of the things of which they suspected him.

"With a bit of luck we'll get it on tape".

Just then Audrey's mobile rang again. It was the detective inspector from Perth saying something had happened up at Balmuir. Gerry turned his car around and headed in that direction. As Gerry turned into the driveway they almost collided with a taxi containing Reginald McLeod and Miss Van Groot. As they reached the front door and stopped, they were met by a tearful butler. All he could say was

"The master's dead, the master's dead."

Gerry and Audrey made their way indoors, where they met James Henshaw and asked him what was going on.

"God knows," he replied. " This morning out of the blue the whole house has gone crazy. Apparently my father has been arguing with my brother William and Reginald McLeod. They have left with their women. Mother has taken to her room and I can't find Christine anywhere. Now the butler has just informed me that my father is dead."

Just at that moment there was a screech of tyres and a car sped off down the driveway. James said it looked like Christine's car.

On entering the study, Gerry and Audrey did indeed find Lord Dunbeth slumped in his chair behind his desk. He had a grotesque look upon his face as though he had died in agony. The butler was right, he was dead, Gerry checked for a pulse, just in case, but there was nothing. They left the room, locked the door behind them and retained the key. It was now a murder scene.

A short time later the place was crawling with police officers, including the DI from Perth and a SOCO team who were now going over the study with a fine tooth comb. The DI had retrieved the recording from the listening device which Audrey had planted. He sat in his car with Gerry and Audrey listening to the recording. What they heard explained all.

From when Audrey had first planted the device on Saturday morning there was nothing much of interest. Sunday morning was completely different. Reginald McLeod was heard bursting into the room around 8.30am. He was livid and started shouting at Dunbeth about the way he had treated Miss Van Groot the night before. He got nothing back from Dunbeth but abuse reminding him that he was boss around these parts. Eventually Dunbeth tried reasoning with his old school chum.

"Come on Reggie," Dunbeth said, "you know the rules, any bit of skirt is fair game. It's not like you are going to marry the tart are you?"

"That's not the point, Maurice," Reginald retorted. "It's just not fair that you can go around abusing Archie Buchanan's niece and the like and always get away with it. Then turn your attention to our women whenever the fancy takes you."

Dunbeth then reminded Reggie McLeod that he too had to shoulder blame and dragged up his part in the Calum McCall incident. And pointed out that only he had the bottle to hang the poof.

The tape was quiet and the three listening sensed that Dunbeth was fed up talking to Reggie McLeod. Then he spoke again.

"Look, young Buchanan got exactly what she deserved and hell mend her. She was asking for it but Reggie, I will not have you coming into my study and lecturing me on my conduct. Now... GET OUT. "

No more was said and it appeared that Reginald McLeod had left the room. It was quiet for around fifteen minutes and then the trio heard the voice of William Henshaw. He also argued with his father telling him that his conduct was reprehensible and just not on.

"You just cannot treat people in this fashion" he said.

"I'll do whatever I damn well please," Dunbeth had told his son. " Now get out of this house and take that tart of a wife with you".

The study door slammed shut. Not long afterwards there was another knock at the door and Dunbeth was heard to say under his breath.

"Who the hell now.... come in."

It was quiet for a moment and they could hear the door opening. Dunbeth spoke and his mood had completely changed.

"Come in my dear, how nice to see you."

Gerry and Audrey were then surprised to hear another voice they recognised, Christine Montgomery. What could she possibly want with Dunbeth?

"Hello my Lord, I've come to give you what you asked for last night."

The trio listening all thought the same, that he must have propositioned her the previous evening.

"Come here, you naughty girl," Dunbeth said and then continued, "What's that?"

There was a rustling sound on tape and then silence for a few seconds before Christine Montgomery spoke again.

"Well Lord Dunbeth, I've just given you a small injection of something similar to curare, to keep you quiet while I tell you a story. I hope you are sitting comfortably.

"It's 1985 and a young woman was working as a typist at the High Court in Aberdeen. She meets this distinguished lawyer. Although he is much older than her and married she is flattered by his attentions. He takes her for a drink, gets her drunk and then drugs and rapes her. She has a baby girl but the shame won't go away and so she takes her own life. The girl is raised by her aunt and uncle and goes on to study chemistry . When she is old enough her aunt gives her a letter which her mum wrote to her to tell her who her father is.

"Well here I am and I'm just back from a wee holiday in South America where I obtained some venom from a Dart Frog. It's very poisonous and if humans come into contact with it they die in agony. I can see by the look on your face that you don't believe me. Here you are then, Daddy dear, try some."

The next sound on the tape was the butler trying to revive Dunbeth without success.

Gerry and Audrey went back to Woodcroft House and told everyone what had happened. Not surprisingly they were dumbfounded. Archie Buchanan then spoke. "I don't know if it is wrong for me to say this but I get the feeling that the world has just become a better place."

Nobody could disagree with that sentiment.

Once the police had completed their enquiries, the body of Lord Dunbeth was taken to Perth for post mortem examination. The subsequent findings were exactly what were expected. He had been drugged and died in agony. The hunt was on for his killer.

Meanwhile Maurice Henshaw was laid to rest in a private ceremony. He was buried in the family vault within the grounds of the Balmuir estate. His death caused a by-election in the constituency of East Perthshire and a candidate from the Scottish National Party was elected.

It would be another three years before Christine Montgomery was back in Scotland. After a long battle against extradition, she was returned from Brazil. She subsequently pled guilty at the High Court in Edinburgh and was sentenced to life imprisonment for the murder of Maurice Henshaw. There was no doubt that what she had done was premeditated, but many had sympathy for her. At the end of the day she was just another victim.

CHAPTER FORTY-TWO

Once back in Glasgow, Audrey began the process of moving in with Gerry. She put her flat up for sale and brought a couple of car loads of clothes to his flat. It was her intention to live between the two flats until hers sold. They had agreed that this was only a temporary arrangement until they could find a house.. A soon as they had done that they were going to get married. Gerry hoped it was only temporary as already he couldn't find anything in his flat and knew it would only get worse.

Sandy and Jean Morton had returned from their cruise and were delighted to hear their news. All Sandy had said to Gerry was "About bloody time," echoing the sentiments of all their old colleagues. What Gerry really wanted to know was Sandy's decision regarding forming a partnership.

Over a coffee in his office, Gerry was just about to find out. After telling Gerry all about the cruise, and how Jean had sent an author on his way when he had found out Sandy was a famous detective and wanted to write his biography, they got down to business.

"Well Gerry" Sandy began "as I promised, I have spoken at length to Jean. As you know she doesn't want me under her feet. She already knew about the other job offers I had received and knew they weren't for me. I told her about the offer you'd made me and her reply was and I quote, 'What are you waiting for' man? I would have snapped his hand off. It will suit you down to the ground.' So that was the end of our discussion. When do I start?"

Gerry couldn't believe it, and jumped out of his seat to shake his old gaffer's hand. This would be an enormous boost for the company, as well as on a personal level for Gerry. It did not take long for Gerry to outline his plans, all of which Sandy agreed with, and they also reached terms amicably. There was nothing left but to go downstairs and have Sandy sign the appropriate paperwork in Tom Kane's office. He would arrange to have Sandy added to the signatories of the bank account.

It was Sandy's intention to start bright and early the following morning. The two men shook hands again and Sandy said,

"See you in the morning, Gaffer."

"No, no," Gerry replied, "we are partners now and you will always be THE gaffer".

Next morning Gerry seemed to fly around Alexandra Park on his run. He couldn't wait to get to work, he was so excited. Immediately both men sat down to discuss the way forward. One change they decided to make was to the name of the company. After much thought and many different suggestions it was now to be known as QLM Investigations Ltd. (Quinn, Lynch and Morton). Everyone seemed happy with that.

Sandy settled in really quickly and just lifted the place by the quiet way he went assuredly about his business. Gerry's prediction was also correct. Once word got out of Sandy's involvement in the company, jobs came pouring in. This saw a need to increase staffing levels, something that both partners agreed on.

They addressed this by immediately employing two former CID officers, one male and one female. They had decided to recruit people who had worked for a police force. The reason for this was because any applicant's background could be easily checked and they knew then what they were getting. Still the work kept coming in and soon they would need more staff. This brought with it another problem; space or, rather, the lack of it. They needed either to extend the existing premises, which was a non starter or get new premises. As it happened the problem was solved for them.

Tom Kane and Sam Bryson had decided to relocate their own office, across the water, to be nearer to Glasgow Sheriff Court. This was where they carried out the majority of their business. They approached Gerry and Sandy to see if they wished to take up the option to rent the offices downstairs. They made them a better offer. They bought the whole building. The two solicitors were delighted to accept their proposal.

Before anything else though there was the little matter of William Robertson's trial. It had originally been due to commence in August at the High Court in Glasgow. The proceeding had to be delayed due to the death of Robertson's defence council, none other than Maurice Henshaw QC, confirmation, if any were needed, that Robertson was the Graham family's man. He was now defended by Walter Campbell QC who had asked for time to review the case papers. Now everything was set and the trial began. Robertson entered a plea of not guilty to all charges. It seemed he was enjoying his day in the spotlight.

The strategy with regard to the Josie Jardine incident was to try and refute the findings of DNA samples taken from the deceased clothing. Back when the murder had occurred DNA had not been heard of but it was now a more than useful tool in the modern age. Because the case was unsolved all the productions in the case, such as Josie's clothing, had been stored for all these years.

Campbell tried to persuade the jury that it was quite feasible for the then Police Constable Robertson's own DNA to be on the deceased's clothing. He had after all, been in contact with any amount of common prostitutes in that particular area of Glasgow on any given day. The Lord Advocate acting for the Crown soon put a stop to that ploy, pointing out that Robertson's DNA was only found on items of the deceased's under garments.

This did not prevent Campbell from arguing loud and long over just about every piece of the prosecution's evidence. His usual method, plenty of bluster. All this resulted in was a very long trial, at the end of which the outcome was never in doubt. All the bluster in the world could not save Robertson. The jury did not take too long before returning with their verdict.

Guilty on all five charges of murder, guilty of numerous charges of a sexual nature, guilty of numerous charges of perverting the course of justice, and guilty of numerous charges of being concerned in the sale and supply of controlled drugs under the Misuse of Drugs Act.

Throughout the whole process Robertson sat impassively in the Dock , quite impervious to the business going on about him in the court. He smiled over towards the public benches sending shivers down the spines of those present. Without doubt he was simply lapping up the notoriety.

Also, for some unknown reason and much against the wishes of his defence council, Robertson had insisted on giving evidence on his own behalf. He just wanted to be the centre of attention. In the end he just dug a hole for himself, so perhaps he was not as clever as he thought.

Once the proceeding were at an end, all that was left was the sentencing and that, Lord Erskine informed the Court, would take place in three weeks, after social and background reports had been prepared.

Robertson was taken back to Barlinnie prison. Once in the prison van he broke out into a sweat. For weeks he had put on a brave face whilst all the time he had been frantically trying to make contact with Billy and Bobby Graham.

He wanted to let them know their secrets were safe with him and that he was not a threat. Robertson was petrified of prison. It went without saying that as an ex cop, even a bent one, he was a target and so was looking for some protection from the Graham family. He was being kept in segregation away from the general prison population but that would not last forever.

Exactly three weeks later, having previously been found guilty, William Robertson had returned to the High Court in Glasgow to learn his fate. It was not good. At his sentencing hearing Lord Erskine handed down the longest sentence in Scottish legal history. Robertson would spent the rest of his life behind bars.

It was cause for celebration at the offices of QLM Ltd. Gerry had opened a bottle of champagne, and Sandy, Brenda and Jenny had a glass while Gerry sipped on a malt whisky. Nothing much was said but all had the same thoughts. Several victims had at last had justice. No doubt Jimmy Quinn would have been happy with that.

One person missing from the gathering was Matty McGowan. In the past couple of weeks Gerry had seen very little of him. He knew he was still about as he had seen him and his beat up old car, in the area but wondered how he was managing now that he no longer worked at the taxi office. Gerry had thought that he looked a bit run down.

After all the excitement of the chase and then the trial suddenly everything slowed down and people were getting back to normality. Gerry had fully recovered from his broken arm and was back in training with a vengeance. He had been more than disappointed to hear of the demise of two of his assailants. Matty had been unable to discover the identity of the other two men. Gerry had been looking forward to tracking them down and meting out some punishment of his own by way of revenge but it was seemed it was not to be.

In prison, William Robertson was just about beside himself with worry. He had never been fat but was now just skin and bone . He had heard nothing from the Graham family. Over the years he had pissed off a lot of people. Someone would be looking for payback. As an ex cop he would be a big feather in somebody's cap. He had known it was coming and it did, despite supposedly being in segregation.

The first attack took place in the queue for dinner. He was stabbed in the back. Fortunately he wasn't badly hurt and after a night in the prison infirmary and a few stitches he was back out into the segregation wing. As to the stabbing, there were no witnesses traced. Even if there had been witnesses they would not come forward, because nobody grasses in prison.

The second assault came soon afterwards. He was going downstairs to the lower landing when he was pushed or tripped up from behind. Again no witnesses and no culprit was traced. Robertson was lucky he didn't break his neck in the fall as it was a long way down. All he sustained were a few bruises and ligament damage to one leg.

By now he was basically petrified. All his bravado and bluster in public was gone. When it came down to it William Robertson was a coward.

CHAPTER FORTY-THREE

Billy and Bobby Graham had been laying low at the farm near Eaglesham for quite a few weeks now. The police were nowhere near catching up with them. They had seen the news, all about Willie Robertson's trial and conviction. That didn't really worry them as he wouldn't speak up and if he even thought about doing so, he would be dealt with.

The twins were frustrated at being cooped up and wanted to know why they couldn't run the family business. After all, apart from Margaret, who was left? They were constantly on the phone to their sister moaning about one thing or another. If something didn't happen soon they were going to come out of hiding and go mental. There was no way they were going to spend the winter stuck up on Fenwick Moor.

Meadow Farm had originally been in the hands of the same family for years. They had kept Clydesdale horses and had a fairly large stable block and adjoining smithy. Once it passed into the hands of the son though things went pear shaped. He had no interest in hard work and became involved in the sale and supply of drugs. Anything for an easy buck, or so he thought. Before he knew it he had lost everything, including the farm, to the Graham family. He had taken his own life some years ago.

As night began to fall the twins heard, and then saw, a vehicle coming along the rough roadway up towards the farmhouse. Both were poised with their guns at the ready. As the car drew nearer they recognised the vehicle and its driver, and relaxed. Margaret had obviously sent them some much needed cocaine, just to take the edge off.

The driver of the car entered the farmhouse and all that was heard after that was a short burst of gunfire. Not that anyone was likely to have heard anything. The farm was well off the main road in a very secluded spot, which was not good news for the twins.

Their assailant had shot both of the brothers to incapacitate them. He had then literally dragged them both across the farm yard to the smithy, using chains attached to the bumper of his car. Once at the smithy, the twins were winched side by side above the furnace which was then lit. Eventually the heat built up until it was unbearably hot.

Both Billy and Bobby were screaming obscenities and abuse at their attacker. All that got them was another bullet wound in either an arm or a leg. Over the next twelve hours or so the assailant asked specific questions of the twins. Obviously at first there was no way they were answering any questions but the more bullet wounds they received and the lower they were winched nearer to the furnace, their demeanour changed.

As the red hot flames seared their skin even they could not hold out any longer. They told the man everything he wanted to know. Both knew exactly what the other was thinking. Their attacker was going to die, very slowly, they would make sure of that. Once they escaped...

The man lowered them nearer to the furnace. The pain was unbearable, and it was then they realised. There was no escape. Each let out a blood chilling scream of agony before lapsing into merciful unconsciousness from which they would never awaken.

It was the next day that somebody had noticed smoke coming from the smithy chimney.

As the farm was supposed to be empty they phoned the local police.

Gerry was up as usual at 6am. It would soon be winter. As he jogged along the pathway, he resolved to seek out Matty McGowan, because he wanted to make sure he was alright. His old wine coloured Fiat car wasn't parked in its usual spot either.

The business had been turned upside down with the arrival of Sandy and several serious crimes had been solved. The publicity they had generated didn't do the firm much harm either. There were one or two things still outstanding but generally life was good again.

As he stood under the shower he could think of only one thing: Audrey. She had been under real pressure at work of late and he had not seen her for a couple of days. It had been easier to stay in her own flat which had, surprisingly, not yet sold. Immediately when Gerry got into work Sandy wanted a word regarding the architects drawings for the renovation of downstairs. The next time Gerry looked up it was almost lunchtime. He was just about to phone his fiancée when she phoned him.

Audrey had an urgency in her voice and said, "Gerry, what were you doing last night?"

"Why, Audrey, what's wrong ?" he replied, realising there was something in her voice.

"Have you seen the news today?" she asked "Turn your television on."

He grabbed the remote control and switched on the news channel. It showed a male reporter standing at the gateway of what appeared to be farm buildings. Gerry turned up the sound.

"... and a police spokesperson here at Meadow Farm, on the outskirts of Eaglesham, has confirmed that the bodies of two badly burnt males have been discovered on the premises. The police have not, as yet, identified the deceased but have confirmed they are treating the incident as murder."

"What is going on?" Gerry asked,

"It's the twins," Audrey replied. "They have been shot, and tortured before being set on fire. It appears they were slowly roasted over a fire. There isn't much left of them. It's horrible."

Both were silent for a moment before Audrey asked, "When I get finished can I come over to yours?"

"Of course you can," Gerry replied, "it's yours as well remember."

"Thanks," was all Audrey could say before ending the call.

Gerry sat quietly with his own thoughts for a minute or two, then went to tell Sandy and Jenny what had happened.

"I'll be expecting DI Samson and his sidekick any time now he joked, just send them through to my office."

Twenty minutes later the internal phone rang. It was Jenny.

"Detectives Samson and Lorimer to see you Mr Lynch," she said, very businesslike.

"Just send them through Jenny."

Let the games begin again. Gerry didn't want to get Audrey in any trouble and so acted dumb. He was good at it. At the request of DI Samson he once again accompanied the officers to Baird Street Police Office. He remained there for nearly two hours answering their questions.

Unfortunately the previous night he had been alone in his flat and hadn't seen or contacted anyone. Not having an alibi, for once, was meat and drink to Samson, but eventually even he realised he was flogging a dead horse. When would the penny drop that there was not a chance in hell of getting anything out of Gerry Lynch?

Gerry was more than helpful, even submitting to being examined for firearm residue, fingerprints and DNA. He felt no need to contact his solicitor and around 3pm he was released.

Fifteen minutes later he was back in his office, finishing off the paperwork.

He left work bang on 5pm and made his way to the flat. Out came the vacuum cleaner and duster as he quickly tried to tidy up the place before Audrey arrived. He gathered all his dirty clothes and fired them into the washing basket. Finally, he made the bed, just to be tidy. He had a quick shower and changed into a polo shirt and chinos. Once he'd finished he looked around the flat. It didn't look any different to him. It was still a tip with Audrey's stuff everywhere. He really had to do something about getting a house.

Checking that there was a nice bottle of Chardonnay cooling in the fridge he tried to settle down and catch an update on the murder on television. The reporter was still at the farm but there was nothing to add from the midday transmission.

It was 6.30pm when a tired looking Audrey poured herself into the flat. She headed straight for the settee, sat down and took off her shoes. When Gerry returned with a large glass of wine she was massaging her feet. After taking a long drink she sighed,

"Ah, that's better".

She smiled and Gerry melted. He was like a small boy, all tongue tied and awkward.

"Do you want to go out for something to eat?" he asked, "Or shall I order in?"

"Just order in please Gerry. I'll have a sweet and sour if you're getting a Chinese," she said.

Gerry was straight on the phone to the Red Dragon and twenty minutes later their meal arrived. As they ate Audrey explained that it was definitely Billy and Bobby Graham that had been found at the farm. It turned out that both had been shot in the arms, legs and body, then they had been tortured for some hours. They appeared to have been roasted over a fire and their feet and lower legs had simply melted away.

Gerry wouldn't lose any sleep over either of them but they appeared to have endured an agonising death. Audrey then explained that the really strange thing about the whole thing was that when officers went to their flat down by the River Clyde it had been stripped bare. The furniture, ornaments and paintings were missing and both their top of the range cars, an Audi and a Mercedes Benz were gone. The safe was lying open and empty and someone had

been to their bank and emptied their account including the safety deposit box. The police were checking CCTV at the flat and the bank to see what came up.

They would find that at both locations the cameras had mysteriously failed for a time and nothing untoward was seen on either system. Whoever was responsible had certainly done a job on them.

Audrey had been over twelve hours at the scene and was shattered. After completing their meal and the Chardonnay, she fell asleep on the settee. Gerry lifted her feet and laid her flat covering her with the duvet from the bed in the spare bedroom. He sat watching her for a while before retiring for the night himself. He had never even told her about being detained by Delilah again.

Next morning Gerry was up early as usual and out for his run into Alexandra Park. He had visions of returning home to find Audrey cooking scrambled egg and toast. He was sadly disappointed.

When he returned home there was a note on the coffee table. '*Thanks for taking care of me, I'll ring you. Audrey xx*'

The news regarding the demise of the twins travelled around the prison like wild fire. The last of the Graham family had been eliminated and it would now be open season on their territory. The drugs trade alone was worth millions. William Robertson lay on his bed in the segregation unit. He didn't know what to think. What would their deaths mean for him?

The next morning he stepped into the communal shower which was empty while he used it. The tepid water had the desired effect of waking him up. He had slept poorly with his thoughts flitting between the Graham family and the young eastern European girl he had abused on his last visit to Spain.

Suddenly he felt something warm running down his chest and dripping onto the floor of the shower. At first he thought that somebody had turned the hot water on and then he looked again.

It was blood, his blood. He began to panic. Someone unseen had slipped into the shower room and slit his throat from ear to ear. He grabbed at his throat as he slid down the wall. He tried to cry for help but couldn't. For a moment he stared up at the ceiling. His one last thought was a simple one, "How could this have happened to me?"

Gerry was in his office when he got the news from Sandy Morton, as one of his pals still in the job had phoned to let him know. Neither man felt any remorse but in some ways they were angry.

Gerry had been unable to exact revenge on any of the Graham family himself. Even two of the hoods who had been sent to beat him up were dead, and now this.

Robertson had only served a few months in jail. He had deserved to suffer far more for the mayhem he had wreaked upon society. Gerry's overriding feeling was jealousy. He would have liked to have struck the fatal blow to avenge his old friend Paul or perhaps to finally expunge the nightmare he had suffered blaming himself for Paul's death and those of his parents. The doctor had been right, he didn't have the nightmare any more but still part of him would have liked to see Robertson breathing his last.

As Sandy said, there would, of course, be a murder investigation within the prison. That would be a complete and utter waste of time. There would be no witnesses. Sandy doubted that the police would try very hard in this instance anyway. Robertson had disgraced the whole service. He was an embarrassment, so good riddance.

CHAPTER FORTY-FOUR

Gerry and Sandy got back to running their business. Plans were well under way to start the renovations downstairs. Gerry would yet again employed his favourite builder to carry out the work. Sandy was sifting through a mountain of job application forms. He wanted people in place once the new offices were ready.

All the mayhem of the past few months had died down. News had filtered out that Margaret Graham had sold the Crooked Man and would be soon moving to Spain to open a bar in Alicante. Now her family was no more Gerry was not expecting any more trouble. But as the saying goes, 'Be careful what you wish for.'

Audrey was still busy at work but two or three people had shown some more interest in her property. She had decided to stay over in the West End and do a bit of decorating in an effort to spruce up her flat.

Gerry and Sandy had been out all day at a business meeting with prospective clients. Gerry had left his BMW park outside his flat and travelled with Sandy in his new Jaguar. It was quite late when they got back to Dennistoun and as they approached Gerry's street the road was blocked with a fire engine. It was only when he got out of the Jaguar that Gerry realised they were attending a fire at his flat. Someone had poured petrol or something similar through the letter-box and ignited it. The front door was a write off and there was some damage internally to the floor. Thankfully some-one had contacted the fire brigade, who had arrived quite quickly.

Gerry had a strange feeling. It obviously wasn't an acci-dent and either someone had a macabre sense of humour or this was a copycat of the fires at both his parents home and the home of Frank and Agnes Graham. It was anything but funny and threw up the question of who could do this. Having secured the door as best they could Gerry went to stay the night with Sandy and Jean as he didn't want to worry Audrey.

Sandy and Gerry discussed the implications of the fire. All they could think was that it was either just kids lark-ing about or it was just an unhappy coincidence. What else could they say?

The next morning Gerry arranged for the repairs to be carried out. A new door was fitted and the damage within sorted. The flat looked as good as new. By the end of the day everything was back to normal, except Gerry had this nagging doubt in his mind. His car had been parked outside his home just like when his mum and dad were killed. Surely someone else wasn't trying to kill him?

That evening Gerry was on his way home when he got a phone call from a uniform policeman over in the west end of Glasgow. He was at the Western Infirmary with Audrey who it seemed had been involved in a road traffic accident. She was being examined as they spoke.

Gerry hung up and turned his car around. He made it to the hospital in record time. Audrey was just returning to the A& E reception having been treated. She had a fractured right wrist a broken left ankle, and a couple of nasty bruises on her face. Gerry thanked the cop had phoned to let him know and told him that if they needed to speak to Audrey she would be at his place.

They drove straight to his flat and en route Audrey never spoke. It was only once he had wheeled her, in the wheelchair borrowed from the hospital, into the flat that she showed any emotion. She burst into tears and as he bent down to comfort her she put her arms around his neck.

"Oh Gerry," she sobbed, "I'm so glad to see you."

Gerry thought it was best if she rested and they could talk later. He took her through to the bedroom and put her to bed. Within minutes she was out like a light. Much later Audrey awakened and told Gerry all about her ordeal.

After work she had gone to her solicitors to sign documents, the good news being that she had, at last, sold her flat. She was going back to her car to phone Gerry with the good news. As she was walking across the road a van sped towards her causing her to almost jump across the bonnet of her own car. The van clipped her on the left ankle and as she fell she put out her hand to break the fall and this resulted in a broken wrist. The bruises which had now risen had been caused by her landing in the roadway. The van did not make any attempt to stop. Audrey was adamant that it was deliberate.

This put a different complexion on things. Gerry phoned Sandy and told him what happened. They both agreed the culprit, for probably both incidents, must have something against either Gerry or Audrey, or both. Tomorrow morning

Sandy would come round to the flat and they would try to work out who that could be.

By midday they had all racked their brains to no avail. They were no further forward. While Audrey was laid up in the flat and would be for several weeks, Gerry was a very busy man. He only had just over a week to empty Audrey's flat and find somewhere to store her furniture. Finding a house had now become urgent. The offices were upside down with renovation work. It was going to last for months as the building was so old, the downstairs needed to be completely ripped out and rebuilt from bare brick. Also the Christmas and New Year Holidays would get in the way. On top of all that he was still trying to figure out if his suspicions about the two incidents had any merit or not.

With his head full of all this nonsense Gerry finally caught up with Matty. He was coming out of the local bookmakers. Gerry hadn't seen him for several weeks even although he lived just across the hall.

"Any luck?" he asked.

"None at all, Mr Lynch," Matty replied sadly.

He didn't look too well and Gerry asked if he was alright. What Matty told him next stopped him in his tracks. At first Gerry thought he had misheard, or that he was joking but then Matty never joked.

Matty was dying.

The pair went back to Gerry's office and over a malt whisky Matty told Gerry as best he could the whole sad tale.

At first he had been experiencing trouble going to the toilet and had terrible stomach pain. His doctor thought that he may have irritable bowel syndrome and had prescribed the appropriate medication. This made no difference at all and Matty had also suffered terrible night sweats and itching.

Matty explained that the night they had visited Ann Marie Docherty and he had vomited in the street, it was not so much what she had revealed that had upset him, although obviously it had, it was just because he was ill.

He admitted that he had previously vomited on several other occasions. Finally his doctor sent him to hospital for blood tests and an ultrasound examination. They had seen something that they weren't too happy about and he then had to undergo a CT scan. The results were not good. It turned out that Matty had pancreatic cancer and only six months, at best, to live.

"The doc told me it could have been caused by my drug addiction and alcohol years ago" Matty said "You know Mr Lynch, I was never the brightest. I cannae even pronounce what it is I've got, never mind spell it. It's just my luck, I finally get free fae the Graham's and I'm gonnae die."

Gerry was speechless. He could see the irony in Matty's words.

"I've to go for chemo at the hospital and then I'll need to go to the hospice in Springburn."

"When do you have to go there?" Gerry asked.

"In just a couple of months I think, I'm no really sure," Matty replied.

Everybody rallied aound to make Matty's last few weeks in the community as comfortable as possible. None more so than Brenda and Gerry. Brenda visited Matty everyday to make sure he was getting something to eat. Gerry took him back and forth to hospital for his chemotherapy treatment. Sometimes afterwards Matty felt alright, sometimes he didn't. Matty had never been fat, but now he was skin and bone and his hair was falling out. It depressed Gerry to see him disintegrating before his eyes.

Only one month later, Matty left his flat for the last time to enter the hospice. In such a short space of time his general health had gone downhill and he looked terrible. Gerry insisted on driving him to Springburn.

He visited every day and tried to put on a happy face to cheer Matty up. Sadie Gleason also came as often as she could. Occasionally Jenny and Brenda also went with Sophie. Matty liked all the attention, although by now he was very weak. Sometimes after a dose of medication he would get mixed up thinking Sophie was his old girlfriend's daughter, Cheryl.

On one visit when Gerry was alone, Matty explained to him that all the arrangements were in place for his funeral. He was going to be buried alongside his girlfriend Shirley Carr and her wee daughter Cheryl in Sighthill Cemetery. Not too far from his old friend Jimmy Quinn. He had arranged with the Stuarts at the Cross Keys to put on a buffet and drink for those who were kind enough to attend. Matty had also made provision with Tom Kane to pay off all his outstanding bills. The one thing Gerry could not understand was how Matty could afford to pay for all these arrangements, but he didn't like to ask.

On listening to Matty outlining his own funeral arrangements Gerry could be nothing but amazed and full of admiration. Here was a man who, by his own admission, was not the brightest, who had from the start, hardly been dealt the best hand. He had suffered tragedy after tragedy, been abused in so many ways and yet had come out the other side a giant. It was Gerry's honour to know him.

The staff at the hospice did a wonderful job. They were always bright and cheerful and smiled in the face of adversity. The treatment Matty had received was called palliative chemotherapy. Some days he seemed much better afterwards, other days not so good. Gerry was impressed by how the staff made every patient feel special. Throughout Matty had borne his fate manfully. He had only been at the hospice a few short weeks but, as Gerry was leaving one day, he had the feeling that he would not see Matty again. On reaching the door he turned and saw Matty looking towards him. Despite being quite frail Matty waved and said, "Thanks for coming, Mr Lynch. Thanks for everything."

Gerry left with tears in his eyes. Matty McGowan passed away that night.

There were more people at Matty's funeral than you might imagine. All the local businesses were represented just as they had been at Jimmy Quinn's passing. Sadie Gleason was amongst the mourners.

Once more the Stuarts put on a very nice spread back at the Cross Keys. It was left to Gerry to say a few words. He mentioned how he'd first come across a young lad in Springburn and how they had met once more all those years later. How Matty had been befriended by Jimmy Quinn and what a great help he had been when Gerry was in need and trying to build his business. He ended by saying how he had come to admire Matty and the bravery he had shown, knowing that he was to die.

The gathering remained silent for a few moments when Gerry finished speaking. All that could be heard was Sadie Gleason sobbing in the corner. Gerry understood: she had lost her friend so many years before, then Tommy and Matty, her surrogate sons. Now she was left alone.

Before leaving Tom Kane asked if Gerry would call and see him at his new office the next morning. Gerry said he would be there, expecting it would be work related.

As the group began to make their way home, Gerry had just one more task left to perform. Somehow he had to get Sadie Gleason into his car and drive her home, down to Saltmarket. Not as simple as it sounded. Sadie was beyond drunk and was a lady of ample proportions, so it wasn't an easy task. Jenny and Brenda had to give him a hand and suffer listening to Sadie's patter as they did so.

"You know you'se pair are bonnie lassies, so you'se are" she had said "Do you'se no fancy goin' on the game? You'se would make a fortune, so you'se would." Flattered they weren't and were glad to see Gerry's car disappearing towards High Street.

He could get her out at the other end himself.

CHAPTER FORTY-FIVE

The very next morning Gerry was struggling to get out of his bed. It had already been a long few weeks looking after not only Matty but also Audrey as well. Thankfully she was now fully recovered and biting his ear off about a new house. Gerry would also have to thank Sandy Morton as he had shouldered much of the work in recent weeks. Gerry for once contemplating whether or not to give his daily morning run a miss for once. No chance.

He jumped out of bed and quickly donned his tracksuit and trainers and headed out into the early morning. He started slowly and gradually increased his speed until he sprinted out of the park and onto Alexandra Parade.

Straight after breakfast he had an appointment with Tom Kane. He had no idea what Tom wanted but it was usually work related. Today he was in for a surprise. Gerry drove across the River Clyde and down beside Glasgow Sheriff Court. There he found Tom Kane beavering away in his posh new office. Tom put aside what he was working on and offered Gerry a seat before getting straight down to business.

"Gerry as you know, Matty McGowan asked me to act on his behalf with regard to his estate. He requested that I see to payment for his funeral as well as the purvey at the Cross Keys afterwards. I have complied with these wishes. He then asked if I would be executor of his last will and testament, such as it is. You may be wondering what this has to do with you? He named only two beneficiaries, Sadie Gleason and yourself."

Gerry was amazed, he could understand Matty leaving something to Sadie but not himself and anyway, what was he leaving? He had nothing. It was something that had bothered Gerry since Matty told him he had already made all his own funeral arrangements, "How had he been able to pay for it all?".

He was about to find out.

Tom Kane told him that Matty had obtained the cost of both his funeral and the purvey and had left the exact sum in cash for him to pay the bills. Also, despite having been homeless when Jimmy had found him, it turned out that Matty owned his own flat, bought and paid for. He had instructed that Tom Kane sell the property and Sadie Gleason was to inherit all the capital from the sale. Gerry was surprised to learn Matty had owned the flat, but thought that it was a wonderful gesture to help Sadie Gleason financially.

Gerry was now intrigued what Matty could have possibly have left to him. Tom Kane had a large sealed envelope.

"I have very strict instructions with regard to this envelope," he said in a somewhat solemn manner. "Matty was quite explicit that I should hand this to you, and you alone, unopened with the request that you read its contents in private. He asks that you give the contents due consideration and thereafter take whatever action you deem to be appropriate. I might add that I have no knowledge of its contents." With that Tom handed Gerry the envelope.

Gerry left and walked back to his car clutching the unopened envelope. He drove straight back to Dennistoun. Entering his office he told Jenny he wasn't to be disturbed under any circumstances.

Sitting at his desk, Gerry laid the envelope down and stared at it for some time. He was intrigued as to its contents. There was only one way to find out. Eventually he opened the envelope. Inside he discovered that it contained a letter and what looked like the key to a padlock. The letter had been handwritten by Matty. Gerry read slowly trying to decipher Matty's spelling and terrible handwriting.

mr lynch

Am sorry to put all this on youse but yur ma one freind. I hope wit I tell ya will no make yu two angery wi me. Youse and mr Corigan wis the only two polis ta treat me gud when shirley and wee cheryl dyed.

When me an me bruver tam wis wee da used to gie us sum doins he had a thick lether belt wi studs in an it didnae mater if he wis foo o drink or no he used to lether us. I think that wis how come I endet up a wee bit slow

Anyhow when Ma was kilt he came hame roarin drunk an we wis in for it butt tam stabbed the bastert and we shuvved him in the clyde.

Sadie was good tae us an so I telt mr kane to sell ma place an gie her the money. Jimmy had got the place for his son Dan but when he dyed he gied it ta me. Jimmy wis loaded then afore he hit the bevvy.

I dunno how ta tell youse the next part. I no the polis gie you a hard time ower aw they grahams bein kilt. At first I thought it wis you what dun it but youse is no like them. I wish I had dun it ta help youse.

I hope youse arny angery wi me butt I kilt they twins. maggie let slip in the pub one nite when she was foo where they wis hidin. I hated them they an old frank kilt ma bruver tam an gie me a kickin the night shirley dyed.

It was easyer than I thought. They was jist cowhards, I shot both of em and pulled them to the barn. Hung em over a fire. They sqwheeled like pigs an telt me the numbers for the safe and the bank. I emptied everything out even the cars and selt it all. I no am slow but I lerned how ta fix cctv so nobody cud see me.

The key is for lockup g14 at fruit merket in blockairn road. I thought you could help mrs corigan an her boy an the 3 lassies what wis hurt by the twins.

May be help people like jim did in the parade an help run ur bisness. Youse is a good man an will do the right thing.

Thank you for bein ma friend
matty

Gerry read the letter several times. He sat in a trance, tears running down his cheeks. The letter explained so much, yet left many questions unanswered.

Matty had admitted to killing Billy and Bobby Graham in retaliation for the death of his brother, Thomas. The fact that the twins had died in agony was strangely quite pleasing as far as Gerry was concerned. Gerry knew exactly what it was like to hate the Graham family. It was obvious that Matty felt exactly the same.

Interestingly Matty had, at first, thought that Gerry may have been responsible for the murders. There was a time when Gerry had felt the exact opposite and that Matty had been the likely culprit. Who was it then, perhaps the Chinese triads after all?

One thing that did strike Gerry was that in all the time he had known Matty, he had never called him Gerry - it had always been Mr Lynch.

After some time Gerry opened his safe and deposited the letter inside but kept the key. He would need to give some serious thought to this matter. He emerged from his office and Jenny could see that he was visibly upset.

"Anything I can do?" she asked.

"No thanks, Jenny," he replied, "unless you know when Sandy will be in."

Gerry then left the office saying he would not be long. He was carrying an empty holdall. About thirty minutes later he returned, the holdall was now obviously full. He mysteriously locked himself in his office only to re emerge several hours later.

It was almost time to go home for the night when Sandy arrived back at the office. He had been out making some enquiries about prospective employees he and Gerry would need to interview. When he heard him arriving back Gerry invited him into his office and told Jenny to get herself off home.

Sandy sat down as he knew by the look on Gerry's face something was wrong. Gerry went into his safe and brought out Matty's letter. He handed it to Sandy and said,

"What do you make of this?"

Sandy took his time to read the letter. The spelling and grammar left a lot to be desired. It was hard to understand in parts. Gerry watched closely as his old gaffer read on impassively. Eventually Sandy came to the end, puffed out his cheeks and simply exclaimed, "WOW!"

He seemed to mull things over in his mind for a couple of minutes and then spoke.

"Do you know what Gerry? A few weeks ago when I was still a DCI with Strathclyde Police, if I had seen this document then, you know exactly what I would have done with it. Today I'm just an ordinary member of the public but with an insight into some of the events mentioned. On balance, what would I do today? How much cash are we talking about?"

Gerry went back to the safe and brought out the holdall which was rammed full of money. He handed Sandy a slip of paper with the amount written on it. Sandy read it and it caused him to raise his eyebrows in astonishment.

"That is a serious amount of money, Gerry".

His remark was an understatement. £1,305,569.42 was indeed a serious amount of money. Gerry nodded and waited for Sandy's conclusion. He didn't get it.

"Leave it with me Gerry," Sandy said. "I swear this is only between you and me. I'll have an answer for you in the morning."

That was fair enough, as Gerry still had more thinking to do on the subject anyway. The next

morning Sandy strode into Gerry office and shut the door.

"I'll not beat about the bush," he said. "Give me the letter."

Gerry took the letter from the safe and handed it to Sandy who simply said,

"I've done all the talking about this subject apart from one thing. How Matty managed to get that amount of money out of the bank without being caught on CCTV, and empty the twins' flat, again without being picked up on CCTV, beggars belief. Somehow he accomplished exactly that. I made some enquiries and apparently there was some sort of power surge at both premises which rendered the CCTV inoperable for a time. It seems to me that your friend Matty was cleverer than a lot of us people gave him credit for. I have given the situation a great amount of thought and have come to this conclusion. It 's time to move on and think of the future son."

Without further ado Sandy produced a lighter from his pocket and set fire to the letter. Dropping it into Gerry's empty waste bin he walked towards the door.

"I'll be in my office when you need me Gaffer."

Gerry was quite happy. Sandy had come up with exactly the same result to the problem as he had. It was time to make the money work for the community.

CHAPTER FORTY-SIX

From the start Sandy and Gerry had an almost telepathic understanding. They both thought that Matty's wishes should be addressed first. Sandy wrote to Jackie Corrigan and enclosed a cheque for a rather sizeable amount of cash. He told her a little white lie, that it was from the police by way of compensation for the loss of Paul.

Carol Duffy, Ann Marie Docherty and Sarah McCarty all received large sums too. In Carol's case it would help in raising her family. After throwing out her useless boyfriend, Ann Marie quit the streets for good and enrolled at college. She wanted to help others who had suffered in the same way as herself.

In the case of Sarah McCarty, Gerry took a special interest, probably because she was part of the Alexandra Parade family, and also to fulfil his silent promise to Jimmy Quinn. He made sure that she went into rehabilitation to kick her addictions. Once that was completed he had her fitted with a new eye and dentures. It was a new woman, who looked years younger, that came to see him once all her treatments were done and dusted. He explained to Sarah how he and Sandy but more especially Jenny were under pressure in the office and wondered, given that she was a trained typist, if she would consider coming to work for him. Sarah was ecstatic and promised she would never let him down.

Later that same week Sandy and Gerry interviewed four more candidates for positions with the company. All that needed to happen now was for the renovations to be completed. Downstairs was looking much better, and the builder reckoned another two weeks would see an end to it.

One last big job was the staircase. A new internal one was to be fitted from the ground floor up to the first floor where Gerry and Sandy's offices were situated. At present they were having to share and were on top of one another. A temporary plasterboard wall had been erected between the office and the hole where the staircase would be.

All this cramped existence only reminded Gerry that he still had not found a house for Audrey and himself. Until he did there would be no wedding. He had kept hold of the lock up which Matty had hired at the Blochairn market. It was now full of Audrey's furniture.

In the office it was also Gerry's hope to create a display on the wall at the top of the staircase. He wanted to show off Jimmy Quinn's citation for bravery and his medals, incorporating the bayonet he had found in the flat when he and Jenny had cleared it out. Sandy had wholeheartedly agreed. The company was after all Quinn, Lynch and Morton.

At 3pm the following day Gerry and Sandy were to hold a meeting with the CEO of a large American company. If all went well and they gained a contract, they would be placing their business on another level altogether and indeed be moving them in a different direction. The meeting was to take place in a Glasgow hotel as their offices were still a work in progress.

At exactly 3pm Gerry and Sandy were shown into a suite at the hotel. There waiting for them was Ralph Steinberg. He seemed to be young to be the CEO of such a large company, however being the grandson of the founder always helped. Ralph was in fact, thirty-five years old, very smartly dressed and possessed a pleasing disposition. Having studied commerce at university he was also a very shrewd businessman. After refusing coffee they got down to the business at hand.

Mr Steinberg explained that his company, Steinberg &Williams, was huge. It had outlets in almost every state in America. In the last six months they had moved to the UK and had established stores in London, Birmingham, Manchester and Leeds. There were plans to extend to more cities in England. Up in Scotland at the present time they had two stores. One in the St. Enoch centre in Glasgow and a second in the Central Retail Park in Falkirk. It was hoped that new premises would soon be opening in Stirling, Aberdeen and Inverness. It seemed that the British really liked the type of clothing that they were selling.

There was, however, a problem. Stock was disappearing from the Glasgow store. Not just one or two items but quite large quantities. It also appeared that the problem was nothing to do with shoplifters and that it was in house.

Steinberg went on to explain that the Scottish stores were supplied from a central warehouse in Cumbernauld. Orders appeared to have been dispatched but a stock take at the Glasgow store had detected a large discrepancy. Mainly in small goods which were delivered in boxes. It seemed that the correct number of boxes were being despatched and received but stock was missing. Quite simply their own security personnel could not solve the problem and so it was that Mr Steinberg was turning to QLM Investigations to try and solve the mystery for him.

Sandy Morton asked, "Tell me, why did you pick our company to help you, Mr Steinberg?"

"Well to tell you the truth Mr Morton, we don't do anything without checking people out first. There were two reasons. Firstly, your personal reputation as a detective in this city is second to none. Secondly your firm was recommended by Richard Jonson, a good friend of mine and a top businessman, back in the States".

Gerry must thank Richard the next time they met.

Steinberg informed the partners that their company would be well rewarded for their efforts and should they manage to solve the problem it may lead to them being awarded a huge contract to act as security consultants throughout Scotland for Steinberg & Williams.

It went without saying that this would entail a great amount of work on the part of QLM. Gerry and Sandy told Steinberg they were more than interested in his proposal but requested twenty four hours to think matters over. Steinberg was happy with this and looked forward to hearing from them the next day.

Gerry and Sandy left the hotel on cloud nine. They were already setting out their plan. At 10am the next morning all the staff would be brainstorming in a meeting at Alexandra Parade. It was only fair as it was the staff who would have to make it work. If things went as planned they would all be on a big bonus.

Before leaving the city centre, Sandy stopped off at the Argyle Arcade. He had to pop in and pick up a piece of jewellery he had commissioned for Jean. It was their wedding anniversary that night and he was taking her out for dinner.

He was only gone a few minutes as the shop was about to close but it would likely take twice as long to drive back to Dennistoun as they were now stuck in the rush hour traffic. Neither man cared. Their meeting had gone on longer than they anticipated but went fantastically well.

It was dark when Sandy dropped Gerry off at the office. He headed off to take Jean out while Gerry was dropping off some documents. No doubt Audrey would be waiting to take him back out and about to see some houses. To be fair she was right as it was now urgent.

CHAPTER FORTY-SEVEN

Gerry found his key to the office and inserted it in the lock. The door was insecure. That was odd. Either someone had forgotten to lock up or somebody was working late because it was now well after six. He entered the building and shouted,

"Hello, anybody there?"

He got no reply. That was really odd. He had expected that Jenny would have locked up before leaving, as she was so reliable. Thinking nothing else about it, Gerry climbed the new staircase which led to the first floor and his office. He opened the door and was confronted by a man he thought he had seen before.

"Who the hell are you?" he asked.

"Good evening Mr Lynch," the man said, "how good of you to join me. Please take a seat."

He indicated for Gerry to sit in his own chair behind the desk. The man remained standing. Seeing as the man was holding a handgun fitted with a silencer Gerry couldn't really refuse. His mind was racing. "Who was this guy?"

It seemed to Gerry that the man facing him was in his early to mid twenties, not too tall but stockily built. He was sure he had seen him before but couldn't place him. For his part the man was as cool as a cucumber, helping himself to two glasses of malt whisky, one of which he handed one to Gerry. Having taken a drink he looked at Gerry, raised his glass, looked at it and remarked,

"Nice," Then he continued, "Now, Mr Lynch, shall we continue?"

Gerry had a strange feeling; this was such a surreal situation. It was almost like some old gangster movie, when the bad guy explains what he has done to the good guy, before going to do away with him. But that never happened in the movies. The good guy always managed to get out of the tight corner. How was Gerry going to get out of this situation? His opponent was a fit, young man who had a handgun and was standing. He was sat behind a desk, his avenue of attack diminished. He had to tell himself to keep calm and await his chance. Gerry certainly didn't want to say much in case he antagonised the guy.

The man finished his drink and was now ready to tell all.

"You are looking at me as though you know me but you don't. You do, however know my dad."

Gerry was still struggling.

"My father is Kevin 'the Cat' McCormack," the man said.

Gerry immediately knew who he was talking to, "You're his son Derek?" Gerry said.

"That's right," Derek replied.

The name threw Gerry's memory almost back to the beginning of his police career. In 1994 he and Paul Corrigan had just finished their two year probation and been given their own beat. In Springburn Kevin McCormack had been a legend. He was known as one of the very best cat burglars in the city. That was where he got the nickname from.

Apparently fearless, he was known to climb to places that others would never contemplate attempting. He was also a renowned safe breaker.

At some point in his criminal career something happened to McCormack. The word was that he had lost his bottle and had taken to drinking. Being drunk all the time was not conducive to being a top criminal. No one ever got to the bottom of his story. All that was known was that one evening after a particularly lengthy drinking session he came home drunk. In the house were his wife Olive and his best friend Ian Coyle, who had called round to see him. Whatever got into McCormack's head, he accused his wife and friend of engaging in an affair.

Despite their denials he set about them with a claw hammer and beat them both to death. At his trial he was found guilty and was sentenced to twenty-five years imprisonment. He was just over half way through the sentence now. For some reason he had always blamed the two officers who had arrested him for all his woes. It was Gerry and Paul Corrigan who had arrested him.

Derek McCormack was speaking and this brought Gerry's attention back to the present.

"You must be like a cat, Lynch. Do you have nine lives?"

"What do you mean?" Gerry asked.

"Do you have nine lives? Every time I killed one of the Grahams the polis gave you the jail but then you got back out again. I set fire to the parents flat just like they did to your house up

in Easterhouse. It was a copycat killing and still the polis didnae charge you. Just two days later I blew up Jamie's car and they never even spoke to you about it".

"Why did you do that?" Gerry asked.

"Well it was my dad's idea. He reckoned that if I blew up Jamie's Mercedes, then being so security minded he would get a bomb proof car. That's just what he did but they weigh a ton and so when I rammed it into the canal at Bishopbriggs, it sank like a stone. The polis done the same again, let you go without charge, even though it was just like how Moira Clarkson died. Then I done Frank and Cammy. My dad got me in with the Grahams but they always treated me like an idiot. Used to send me on silly errands and called me 'Dumb Derek' and other names. I just went to the pub when I knew it would be quiet and shot the pair of them. I might be dumb but I've found out I'm quite good at killing people."

McCormack paused to pour himself another drink and then continued. Sweat had soaked Gerry's shirt and he knew McCormack was nearing the end of his narrative. If he was to do anything it would need to be soon.

"That is until you, Mr Lynch," he said, sipping the malt. "I set fire to your door cos' I thought you were at home, what with your car being outside. A schoolboy error that one. I was so angry I followed your woman for a couple of days and knocked her over. She's a fit one though, jumping on the car saved her a lot of grief. Anyway, here we are at last. I think it's time, don't you?"

With that McCormack raised the handgun and pointed it at Gerry. He was just about to shoot when he was interrupted.

"I wouldn't do that." It was Sandy Morton.

McCormack turned to face Sandy and as he did so Gerry moved swiftly from behind the desk with the intention of trying to strike him. McCormack was much too quick. He fired twice, both bullets penetrated Gerry's chest sending him flying backwards.

McCormack fired again and Sandy fell to the floor.

Believing that McCormack had killed his old friend, Gerry grabbed Jimmy Quinn's old bayonet and leapt upon the gunman. He thrust outwards with the bayonet and was successful in hitting the mark. His momentum meant that the two men collided and fell against the plasterboard wall. This gave way under the weight and they fell down onto the staircase below. The last thing Gerry saw was the newel of the banister coming towards his head.

The following morning Kevin McCormack was sat on his bed in 'C' Hall, HMP Barlinnie. He'd had his breakfast and was just waiting to be escorted to his job in the carpentry shop. Later he was expecting a visit from his son. He was really looking forward to that. Nothing like a bit of good news to cheer you up.

A prison officer appeared at the door of his cell, but he wasn't there to escort him to the carpentry shop. He was taken to an interview room where two CID officers were waiting to speak to him. It was a very forlorn looking prisoner who accompanied the two policemen to their car. He had was being taken to the City Mortuary to identify the remains of his son Derek. Once the police enquiry was completed he might have to face some criminal charges.

CHAPTER FORTY-EIGHT

Gerry Lynch had been a very lucky boy. He had fractured his skull on the newel of the staircase. Two bullets had been removed from his chest. Thankfully no vital organs had been damaged. He had been in hospital for nearly three weeks and was desperate to get out. He was sat up in bed listening to Sandy Morton. He saw his friend still had a bandaged right shoulder and his arm in a sling for support.

This was the first time they had seen each other since the incident, although they had spoken briefly on the phone.

"I've got lots to tell you." Sandy said "But the doctor says I shouldn't really stay too long, in case I tire you out.

"That night I came back to the office because I had left my anniversary card for Jean on my desk and had to get it before we went out. In a way then I suppose you could say it was pure luck.

"Anyway when I got to the office I saw the door wasn't locked and then I heard voices. I stood outside the door as long as I could, then had to intervene, because he was about to shoot you. Well, he did anyway and then aimed at me. The shot hit me in the shoulder and knocked me over. The next think I know you and he are disappearing through the wall.

"You ran him through with Jimmy's bayonet and he was impaled on the stairs. He was dead on impact. I think a big lump like you landing on top of him, probably broke every bone in his body. You knocked yourself out and fractured your skull. I just managed to phone for the cavalry before blacking out myself."

Gerry knew somehow they'd both had a miraculous escape. Perhaps Derek McCormack had been right and he did have nine lives. Sandy told him that the police enquiry was now complete. This meant that the office was no longer a crime scene, so the builder could finish the staircase and of course Jimmy's display.

"They didn't say if we were getting the bayonet back, I'll have to ask about that". Sandy said.

Because of his past position in the job, Sandy had been able to learn a little more probably

than a different person might have been told.

Gerry knew all about Kevin McCormack. But he didn't know too much about his son Derek. Back in 1994 when his father was imprisoned for the murder of his mother and his best friend, ten year old Derek had gone to live with his grandparents in Drongan in Ayrshire. It was a small community about eight miles outside Ayr, a million miles from his upbringing and what he was used to in Springburn.

He was bullied at school, taunted because his father was a murderer. He rebelled and came to the attention of the local police. As soon as he could, Derek made his way back to Springburn, and became involved in drugs and therefore the Graham family. His father had known Frank Snr. so as a favour he had told his family to find Derek something to do.

It turned out he wasn't very good at much and eventually was mainly used as a message boy.

He had not escaped the bullying either. On an almost daily basis he was called all sorts of derogatory names which really made him mad. It wasn't just school kids that could be really annoying, criminals were the same. Derek took to visiting his father in prison on a regular basis, because he was the only person he could speak to.

It would appear that Kevin had devised a plan which would benefit both of them. He wanted to get back at Lynch and Corrigan, the two policemen who had arrested him. For some reason, known only to him, he blamed them for his present predicament and wanted revenge. Derek wanted to hurt the Graham family for taunting him all the time.

Kevin knew about the Grahams' attacks upon the cops who had jailed Frank Jnr., and that Corrigan was already dead but what better way to get back at Lynch. Carry out copycat attacks on the Graham family and that would make Lynch the prime suspect.

As it turned out their plan was delayed as Gerry had been hospitalised. This gave Kevin time to speak to his son and teach him certain skills. By the time Gerry was released from hospital in Argyll, Derek McCormack had found his true vocation. He may have been a rubbish run of the mill criminal. Now he could make bombs, open just about any lock and best of all, just like his father, he was about to become a killer.

Since the death of Derek McCormack, his father Kevin had been moved from HMP Barlinnie. He had totally gone off the rails. He would serve the rest of his sentence in the state hospital at Carstairs. The Crown were mulling over charges against him in relation to his son's activities, but whether it was worth charging him was another matter.

As far as Gerry was concerned he was now where he should have been since 1994. It was not a sane person who had inflicted such horrific injuries on Olive McCormack and Ian Coyle.

Anyway, enough of all that. Gerry wanted to change the subject and so asked about the Steinberg job.

"No problem. Despite being at the hospital most of the night with Jean and Audrey, Jenny gathered the troops and they came up trumps. They are carrying out surveillance as we speak. We were right employing people who were ex job. They know exactly what is required. They told Jenny what they needed and she saw they got it. Ralph Steinberg has been fully appraised of our situation and is more than happy for us to continue. He sends his best wishes by the way.

"Just one more thing quickly before Audrey comes back. I have let the estate agent in Baillieston know about your interest in the house around the corner from me. I explained you were in hospital but they reckon you are the only one interested in the place anyway, so the quicker you are out of here the quicker you can seal the deal.".

Gerry thanked his old friend and suddenly felt a wave of tiredness wash over him. Perhaps he should listen more to the doctors. He must have closed his eyes as he wasn't even aware of Sandy leaving or Audrey coming into the room. They didn't speak, she just smiled a tired smile and lay her head on the pillow next to him. It was a great comfort to know she was there.

There had been one last thing which Sandy had not bothered to mention to Gerry, well two really. That very day the funeral of Billy and Bobby Graham had taken place at Daldowie Crematorium. No one attended. The last sibling, Margaret had moved to Spain. Not one associate of the Graham family appeared and no other members of the criminal fraternity. It seemed that the twins and their bullying ways would not be missed.

The other thing was that Delilah, DI Samson, was really pissed off, but then why wouldn't he be. His prime suspect had only gone and solved all the outstanding murders on his patch, then killed the culprit into the bargain. Sandy had it on good authority that he was fuming. Perhaps he would tell Gerry later.

CHAPTER FORTY-NINE

With Gerry in hospital and Sandy at home under the strict supervision of Jean. In their absence, it fell to Jenny Galloway to run the show. Under her leadership, the QLM team soon solved the mystery of the stolen clothing. It turned out that the dispatch manager at the depot in Cumbernauld and the manager in charge of deliveries at the Glasgow store were related through marriage, and had set up a scheme, whereby two or three empty boxes were dispatched. The clothing from these boxes was then smuggled off the premises, taken to their homes and sold at local markets at the weekends. It was not difficult for such a highly trained team to pick up on this. It seemed it had all started because the manager in Glasgow had been overlooked, so he thought, for promotion and held a grudge against the company. Both were now in police custody awaiting trial.

Needless to say Ralph Steinberg was more than pleased and awarded QLM the promised contract. This would mean much more work for Gerry and Sandy. More staff to recruit.

Gerry was sent home from hospital with orders to take things easy. He still had to visit a physiotherapist twice a week as he had some stiffness in his right arm plus he had to remember he had fractured his skull. No heading newel posts allowed.

He asked Audrey if she would drive him to Baillieston, and she stopped at his direction in a quiet cul de sac. Sandy Morton had told him about a detached house just around the corner from his own home that was for sale. A lot of people had been put off as the previous occupant had been an elderly lady who kept cats, dozens of them.

The result was that when she had passed away her long lost relatives came to claim their inheritance only to find a stinking mess overrun by cats. Although the house had now been cleared it would need, at the very least, a complete makeover.

Knowing the extension that Gerry had built at his parents' home under his father's guidance, Sandy knew it was probably be an ideal project for Gerry, which he would no doubt relish. He also knew he could call on the builders who had worked for him in the past, most recently on their own offices.

The main thing which attracted Gerry to the property was its price. Because of its condition it was going cheap. Even so he knew the estate agents were having trouble getting rid of it off their books.

Gerry took two pairs of Wellington boots from the boot of his car. He and Audrey ventured into the jungle that was the garden. They wandered about for fifteen minutes or so and Audrey counted how many times Gerry said,

"You just have to look past the mess".

They got back into the car. Audrey was looking less than interested.

It was Gerry who spoke first, "Look Audrey, I know what we agreed. We would get a house and then get married but things have changed. You've sold your flat and we are both crammed into my place. I know that's not ideal but I can stand it if you can, as long as we are together.

Why don't we buy this place and flatten the whole lot, clear the ground and then have architects design the house of our dreams, one to spend the rest of our lives in?"

"Perhaps you're right," Audrey said. "I know I'm sick to death of viewing houses that are overpriced and nothing I've seen so far has rocked my boat. Okay, phone the estate agent with an offer."

Gerry was ecstatic, he kissed her and stared into her face. "Are you serious?"

"Of course I am," she replied "go on, phone and make a bid."

Gerry reached for his mobile and grunted as he tweaked his sore arm. He just ignored it as he was so happy. He had the phone number on speed dial and it only rang a couple of times before being answered. His face suddenly changed from joy to gloom and he hung up.

"What's wrong?" Audrey asked,

"Someone's already bought it," he replied sadly. "They told me I would get it, no problem".

He was so crestfallen he couldn't speak. Eventually he thumped the dashboard and said,

"I offered £100,000 for the site and they said they had sold it yesterday to some woman for £97,500."

"That's right," Audrey laughed, "that woman was me",

"What are you on about Audrey Jennings? It was me who got the bang on the head."

"Yes, but it didn't galvanise you into action, did it? Jean Morton told me about this place weeks ago and unbeknown to each other we have both been trying to buy the same place, because we have the same idea and no, the way we are living just now is not ideal, but at least we are living. I thought that I was going to lose you again the other week and I swore that's not going to happen again. Not only have I bought this place but I hope you're not doing anything next Saturday at 2pm? "

"Why?" Gerry asked meekly.

"Because we are getting married".

CHAPTER FIFTY

It was Saturday morning, the day of the wedding. Gerry had stayed overnight with his friend and mentor, Sandy Morton. His wife Jean had been with Audrey at the flat in Dennistoun.

Sandy was going to be a very busy man today. Not only was he carrying out the duties as best man but also giving the bride away. That was what the couple wanted. Ideally Gerry wished his old pal Paul Corrigan was there to be his best man but that could not be.

Gerry had just stepped out of the shower and was sitting in a towelling dressing gown. There was a knock at the bedroom door and he shouted come in, expecting it to be Sandy. The door opened and there stood a tall, handsome red headed young man, dressed in a kilt.

Gerry nearly fainted. To all intents and purposes he was looking at his old pal Paul Corrigan. Actually it was his now seventeen year old son Scott. He was Sandy's first surprise of the day. Sandy was right behind the lad and smiled at Gerry.

"Scott is here to be your best man. I cannae do everything, you know".

Gerry was so happy, he could not speak. He just hugged the lad. His father would be so proud of him, he thought, as he began to dress himself, in the Lynch tartan kilt.

The two of them chatted away about everything and nothing until the time had arrived to leave for the ceremony. Scott had already warned Gerry that his mum Jackie had also come up from England with him for the ceremony. She had said it's what Paul would have wanted.

Five minutes later a limousine arrived to take Gerry and Scott to the Registry Office at 22 Park Circus in Glasgow. It was a beautiful 19th century building which had originally been commissioned by a famous industrialist and in a former life had been the Italian consulate. Each room was as magnificent as the next bedecked in gold with beautifully ornate vaulted ceilings. Overlooking Kelvingrove Park as it did, it was a stunning location.

As they alighted from the car a piper burst into tune. Yet another of Sandy's surprises. He had managed to secure the services of members from the Strathclyde Police pipe band.

Gerry and Scott entered the building and found the right room. They stood nervously for what seemed an age, until they heard the piper outside strike up again.

Moments later Jean Morton slipped through the front door and sat next to Jackie Corrigan. Just a few seconds later there was Audrey. Stunning in her silk wedding dress, her hair and makeup done to perfection, carrying a bouquet of red and white flowers. Next to her Sandy Morton resplendent in his kilt and looking as proud as punch to be giving Audrey away.

Just when Gerry thought the day couldn't get any better, he then saw that Jenny and Sophie Galloway were also in attendance. Yet another surprise. Both were wearing beautiful silk dresses which matched Audrey's. Jenny was Audrey's bridesmaid and Sophie her flower girl.

The ceremony itself seemed to be over in a flash. Everyone found themselves back outside

being serenaded by several pipers. Gerry kept staring at the wedding ring on his finger. He was actually married.

All too soon the limousines returned for them to take them on to the reception. This was to be held in a hotel in the centre of town. Gerry was flabbergasted that Audrey had managed to make all these arrangements without him knowing a thing. But then he had been in hospital.

The function suite at the hotel was packed with lots of friends from Alexandra Parade, and the police. After the meal Sandy stood and made a speech. He kept it short but would have been failing in his duty if he hadn't mentioned it was long overdue. As his duties dictated Scott, as best man, read out all the cards of congratulations. He then made a short speech in which he mentioned his pride in standing in for his father on the occasion of his best friend's wedding. There wasn't a dry eye in the house.

Gerry spoke about his stupidity in not realising sooner what a wonderful woman he had and how proud he was.

Later as they were about to leave for a quiet honeymoon in Perthshire a surprise guest arrived.

Richard Jonson had flown in especially from the Caribbean.

"Hi guys," he said, "massive congratulations on your wedding. I'm sorry Aimi couldn't be here, as you know she is in the middle of arrangements for her own wedding and given her condition the doctors would not let her fly. Still she wanted to send her congratulations and to give you a small present."

Richard handed over a set of keys.

"These are the keys for a beach side villa in Bermuda," he said. "It's being occupied by a couple called Mr & Mrs Lynch for the next two weeks".

In typical Jonson style, Richard had laid on his own private jet to take the couple from Glasgow to Bermuda. Their luggage had already been packed and was on board. Yet another Sandy Morton surprise.

As the plane took off Audrey looked at Gerry. He couldn't stop smiling.

"Not a bad day eh, Mr Lynch," she said.

"Not a bad day at all Mrs Lynch," Gerry replied.

His thoughts turned to his parents and Paul. He would have given anything for them to have been there today, when he had married his wonderful bride. But he'd had all this and still had Richard and Aimi's wedding in Hawaii to look forward to in just a few weeks, at Christmas. He could definitely get used to this.

Tired after a long emotionally charged day and still recovering from his injuries, Gerry knew he would soon fall asleep as the aircraft soared westward, thousands of feet above the ground.

No doubt he would dream but only of the future.

There would be no more dark days.

THE END

AUTHOR

Gordon Waugh was born in Scotland but raised and educated in Yorkshire. Returning to the country of his birth, he served 30 years in the Police before retiring to Spain. He and his wife now live at the foot of the beautiful Campsie Hills. Dark Days is his first book.